AMY JOHNSON

authorHOUSE®

AuthorHouse™
1663 Liberty Drive
Bloomington, IN 47403
www.authorhouse.com
Phone: 1 (800) 839-8640

Published by AuthorHouse 08/16/2017

ISBN: 978-1-5462-0281-3 (sc)
ISBN: 978-1-5462-0279-0 (hc)
ISBN: 978-1-5462-0280-6 (e)

Library of Congress Control Number: 2017911984

Print information available on the last page.

Visit my website!

http://neverletgoamyjohnson.webs.com

o Click on the guest book and tell me what you think will happen in the next book!
o Please leave your reviews and comments about Never Look Back or the other 2 books in the series:

Never Let Go

Never Say Never

o Visit the Never Let Go by Amy Johnson page on Face book and "like" it. Leave your comments and reviews.
o Order copies for family and friends from:
   http://neverletgoamyjohnson.webs.com
   authorhouse.com
   amazon.com
   Google play books or other e-book retailers

Thanks for your support!

Foreword

"Life got in the way," is what I have been telling my family, friends, and fans when they ask me why it took so long to publish another book. Yes, it has been **FIVE years.** Real quick: do me a favor and take a deep breath. Breathe. Inhale. Exhale. Just for a moment, think about your life as it existed five years ago. Breathe. Are you the least bit surprised by how many changes have transpired: how many smiles, how many frowns, how many mistakes, how many wins, how many losses, how many triumphs, how many defeats, how many regrets, how many proud moments, how many embarrassing situations, how many deaths, how many births, how many rebirths, how many thoughts, how many bright ideas, how many heartaches, how many headaches, how many surrenders, how many disappointments, how many opportunities, how many loves, how many hates, how many dreams, how many wishes, how many positives, how many negatives, how many laughs, how many tears, how many prayers and how many blessings. Think about it. Really, who has time to write? Life gets in the way, but my creative juices never stop flooding my brain.

Regardless, my characters have been speaking to me, and they want me to finish their story. Some of them want me to tell more of their stories because I haven't told enough, and some implore me to continue telling their stories. I see and hear them at home, at work, at church, in my community, in the news, on social media, and just about every place that I go. I see Amina in the vulnerable, fragile, yet strong women that I encounter every day. I hear Anthony in my husband's jokes, on television, on the radio, and in random conversations at football games, basketball games and other events that I attend.

For the past few years, when something reminds me of my characters, I have written it down. When I get an idea for a new character, I write it down. Often, people see me writing feverishly, and one would think that I'm trying to finish something for work or something that needed emergency attention. No, I was writing ideas for this book. I have spiral notebooks and composition books filled with complete stories as well as haphazard scribbling that contain only bits, pieces and ideas. Handwritten notes are spilling out of my desk drawer because I have been stuffing them there for years with the promise that someday I would revive my characters with them.

This book is a fulfilled promise: a huge thank you goes to everyone who questioned me about it, those who inspired me, and especially those who encouraged me along the way. I don't even have to list names this time around because you know who you are, and I love you, respect you, and appreciate the fact that you are a part of my life. I am beyond blessed. Thank you Jesus!

Special Thanks to:

My mother and father
My husband and sons
My brothers and sister
My nieces and nephews
My aunts, uncles and cousins
My grandparents (RIP)
My in-laws
My friends and co-workers
My past, present, and future
Believe it or not, you have provided me with an abundance of writing inspiration by living life to the fullest, by living life to the lowest, by being yourself, by being full of pretense, by doing me right, by doing me wrong, by hating me, by loving me, by paying close attention to me, by ignoring me, by encouraging me, by praising me, by degrading me, by angering me, by hurting me, by comforting me and vice versa. I'm not innocent; I have done the same to you. Neither apologies nor thanks are necessary because without you, I would not be me. Without you, I would have no voice, and without a voice, I could not do what gives me ultimate pleasure, peace, satisfaction: **WRITE.**

–1–

The Old Millennium

December 27, 1999

Dr. Branson,

*I*t's hard to believe that a year has passed since that horrendous day when Victoria Miller terrorized me and Anthony at my house only to end with her taking her own life. I'm sure you are seeing all of the anniversary news features on television and in the newspapers. Because it was such a newsworthy story in the usually quiet town of Coronado, Arkansas, it's all anyone wants to talk about. You would think that people are discussing a blockbuster movie or something! The story has grown and even been exaggerated in the media. All I can do is shake my head because it just opens up the hurt all over again at a time when Anthony and I are finally trying to face the reality and get ourselves back on track.

She was your patient. Do you really understand why she did what she did? Not the medical explanation, but the human explanation. Can the brain be so intricately wired to and dependent on chemical balances that it can get screwed up enough to make a woman tirelessly obsess over a man who didn't want her, shoot up the home and vehicle of his innocent girlfriend, and then shoot herself knowing that the child she was carrying would ultimately die? Is the brain really that vulnerable, that sensitive, that complicated?

1

Can missing medication or mixing medicine with alcohol really result in such radical consequences? Are we all simply ticking time bombs waiting for a chemical imbalance to detonate an explosion in our lives?

Do you think that perhaps you missed some warning signs? Do you ever wonder if there was anything else that you could have done? These are questions that Anthony and I have discussed, avoided or argued about in one way or another. Could we have prevented it from happening? Did we exacerbate the situation by ignoring her erratic behavior?

I saw that story on the news about Vickie's cousin Trevor and that other family coming together to file a civil lawsuit against you. I think it is absolutely ridiculous, but I just haven't said anything to you about it because avoiding all mention of her name and that situation seems to work in my mental favor. I am only bringing it up now because all the news stories and focus on it is creepily close to terrifying me. I haven't had a single anxiety attack since she died, and this shows me how mentally damaged I was and how severe my PTSD was. Could I possibly have ended up in her situation? Is there a chance that I could revert back to that fragile state but not be fortunate enough to recover? The possibilities take my breath away.

As much as possible, Anthony avoids all mention of her too. We have basically spent the entire year avoiding the subject as much as possible, working nonstop to keep our minds occupied, pretending that everything is fine in our relationship, and putting on quite a show for our friends and family who are now convinced that everything is truly back to normal with us. They think that we haven't missed a beat, that we are hopelessly in love, that we overcame an incredible obstacle with flying colors, without a scratch, and emerged better than we were before. They couldn't be farther from the truth. Our relationship is in serious trouble, and this time around I am not the only one who needs therapy.

I still see Dr. Branson, but our sessions progressed from weekly to biweekly to monthly to bimonthly to quarterly. Now, that's progress because back when I was seeing her once a week, I was a nervous wreck. In addition to my rapid progress, we ended up being pretty good friends. She joined my exercise group at the CFC – Coronado Fitness Center, and she fit in perfectly with my friends Evelyn and Sasha. Evelyn and Sasha are dispatchers at CPD, and they both knew Vickie quite well. Even in my exercise group, we avoided mention of her.

Although there have been many occasions when we wanted to talk about her, we all give each other a funny "let's not go there" look and change the subject. It's hard not to think about Vickie though, especially since there's a huge memorial plaque with her picture on it in the front lobby of the CFC. The minute you walk into the front door of the gym, there she is staring at you, reminding you that she used this facility quite a bit.

The plaque, courtesy of a benevolent foundation in Coronado, was also followed by a membership drive which awarded three lucky winners an annual free membership to the CFC in Vickie's honor. I never knew she was such a supporter of fitness, but then again, there was a lot that I didn't know about Victoria Miller, but Anthony did, and little by little, this information leaked out and blemished Anthony's heroic reputation.

She knew that he consumed a lot of alcohol, and she was perfectly okay with it. According to rumors, she was quite an alcoholic herself. I witnessed her drunken behavior firsthand on many occasions. As it turns out, Anthony wasn't completely honest with me about their relationship. As it turns out, he was not honest with me about a lot of information, and as I learned more about him, I questioned myself about why I'm with him.

For example, he agreed to attend the plaque dedication ceremony at the CFC. From what I heard, he had some pretty nice things to say about her. I wanted to leave it alone, but I had to ask him why he felt obligated to even attend, much less speak! His answer was one that I expected. "She was a cop, I am a cop. We support our own, no matter what," he explained. It's true that many officers attended that day, but it would not have been an anomaly for him to miss it. *After all, she did try to kill him . . . and me, the so called love of his life, the woman he wants to marry and bear his children.*

So, now every time I walk into the CFC, there she perches like a vulture above the admission desk, the one place where everyone must stop and slide their identification card. You wouldn't believe how fast I zoom into the gym, slide my card, and motor to the dressing rooms when I go there. That plaque is overbearing! It should be at the police department instead of the gym! *Oh wait! There is one at the police department! A big one!* It's like she's watching me from the grave and warning me that she's not finished with her harassment.

An obvious way to avoid that self assured smirk of a smile of hers would be to just go to another gym, but guess what? CFC is the only full service gym in Coronado! Anthony goes to the gym regularly, and he hasn't complained once about the plaque. In fact, he started inviting me to the gym even more after the dedication. Sometimes he acts like the whole ordeal never happened, and other times, he drowns his sorrows in a bottle and it is all he wants to talk about. Long walks in the park were my escape when I couldn't bear to walk into the gym and try to avoid her face.

Dr. Branson, Lanita, invited Anthony and me to Coronado's Christmas with the Arts program. It was an invitation only event and quite a fancy affair. It was nice to get dressed up, go out, and hang with important people. Lanita's husband, Robert, is an orthopedic surgeon. They introduced us to all of their doctor and surgeon friends. We thought that we would go and be out of our element, but we went, we fit in, mingled perfectly, and thoroughly enjoyed ourselves. Robert, Lanita, and most of their professional friends were down to earth, and we got along fabulously. That night out was actually a breath of fresh air for me and Anthony because we had both been working nonstop to keep our minds off of the fact that the anniversary of the ordeal was looming near. That's what we call it: "the ordeal." We loosened up, naturally enjoyed each other's company, and had a great time.

Actually, Anthony had too much of a good time. Doctors, chiropractors, surgeons and many others in the medical field are also quite into the field of alcohol consumption. They drank until the cows came home. The only difference is that many of the other guests were driven to the event by limousines or hired drivers. I begrudgingly drove Anthony home that night, and struggled tremendously when I tried to get him into the house. Once inside, he threw up inside a large decorative vase beside the front door that I used as an umbrella stand. He thought the whole thing was funny, but he lost a lot of cool points with me that night. *Shit, every time that I had to drive his drunk ass home resulted in a loss of cool points. Honestly, Anthony had almost depleted his supply of cool points.*

I really wanted to, but I never gave Lanita that letter, and I have no idea why. Letter writing was the principle way that we communicated. I would write her a letter and confess everything that I might feel embarrassed about saying in therapy, and we would discuss the contents of the letter during our session.

Every time I looked at it, I felt like I was keeping a dirty secret from not only my doctor but also my friend. It would have sparked a great discussion, it would have lifted a heavy weight off my chest, and it might have led to a referral for Anthony, yet I kept it folded in half in the front cover of one of my journals. I repeatedly reread that letter for a variety of reasons: first, to analyze my current status with Anthony. Our relationship had fizzled from somewhat normal to completely weird; second, stare at the fact that perhaps Anthony is not the man of my dreams . . . reality sucks – he has a drinking problem; finally, to remind myself that I should be thankful that things are so much better now regardless of the fact that they are messed up in a new way. *Do I even want to deal with it? Is he even worth it? Why do I feel so bad for wanting to call it quits?*

Perhaps, I should just stick it out and wait for the next guy – the one who doesn't already have a child, the one who doesn't have a drinking problem, the one who didn't have an obsessive girlfriend who tried to kill me? I have two "somethings" trying to tell me what to do.

Something #1 tells me that I need to walk away and continue to concentrate on my career. I'm young, I'm beautiful, I'm free, and the world is waiting for me to make my move and have fun while I'm doing it!

Something #2 tells me that it is too late to back out because my feelings run too deep at this point, my heart would break without him, and he's worth fighting for. Weighing my options is something that I shake my head and smile about now because I never had such an opportunity before that presented so many positive possibilities. I guess it's what one could call growth. I have grown a lot, but obviously, I have a lot more growing to do.

−2−

You Should Have Been There

January 1, 2000

I tiptoed to the bathroom and tried to figure out a way to get rid of the man in my living room. Honesty. I would just tell him the truth. He would certainly understand my change of heart. I walked softly through my bedroom, out into the hallway, and I opened the door to the living room.

My nervousness faded as I stopped to smile at the sight that greeted me. Rashad, stretched out on the couch, was fast asleep and snoring. I listened to him and watched his muscled chest rise and fall. Shaking my head and smiling, I tiptoed back down the hallway to the closet and found a blanket, covered him with it and stared at him for a few seconds before turning off the light. *Yep, he's one fine chocolate specimen. He looks like Morris Chestnut or maybe even Omar Epps?* Heavy sleeper though. He didn't flinch or change positions when I covered him, or when I stood there staring at him like an idiot. Myself, on the other hand, I tossed and turned for the remainder of the night and even laid awake staring into the darkness.

Extremely tired from the busy day and night that seemed to never end, I should have fallen asleep as soon as my head touched the pillow, but that just did not happen. I considered going into the living room to see if Rashad was suddenly lying awake as well, but the bright neon numbers on the clock told me that I should remain exactly where I was. *Plus, after the evening we just shared, I didn't want Rashad to get the wrong idea, which might surely happen with me wanting to talk at this time of the morning!* Finally, I drifted off to sleep and dreamed about the events of that evening.

~+~+~+~+~+~+~+~

"Come on now! There's no reason why you should spend New Year's Eve at home alone!" Rashad coaxed.

"I'm okay with it, really! I can watch other people celebrate on TV. I don't have to be out in it," I answered.

"Amina, when was the last time you went out?"

"Umm . . ." I wondered aloud wanting to avoid mention of that night out last week.

"See! That's too long! Most of our coworkers will be there. At least join us at Boudreaux's for dinner. What ya plan on eating tonight anyway?"

"Popcorn," I mumbled.

"Come on girl! Don't make me beg!"

"You are begging. I already told you no!"

"But I can tell you want to go! What's holding you back?" he pressed.

"I don't know. I always want to ring in the New Year with my boyfriend, and for the past few years, it hasn't happened that way," I explained.

"Well, maybe it's time for you to find a new boyfriend," he suggested slyly.

"Stop!" I giggled, "Okay, I'll go! But, I don't want to stay out too late because I have a lot to do tomorrow," I bargained.

"Okay, no doubt. Me too. Want me to come and pick you up?"

"Oh, you are going to be the DD tonight?"

"Yeah, I can be! That means that I can get you drunk! And you really act up when you get drunk!"

"Aw hell no. I'll drive!"

"Girl, you know I'm joking! I'll come by at 8:30. Will that be good?"

"Sure," I said and envisioned his gangster smile with that gleaming gold crown.

As soon as I got out of the shower, Anthony called. He explained that it would be a busy night at work, but he would call or come by later to check on me. I told him that I was going out with Rashad and some other friends from work.

"On a date?" he asked incredulously.

"No! A group of us from work are going to Boudreaux's for dinner then to the Steppin Out Club to ring in the new year," I explained casually.

"Dinner and dancing, huh? That sounds like a date to me baby," he deduced bluntly.

"Well, it's not," I countered, "we're just hanging out together. I wish I could spend the evening with you."

"Well, duty calls," he answered without emotion, "we went to that nice party last weekend."

"Yes, we did. I guess I'm just greedy," I supplied facetiously.

"Whatever! Behave yourself during your night out with your friends," he cautioned.

"Always baby," I agreed with a smirk. We hung up, and I finished getting ready to go out. I plowed through the closet for thirty minutes looking for something to wear. Nothing seemed appropriate. A dress seemed too sexy, and pants seemed too casual. Finally, I called Katy and Whitney and asked what they were wearing. Whitney wasn't going. Katy said that she was wearing a sweater, jeans, and boots, so I decided to wear the same. I had a cute off the shoulder sweater that looked great with jewelry, jeans, and boots. It was cold enough, so whatever I chose to wear would be covered with my coat anyway!

Dinner was fabulous, but it did seem like Rashad and I were on a date because everyone was paired up with their significant other. When we toasted to our friendships, Rashad was staring a bit too deeply into my eyes. At the club, Rashad kept insisting that we slow dance, but opted to mingle with people in the raucous crowd during the fast songs. Every time a slow song came on, he spotted me, grabbed me, pulled me out to the dance floor, and held me close. Once, he even pulled me away from Devondrick, his good friend and roommate and explained that he couldn't give up any dances with me tonight.

"I'm just doing your boyfriend a favor," he explained when I asked him why I couldn't dance with anyone else.

"Oh really? How is that?"

"He can trust me. I'm not going to be rubbing all over your sexy body or whispering in your ear while we out here slow grinding, but another man would definitely do that to you!" he said as he pushed me back at arm's length just to prove his point. I burst into a fit of giggles, and he smiled, pulled me back close to him, and looked down at me. I stopped laughing and looked up into his intense brown eyes. I thought that I sensed a kiss coming toward me, but thankfully he just smiled down at me, looked away, and continued our dance.

The song ended, and the countdown to the new millennium began. People ran out and crowded the dance floor, and Rashad and I were trapped right in the middle. We were squished together, so Rashad put his arm around me so we could comfortably join in the merriment.

"10, 9, 8, 7, 6, 5, 4, 3, 2, 1 . . . Happy New Year!" With that, it seemed the entire crowd started a kissing, hugging, and alcohol chugging frenzy. Rashad enclosed me in a tight embrace and planted a hot kiss directly on my lips, both catching me by surprise and taking my breath away. One second we were standing side by side with his arm resting on my back and shoulder, and then we were face to face with his arms around me, my body flush against his with his lips devouring mine. The chiseled rigidity of his body shocked me. *Damn! What's under those clothes?* It happened so fast that I didn't have time to think about how nice it felt. Then among the falling confetti and balloons, he hugged me, and whispered, "Happy New Year Amina!" I hugged him back, delighted to wrap myself around his firm body.

Before I could say anything, a crazy bass booming booty shaking song came on, and the crowd on the dance floor seemed to go wild: picking up confetti and balloons and throwing them, shooting silly string, spraying champagne, dancing wildly, and jumping up and down. Our holds on each other relaxed, and we stood there, dumbfounded.

Looking around at the chaos that surrounded us, we both knew that we needed to move immediately.

Soon, it was out of control: a fight erupted in the corner, and chaos ensued. Rashad put his arms back around me protectively, grabbed our coats, and ushered me out to the parking lot. He kept his protective hold on me as we walked to his car, but I didn't mind. Droves of people were leaving quickly, so the parking lot was in disarray too. It was when we got to his car, and he bent down to kiss me again, that I had to pump the brakes on him. I pushed him back slightly, so I could speak.

"The kiss at midnight was very nice," I started and before I could even finish, he had pressed his hard body against me and covered my lips with his. His lips were warm, soft, and inviting. His hot tongue darted between my lips. I was quite tempted, it took everything in me, but I did not reciprocate. I didn't move, and he finally took the hint.

"What?" he whispered into my nonresponsive lips, "You just said that our kiss was nice! I was just going to give you another one!" I inched away from him, so I could speak without his muscled chest, rock hard abs and large erection touching me.

"Rashad! You know that I'm in a relationship!"

"Yeah, you keep telling me that, but I don't see a ring on your finger, and every time I turn around, you are spending time alone, with your friends, or with your family. I don't even see him coming around anymore. You act like you are free as a bird, and baby I'm ready to fly with you. What's the hold up?"

Smiling, I ignored his last comment and question; I was not surprised that he had observed the deterioration of my relationship with Anthony. It was hard not to notice.

"See, now that shows how much you know! Anthony and I went out last weekend!" I replied weakly.

"Oh really? When I asked you earlier, you acted like you couldn't even remember the last time you went out!" The swarm of people leaving the club did not distract us from our discussion. We continued on, unaware that the police had arrived, and the chaos was moving outside.

"Yes, we went to a pretty fancy party last weekend. We had a great time!" I exaggerated.

"Then why are you always so sad and always trying to hide it with working yourself to death?"

"Ummm . . . I have bills to pay! Do your bills make you happy?" I answered obnoxiously and giggled.

"That's the other thing. If y'all are so serious, why aren't you living together? That would solve your bill problem automatically!" *Damn! Rashad is all up in my business! Does he know how long it's been since we had sex too?*

"Because I'm an old fashioned type of girl!"

"Shiiiiittt!" he chuckled, "And my name is Bart!"

I laughed and looked at the full moon in the distance. He stopped laughing, and looked at it with me.

"Full moon. You know what happens on nights with a full moon?" he grinned.

"Yes, all the werewolves, vampires, and other creatures come out searching for their prey," I giggled. He howled loudly, and I burst into cacophonous laughter. Although it was cold and noisy on the parking lot, we made no move to get into his car, and he continued on with his interrogation.

"When he comes to the store to see you, which is damn near not as often as it use to be, you don't always seem so happy to see him," he stated seriously.

"I can't lie and say that we don't have problems every now and then," I answered, "because we have been on a rollercoaster of problems this past year."

"Yeah, I guess so after that crazy bitch, huh?"

"Umm hmm . . . if that's how you want to describe it," I replied evasively.

"There ain't no other way to describe it! That bitch was crazy!" he chuckled. I smiled, reached up impulsively and kissed him on the cheek. He shook his head affirmatively. He understood what that kiss meant, and he concluded his quest to get into my panties.

"Let's get you home girl," he said as he opened the door for me.

We talked about current events and store gossip on the way home. He sprinkled the conversation with silly jokes and hilarious impersonations, and we laughed heartily. He walked me to my door, gave me a warm hug, and waited until I went inside and turned on some lights. I came back out to say goodbye.

"Happy New Year Rashad. I'm glad you talked me into going. I had a great time."

"Happy New Year Amina. I had fun too. See ya later," he said as backed away from me and walked down the steps, down the sidewalk, and to his car. I watched him ruefully. He was super fine: tall, dark, handsome, muscular, broad shoulders, well dressed, history of being a thug, which fascinated me, and he thought that he wanted to be more than friends with me.

No, not a good idea. Yes, we could have an interesting dance in the sack, but then every time he looked at me at work, I would feel extremely guilty. Either that or I would feel extremely horny. *Hmm . . . I bet he likes it rough, and I'm sure he would talk dirty throughout.* Shaking those thoughts from my head, I closed the door, turned on the TV for background noise, and changed out of my clothes into my pajamas.

~+~+~+~+~+~+~+~

Loud banging on the door woke me up from that fitfully surrendered sleep at about 6:30 in the morning. With a throbbing head, I dizzily rolled out of bed, threw a robe over my pajamas and ran to the door.

Rashad sat up on the couch with a perplexed look on his face and asked, "Yo! What's happening? What's up?" Groggily, he looked around confused for a few minutes until he realized where he was.

I peered through the peephole. Anthony. *What the hell was he doing here so early?* He was still dressed in his police officer uniform. He looked furious. He looked straight into the peephole, and he gave me a look that said, "Well?" and he banged on the door again. *Damn! Was this official police business? Glad that I didn't agree and give his ass a key!*

"Amina! Wake up! Open the door. I know you're in there." He banged on the door again. I looked sideways at Rashad, who was rubbing sleep from his eyes, swallowed hard, then took a deep breath before opening the door. The sun and frigid wind attacked me instantly.

"Why are you banging on my door like that?" I asked rudely as I stood in the doorway, looking up at him with one hand on my hip.

Moving forward, he ignored my question, "What's wrong with you? What took you so long? Who's here with you? Whose car is that in your driveway?" he bombarded me with questions.

His face was red, tense with frowns, and his eyebrows were scrunched together. The bright sunlight and bitter cold wind made me scrunch my eyes as well. I shivered against my will. He noticed, but he ignored it when he realized that I was not just going to let him barge in. *What if I had a relative over for the night? This would be an extremely embarrassing situation if that were the case.*

"Hey! What's the problem? Are you going to let me in, or are we just going to stand here looking at each other?" he asked impatiently and put his hands on his hips and looked down at me fiercely. *Damn! Shut the hell up and give me a second to think!* He was tapping his right foot, and I noticed that he was clenching his jaw muscles, and this scared me a little. A tiny knot of anxiety surfaced in my gut and reminded me that I did not like feeling this way.

"Not until you calm down," I firmly told him with a direct look up into his angry eyes. Anger. *Why was he angry? Oh shit! Did someone tell him that they saw me kiss Rashad?* With that, Rashad got up and came to the door to rescue me.

"It's cool man. It's not at all what you think," he tried to soothe. Anthony looked at Rashad, fully clothed then at me with pajamas and a robe, and he seemed to calm down just a pinch. Slowly, I moved aside; he walked in and looked around. His eyes settled on the couch which held the makings of a "crash on the couch." Anthony strode across the room, sat on the loveseat, and shot me an irritated glance. Rashad grabbed the sheet, blanket, and the pillow from the sofa and handed them to me.

During this short, awkward silence, Anthony cleared his throat and looked at his watch. Rashad sat down, put on his shoes, and explained the situation that landed him on my couch, Anthony listened, and I slinked off to the kitchen to make coffee.

I could hear Rashad explaining that the New Year's Eve party last night at the Steppin Out Club became wild and out of control shortly after midnight. The group that we went with decided to leave right after the balloon drop that ushered in the madness. *I love how he made it seem like we stayed with the group the whole time!*

Exhausted, Rashad dropped me off, and he went home. However, Rashad's roommate, Devondrick, continued the wild and out of control behavior at their apartment. They got into a boisterous argument then a fist fight, and Rashad called me and asked if he could sleep on my couch for the night.

Even though I feared this type of mixed up situation with Anthony would arise the next day, I told Rashad that he could. Trying to find a hotel room for the night would have been a fruitless endeavor, and his family lived almost two hours away near Breckinridge. Rashad was a nice man. He was a man though, and he definitely slipped up every now and then, but I wasn't about to tell Anthony that.

Besides, Rashad was a dedicated co-worker and a loyal friend. I met Rashad long before I met Anthony. I thought about my other friends from work: Dottie, Katy, Michelle, Whitney, Liz, Sondra, Glenda and the list goes on. I would have offered them the same spot on the couch without a second thought. He was one of the few men that I considered a close friend, and even though he joked constantly about us moving past friendship, he knew that we never would.

When he walked in, I even thought about telling him that I changed my mind and that he should go because I hadn't spoken to Anthony about it. Additionally, I did not want Rashad to get the wrong impression. *We did share a steamy kiss at midnight, and he stole another one shortly afterwards. It could have turned into something, but it didn't because it was nothing! Oh shit! Surely Rashad knows to leave that little detail out of his recap?* I kept thinking that Anthony would call or stop by for a few minutes last night to wish me a Happy New Year, but he didn't. I considered calling him, but that's not how we operated when he was working. Because he knew when it was a good time for us to talk and when it was not, he did all the calling from work which was fine with me.

Well, my phone did not ring last night, and it surely did not ring this morning before Anthony came and attacked my door with his fist. So, Rashad slept on the couch, I slept in my bed, and Anthony found out about it this morning instead of last night. I angrily surmised that we wouldn't be in this uncomfortable predicament if he took a minute to call me like he usually does. Case closed. *Poor communication incenses me, and it is a sure fire way to get your ass kicked to the curb Anthony!* I glared at him on my way to the kitchen.

They proceeded with their calm discussion, so I figured there was nothing to worry about. As the coffee brewed, I slipped back into the living room and observed Anthony and Rashad in a deep, hushed conversation. It did not seem charged or angry, just quiet and this bothered me because I wanted to know what they were talking about.

"Coffee will be ready in a few. Join me in the kitchen for some when you finish talking, okay?" I softly spoke to their backs. I waited and neither of them said anything, then Anthony turned slightly, "Okay baby, thanks," he said over his shoulder. I stood there for a few seconds hoping that Rashad would look at me, send me a signal or something, but they went back to their quiescent dialogue, and again this worried me slightly.

I went to the kitchen and opened the blinds. Sunlight flooded the wide open space. I walked over to the bar which was within sight of the living room and sat down. The quiet conversation between Anthony and Rashad continued along with my wonders of why they were being so secretive. I poured myself a cup of coffee and looked out the window. It was freezing outside, but it was warm and toasty in the house. I thought about lighting the fireplace, but quickly ruled that out because I would be spending the day at my mother's house helping her dismantle her Christmas decorations.

Soon, only Anthony joined me in the kitchen, and I gave him a puzzled look while trying not to frown. I watched Rashad open the front door and leave without saying goodbye, and I narrowed my eyes.

"Rashad is going home to try to patch up his friendship with

Devondrick," Anthony explained, "It's good that Rashad left his apartment when he did because his roommate's girlfriend, or whoever she was, called the police when Rashad had an advantage in the tussle. Some neighbors broke up the fight, and Rashad left. That was a responsible decision. When the police arrived, Devondrick was wildly out of control, and they were about to arrest him for drunk and disorderly conduct until I heard the call and offered my input," he explained. *Always a hero. What? Do you want a pat on the head or something? Is this what you guys were really talking about? I certainly hope so!*

Despite what I was thinking, I smiled at him as he continued proudly, "I told the arresting officer that it sounded like the guy just needed to go into his apartment and sleep it off. I did not really see the need to arrest him if the fight was over, his roommate had left the scene, and he was just talking a bunch of smack. The neighbors all vouched for Rashad's and Devondrick's good character, so the responding officers just chalked it up to the rowdiness that goes along with ringing in the New Year." *Yep. Add alcohol and the rowdiness is intensified by 1000.*

Anthony continued, "I didn't even know that he was Rashad's roommate until this very moment. I kind of remember him from Thanksgiving dinner at your mom's, but I was just making a judgment call last night that would hopefully keep another man out of jail. Everyone agreed with me as I agreed with them when they made the same decision more than once last night. It was a very busy night baby with many more serious issues that actually warranted arrests. I am so sorry that I did not call. I'm even sorrier that I did not come by last night to check on you. I'm the sorriest for jumping to conclusions. I thought the worst of you, and I shouldn't have because I know that you love me, and I hope with all my heart that you will forgive me. I'm ready to get back to the way we were," he pleaded.

Of course, I forgave him, but things took a very long time to get back to the way they were.

Consequently, Rashad backed off completely after that. Before, he flirted every now and then, gave me sexy looks, and insisted that we would someday get together, but after that situation, he was just business and professional. I was sure that Anthony said something to him that brought about this change. I missed Rashad's flirty jokes, sexy looks, and sweet compliments, but I reasoned that the change was for the best. I guess that talk with Anthony convinced him that we were extremely serious. *Maybe Anthony threatened Rashad's life, safety or freedom? Perhaps his police power has given him a superiority complex, and he thinks he can boss everyone around? There's no telling, and if I keep thinking about it, I could come up with millions of possibilities.*

I still had nagging suspicions about Anthony, and something was keeping me from becoming completely committed. Sometimes, I didn't know what to think about Anthony's behavior or his motivations. It was heartbreaking for me to admit it, but he had become so dependent on alcohol that it was affecting his mood both when he was drunk and when he was sober.

Add to this the now strained relationship that he had with his daughter thanks to the manipulations of his ex-wife, and this only escalated the amount of liquor that he consumed to dull the pain. He's so macho about it that he would never even admit that he was hurting. He would admit that he missed Arielle and wanted to spend more time with her, but just like any other man, he wouldn't admit that a piece of him was broken inside because he did not have custody.

This is why it took so long for us to finally put the wet blanket of Vickie's memory to rest, at least somewhat, because he would never admit how much it hurt. He was a great pretender, and this bothered me to no end. We argued a lot because sometimes I wanted to talk and hash things out, but he wanted to "just leave it alone." It would be easy to leave it alone if we had ever talked about it in the first place rather than pretend it never happened.

—3—

Arguments Abound

It seemed the more comfortable Anthony and I became with each other, the more we irritated each other. The quirks of our personalities surfaced each time we spent more than a couple of days together, and they were annoying. He loathed my occasionally impulsive nature but complained when I overanalyzed situations before making a decision. I hated it when he wanted to talk about things that I did not want to talk about. I hated it even more when he avoided discussion when I wanted to talk. Simply put, we were at a stage in our relationship where we just got on each other's nerves.

He wanted to spend the night. I wanted him to take his ass home. I wanted to go out to eat. He wanted me to cook. He wanted us to go away for the weekend. I wanted to stay home and rest during the weekend. He wanted to hang out at the Blue Light Sports Bar after work. I wanted him to come to my house, snuggle up, watch movies, and eat popcorn. He wanted to watch the news and sports. I wanted to watch soap operas and sitcoms. When I leave him to watch sports in the living room, so I could go watch sitcoms in the bedroom, he tells me that he might as well go home if he's going to watch TV alone. We were not on the same page, we were totally out of sync, and it bothered me with extreme head shaking, exhaling, and eye rolling intensity.

On this particular night, we were relaxing at my house. I was in a pissed off mood because he had won several arguments: instead of going out to eat, I cooked; even though we argued during our time together,

I agreed that he could spend the night; he wanted to watch football, so there I sat beside him, pretending that I was watching as well. I have nothing against football; I'd just prefer to watch the one big game every year and call it even. Despite my objections, we were watching this regular season game, and he was drinking beer. Never mind that he was on #7 of a 12 pack. "It's just beer," he justified.

Before half time, the boredom was strangling me and I couldn't take it anymore, so I excused myself to my bedroom. I pulled out my journal and started writing. The sounds of Anthony cheering and yelling at the TV emanated from the living room, so I moved to the sunroom which was located in the back of the house beside the kitchen. The cordless phone was in the kitchen, and it rang as I was walking by. I answered it on the second ring.

"Hello, Amina Rechelle," a deep masculine voice greeted. It was DeWayne, D for short. Besides my mother, D was the only other person who addressed me by my first and middle name. I cringed when my mother did it, but when I heard him say it, my spirit smiled.

"D! What's up? How have you been?" I answered excitedly. It had been a while since I talked to him. I plopped down on the window seat in the sun room. It was about 10 degrees cooler in there, with all the windows, so I walked quickly through the kitchen, through the dining room, down the hallway back to my bedroom to grab a small blanket to wrap up in.

"When are you coming back in here?" Anthony called when he heard my footsteps.

"I'm not," I answered as I hurried back to the sunroom. His audible objection became just a mumble when I closed the door. I settled myself on the window seat's plush cushion, wrapped the blanket around myself, dropped the journal in my lap, and repositioned the phone in my hand.

D and I had talked for less than ten minutes when Anthony opened the door and mouthed, "Who is that?" I rolled my eyes, shook my head, waved my hand at him, and kept talking. Anthony turned with a huff and went back to the living room. Our conversation continued until we were somewhat caught up. I bragged about my promotions at work and smiled brightly when he congratulated me. He was happily married now, settled into working and establishing himself in his community. I was happy for him, and I told him so.

Talking to him instantly diminished the funky mood that I was in earlier. We chatted for close to an hour, and when we hung up, I immediately started writing in my journal. I heard the garage door open and close, but I didn't bother to get up and see if Anthony left or what. *Surely he would not drive after drinking 7+ beers! Then again, maybe he would. He's done it before. Being a police officer sometimes makes him an arrogant jerk, like he's above the law, and definitely like he's entitled to do things that other people shouldn't do.*

Fifteen minutes later, I heard the garage door open and close again. Once again, I thought nothing of it, and I continued writing. When I write, I lose all sense of time, space, and my surroundings. I only stopped when I needed to go to the bathroom, nearly two hours later. I sauntered through the house to go back up front, satisfied that I was feeling much more positive than I felt when I left. I went to the half bath because it was closest to the living room.

When I finished and walked into the living room, the sight that hit me suddenly transformed my sweet apple smiles to sour lemon frowns. Anthony, wearing nothing but his boxers, was stretched out on the sofa. He had kicked off his shoes in front of the door, his coat was hanging on the hooks beside the door, and his shoes should have been underneath them! His shirt, undershirt and jeans were scattered on the floor as if he undressed as he walked in. In front of him, on the coffee table was a large bottle of vodka still in its brown paper bag, a bottle of cranberry juice, and a red plastic cup. *Why? Why do liquor stores give out those ridiculous cups? Do customers ask for them, or are they just given out with each purchase?* He had finished several cups of the juice and liquor, and his mood was rapidly approaching its vehement stage.

"Oh! Amina Jefferson has entered the room!" he loudly announced and chuckled.

"Anthony, why are you drinking that stuff?" I asked incredulously.

"Because the beer wasn't doing anything for me," he loudly answered in a surprisingly serious tone. I looked at him and frowned.

"Because I needed somebody to keep me company while I watched the game since my woman was so occupied. "Come here!" he swung his legs off the couch, stomped his feet on the floor, and patted the cushion beside him, "Come sit down and watch this game with me baby!"

I rolled my eyes at him as I peered down at the floor littered with his clothes. I longed to pick them up, but I stood there, glued to my spot, paralyzed with disgust. *Who is this man? Why is he in my life?*

"No, I'm going to go back in the sunroom to write," I answered casually. He leaned forward and poured more liquor into the cup followed by a few drops of the cranberry juice. *Umm . . . you got that shit backwards baby! Pour the juice then the liquor!*

"And talk on the phone?" he accused with a raise of his right eyebrow.

"Oh, that was just D," I informed nonchalantly with a casual dismissive wave of my hand.

"So, you're still talking to him?" he huffed after taking a swig of his drink, closing his eyes and shaking his head due to the intensity of the alcohol.

"Yes Anthony. I'll always talk to him. He's my best friend from childhood. Remember, we already talked about this. We've been friends . . ."

"For as long as you can remember. Yadda yadda yadda yah! Yes, I remember talking about the fakery, not the reality. Spare me the got damn theatrics my drama queen!" he sneered. *Oh shit. His full blown buzz is taking effect rather quickly. Then again, I did leave him to it for the past couple of hours. Time for me to disappear.*

"But what we really didn't discuss is the fact that you **fucked** him!" Anthony loudly sputtered. He pronounced that f word with such force that spit sprayed out of his mouth and landed on the coffee table. I was shocked into silence. I raised my foot to move, but his drunken spiel stopped me in my tracks.

"Not only did you fuck him, but you fucked him many many many many many many many times!" he drunkenly exaggerated. He was still patting the spot beside him as if I would actually come and sit down.

Shocked, I stood there with wide eyes and wondered if he had been reading my journals. *Where was all this coming from? Has something happened? He hasn't had a problem with me talking to D before this! Why is it such a problem now?*

"I'm not stupid Amina Jefferson," I can tell when a man has fucked my woman or wants to fuck my woman! Your friend D has fucked you, and your friend Rashad wants to fuck you!" he shouted as if he just announced an earth-shattering revelation.

I just looked at him and wondered how he could possibly get that drunk so fast. *And why do drunk people speak nothing but truth? I had to keep my mouth shut on this one. There was practically nothing that I could say in my defense.* I started walking away, but he got up, stumbled over to me, and blocked my path. The alcohol smell was so strong that it almost gave me a buzz!

"This shit is going to stop! And it's going to stop right here, right now! You are going to have to choose. Either you want me or you want your male friends, but you can't have both!" he roared. As he was yelling down into my face, I winced, not only from the overpowering smell, but also from the realization that he was right, and that it was going to be a difficult decision.

Obviously, our night was ruined. *No romance tonight.* He fell asleep on the couch, and I fell asleep in bed with the door locked.

—4—

She's Number One

Alycia Wallace is Anthony's ex-wife, his daughter Arielle's mother, and sometimes the bane of my existence. From the moment that I met her until now as I keep learning more disturbing information about her from Anthony, his mother, his sister, his daughter and from Alycia herself, I could tell that she was not a dedicated mother.

From the start, I could tell that she was more concerned about herself than she was about her daughter. She loves it when Anthony's mother, Jacinda or sister, Angelique (Angie) takes Arielle away for the weekend, when they pick her up from school, basically when they step in and take care of her. This puzzles me because Anthony wants to be a full time father with full custody, but she won't hear of it. It's like they are fighting over a doll. The girls can play with her, but the boy can't, and when the owner wants her back, nobody gets to play.

Alycia is chronically unemployed, chain smokes cigarettes, drinks like a sailor, has a constant stream of boyfriends, frequently asks for money "for Arielle," and spends it on who knows what. This past year has been the worst. It seems the closer that Anthony and I become, the farther apart he and his daughter become. This is definitely not what either of us wants, but Alycia, with her rude, smug attitude seems to find joy in keeping Anthony and Arielle apart. She loves to brag to Anthony about her "new man" (as if it would make him jealous). Anthony always reacts calmly with her, but blows up a little when he talks to me about

Alycia's boyfriends. Understandably, his main concern was his daughter and what kind of men Alycia was allowing in Arielle's presence.

Predictably, Arielle, now a teenager, seems to be taking some cues from her mother. She is fiercely protective of her mother, and this protection includes withholding information from her father. She and Anthony use to talk two or three times a week. He would drop everything to chat about "what he's missed," and she would delight in telling him everything.

Additionally, she would ask about me and my niece Jade who she met at a Thanksgiving gathering at my mother's home. Anthony and I gave Arielle her first sleepover that night, and Jade was the only girl invited. Arielle and Jade are now pen pals or "email/text pals," and they talk often, but now Arielle seems to only call her father when she wants or needs something.

I'm not sure if he even notices because when he is not being a workaholic, he is being an alcoholic. I notice the purposeful calls though. He is like a bank now, not only spitting out money to Alycia for alimony and child support, but also sending additional money to Arielle for things like clothes, shoes, and food. He bought Arielle a cell phone, and he pays the bill for it.

This created a huge disagreement between Anthony and Alycia, mainly because she wants a new phone too, and she wants him to pay for her phone as well! She has some nerve! She gets a free cell phone from the government with a free set of minutes every month. Alycia will accept handouts, but she's under the impression that she should be given more, and she's not willing to work for it. Somehow, she is getting a monthly disability check for "debilitating migraines." I have never heard of such nonsense, but I'm sure that there's more to it than that.

I was extremely proud of Anthony when he finally told her off after she kept putting Arielle up to hinting about Alycia needing a new phone. He fusses when Alycia asks for extra money, so she figured it out – just get Arielle to ask for various things that she "needs," and he hands it over with no problem. With long acrylic fingernails filed to dangerously sharp points, I want to poke Anthony in his eyeballs to check to see if he is blind and if the rest of his senses are intact.

Of course the extra money that he has been sending was not being spent on Arielle, but whenever she asks for money, he sends it to Alycia. I pointed out that he could send money to his mother or sister for Arielle, and he did a few times, but I'm sure the money still ended up in Alycia's pocket. He wouldn't admit it, but he knew it did too, so why bother with middlemen?

After meeting them only once, I now talk to his mother and his sister occasionally. According to Angie, Arielle is usually poorly groomed, poorly dressed and extremely hungry whenever she drops by to check on her, or when she picks her up after school to come and stay for a weekend. Jacinda says that Arielle goes into a quiet, depressed state whenever it is time for her to return home after a weekend away from home. Even my niece Jade mentioned that Arielle has said often, "I wish I could come and live with you."

Of course, Anthony's mother and sister told him what was going on, but I have not told him everything that Jade has been telling me. Jade thinks it is cute that Arielle wants to be her "cousin", but the other information that Jade provides about Arielle's problems rings severe alarms for me.

Above all, I didn't want to argue with Anthony about this situation; every time we talked about it, I offered my opinion because he asked for it. However, we disagreed on the way to get from point A to point B. I hated arguing with him, and that's exactly what will happen again because this was a subject which we did not see eye to eye on all the delicate points. Delicate. That's exactly how he wants to treat the situation, as if something or someone will break.

On the other hand, I want to move in swiftly and remove Arielle from the situation. Even if she is confused or angry about it at first, she will get over it and realize that she is living in much better circumstances with me and Anthony. Ultimately, I bow out of the conversation because it really isn't any of my business, which Anthony has rudely pointed out more than once, when he was inebriated, of course.

Arielle's reaction to her mother's neglect is fiercely protective. She becomes angry and rebellious if she hears anyone criticize her mother. She once yelled at Anthony, "She's a single mother; thanks to you!

She's doing the best she can Daddy!" He was trying to find out what happened to $50 he sent for her. Arielle knew nothing about the money, and he slipped and accused Alycia of using it for cigarettes, booze, or some other nonsense. Arielle yelled, and he bit his lip rather than discipline her. Oh my gosh! I didn't agree, but I kept my thoughts to myself because we are not married. I'll save that disagreement for when we are *if we ever make it to that point!*

I tried to encourage Anthony to take Alycia to court for full custody because obviously, she was taking advantage of him, but he refused with the excuse that it would hurt Arielle too much. She's lived with only her mother all her life, with the exception of when she was an infant and her parents were together. I reasoned with him that Arielle is old enough now to understand the reality of the situation, so he needed to have that conversation with her to see how she really felt about her living situation.

What did she want? I could see it from both sides, and I understood how Arielle could have a jumble of emotions as far as her mother was concerned, but from everyone who I have talked to about Arielle, her life seems extremely sad and lonely. The only time she seems to be happy is when she is with her grandmother, with her aunt, with the few friends that she has, and definitely when she is with her father. To make matters worse, Anthony's side of the family is the only family that Alycia and Arielle have. Neither Alycia's parents, nor her brother acknowledges that she and her daughter even exist.

Her wealthy parents disowned her as a pregnant teen when she refused to give up her child for adoption. Her racist older brother also disapproved of her relationship with Anthony. When he learned that she was pregnant by her black boyfriend, he tried to convince her to get an abortion. He was going to pay for it and promised not to let their parents know with the condition that she stop seeing Anthony. When she refused, he stopped speaking to her.

When her parents discovered that she was pregnant, they sent her away to a boarding school. Alycia stayed for a few weeks, but then she ran away with the help of a group of friends. Alycia's parent's accused Anthony of helping Alycia leave the boarding school, and they got the police involved. Alycia vanished, and she stayed in the shadows for weeks. Her parents even started thinking that something terrible happened to her.

Of course, Anthony had nothing to do with Alycia's disappearance, but the whole story became quite a scandalous issue once it was covered in the media. Anthony's father who was the chief of police, intervened by hiring a team of private investigators to find Alycia and clear his son's name. They found her, returned her to her parent's home, and for a while her life settled down. Alycia's parents set strict rules for Alycia to follow including staying as far away from Anthony as possible, but they attended the same high school, so they saw each other there until school officials insisted that pregnant Alycia attend the city's alternative school to finish her senior year.

Without Anthony's consent, Alycia agreed to give the baby up for adoption, and this pleased her parents. However, after giving birth, Alycia changed her mind, called Anthony to the hospital, and told her parents that she intended to keep her daughter. She even had a name for her, Arielle, after her favorite princess.

Her parents wanted no parts of this fiasco. They were members of the social elite of Scottsboro, Arizona, and this would certainly sully their respectable reputation. They gave her an ultimatum: give the baby up for adoption, or never return to their home again. Alycia chose the baby. Her parents had her belongings delivered to the Wallace residence the next day. Alycia reacted to their rejection first by rebelling then with indifference. She started looking out for #1 and even though she was a new mother, the baby was not #1.

Consequently, the Wallace family accepted Alycia and Arielle with open arms. Anthony's father wasn't pleased with the situation at first, but he was happy to counsel his son about doing the right thing: legitimizing his family. The day after Alycia's 18th birthday, Anthony and Alycia got married at the justice of the peace's office which was housed in the same building as the Scottsboro police department.

With only the justice of the peace, Mr. and Mrs. James Wallace, Angelique Wallace, and baby Arielle Duchovny (Alycia's maiden name) in attendance, 18 year old Anthony and Alycia were proclaimed husband and wife. From that office, they walked to another office in the building and applied for their baby's name change to Arielle Marlyce Wallace. With that, Alycia legally erased her ties to her family and joined another family all in less than two hours.

Just as his father did at his age, Anthony joined the army and went away to basic training. Alycia did not want him in the military; she wanted him to get a job, find a place for them to live, and immediately start acting like adults. Anthony, however, wanted to accept his parent's help which included living with them, following their rules, working and saving money, and Alycia going to community college or trade school once Arielle was one or two years old. Anthony's mother and sister helped tremendously with raising Arielle to allow for this to happen. Instead, this care enabled Alycia's spoiled, lazy, neglectful, selfish tendencies. She didn't want to go to school, learn a trade, or find a job. She wanted to lie around and get pampered like she was the queen of the castle.

Up until this point, Alycia and Angie were somewhat friendly towards each other, but something happened between them while Anthony was away, and their relationship went cold. Angie declared that she never wanted to talk about it, and Alycia became adamant about moving out of the Wallace home; she wanted a place of her own. Angie adored Arielle and abhorred Alycia.

Eventually, Anthony and Alycia moved out of his parent's home and into the apartment complex where Alycia and Arielle still live today. The marriage barely lasted two years, and soon Anthony was living at his parent's home again. With Anthony away on active duty, it took a while for the divorce to finalize, but when it was final, Alycia came out on top, or so she thought. She got custody of Arielle, monthly alimony, monthly government assistance, and the medical declaration that she was disabled and could not work which resulted in additional assistance from the government.

Now, this arrangement might have been ideal when Arielle was a child, but now that she is a teenager and times have changed as well as the monetary requirements to keep up with that change, Alycia needs more, wants more, and uses her daughter as an excuse whenever she can.

I've spent quite a bit of time with Anthony and Arielle, and she is simply precious to me. Just as the desert sands crave the rain, so does Arielle crave attention and affection. Based on research, I tried to explain to Anthony that a neglectful mother plus an absent father equaled Arielle seeking love, affection and attention in all the wrong places. He stopped listening to me and took offense when he heard "absent father." We had an extremely ridiculous argument about my choice of words, and he went home and drowned his sorrows in a bottle.

So, the subject of pursuing joint custody was off limits. The information that Jade shared with me about Arielle bothered me to the core, and I felt deceitful keeping it from him, but I will do damn near anything to avoid arguing with him. *Enough was e damn nough.*

Speaking of avoiding arguments, another one of our hot button issues was the amount of alcohol he now consumes and why the hell I care enough to put up with it. Being a cop didn't help the matter either. Anthony has a predictable pattern of working long hours, and then spending long hours afterward at the Blue Light Sports Bar, the spot for alcoholic cops, firemen, paramedics, security guards and military personnel. At first, I hung out with Anthony and his cop buddies at the Blue Light, but that got old faster than a loaf of bread on a supermarket shelf. Loud, drunk, obnoxious cops were definitely a turn off.

Anthony has several moods when he is drunk and they all depend on what he is drinking: beer – harmless, but loud and obnoxious; wine/ mixed drinks – cheerful, laid back, and easy going; hard liquor – either extremely argumentative or extremely horny. I could only deal with him during and after drinking wine or mixed drinks. Otherwise, I didn't want to be anywhere near him. It was during his inebriated moments that I seriously contemplated breaking up with him. I did not sign up for this type of relationship! This was the type of shit that I so desperately wanted to get away from!

The Anthony that I fell for had some baggage, yes, but otherwise he had his shit together! He still worked out regularly, but the increase of alcohol consumption was taking a toll on him physically. He looked like an entirely different person after drinking, and for days later he even smelled different! Alcohol consumption was making him slower and sluggish, and he became frustrated more easily because he was so accustomed to being completely on top of everything.

It was very difficult for me to see him perform at less than his best because I've only seen him at his best. He has become everything to me, and I certainly thought that we would make it. It took such a long time for me to give in and recognize our relationship as a commitment, and now I was having serious doubts. I love him with all my heart though, no doubts about that.

There are no other men standing in his way as there was Clayton in the past. At times, I not only have to convince myself, but I also have to convince Anthony that I only want to be with him. It's easy to understand why with the way our relationship started, the way it progressed, and the incredible obstacles that almost tore us apart.

Alcoholism. Is this just another obstacle that we must face and overcome together? Why couldn't our relationship just be problem free? I sat thinking about this the other day, and it led me to some of my other worries that are hard to ignore.

Anthony has some passive aggressive tendencies that are kind of scary when I closely analyze them. One day, I feel, he is going to snap, and I don't want to be anywhere near when it happens. When I start thinking this way, I can't help but compare his behavior to the overtly aggressive tendencies of my ex-husband. My experiences with him caused me to have severe anxiety attacks for months after he died. I sit and think and actually over analyze these thoughts. I try to remember if I ever had these uneasy feelings when I was with Clayton or D.

As much as I analyzed it, the answer was always the same. No. Even though our relationships were short lived and fraught with problems, there was never anything about either man that I could possibly compare to Tim's behavior and nothing about them ever made me feel uneasy or anxious. I can't say the same about Anthony. It's the alcohol. It's the one thing that Anthony and Tim have in common. This alcoholism exacerbates everything: his ticking time bomb temper, passive aggressiveness, control freak tendencies, and something else that I still, to this day, have not been able to solve.

This brings me back to Alycia. Miss "Always #1". One of our most recent arguments involving Alycia brought out his hot temper. How I got caught in the middle still incenses me, and I'm pretty sure Alycia planned it that way. She called me, and tried to recruit me in her quest to get more money from Anthony.

~+~+~+~+~+~+~+~+~

"Really Alycia? You should be talking to him, not me. I don't control his money, and I can't influence him to do anything with it," I explained. I was simply amazed that she would ask for my help.

"Well, every time I ask, he makes it into a big deal. Then, even when Arielle asks for his help, he acts either suspicious or angry. I told him that we could send receipts if he did not believe us. Don't you think that's a good idea?" I rolled my eyes. I wanted to hang up, but that would just be downright rude.

"Yes, receipts would provide him with proof, but you need to talk to him about that, not me," I explained again, trying to keep my voice neutral.

"I'm asking for your help to convince him that we need a bit more. He'll listen to you. You know how much food, clothes and shoes cost. Arielle is growing like a weed, and she eats like a grown up. Things are really tight here, and I need more money per month to make ends meet," she requested. *Then get a damn job! Do something to help yourself! Quit asking for handouts!* I remained silent because I didn't know what to say.

"It's hard for me to do without things that I need, but it breaks my heart that Arielle has to go without things that she needs," Alycia sighed.

"Yes, I can definitely understand that," I agreed.

"But wait! You don't have any children, do you?" she sarcastically inquired. I could see the smirk on her face, and I immediately wanted to slap it off.

"No, I don't, but I grew up knowing what it felt like to not have things that I needed and especially things that I wanted. Sometimes, the "wants" were just a lost cause. You may want something, but you needed something even more. I don't have to be a mother to understand that concept," I threw back at her with a definite hint of attitude. This conversation needed to end now. *Silly bitch. Talk to him about this!*

"Well, I was wondering if maybe you could help? I know that's a lot to ask, but I have to do something," she desperately pleaded. *Is this bitch for real? Is she seriously now asking ME to send her ass some money? She must be on something! Whatever it is, it's draining her pockets dry and scrambling her brain.*

"Alycia, I would love to help. I really would, but can't you see how my involvement in this matter might cause all types of problems between me and Anthony?"

"Yeah, I guess you're right," she sighed.

I exhaled a sigh of relief because I was sure that she would ask me to keep it a secret from him. That surely would have caused an angry reaction from me.

"I've asked him to just send a certain extra amount every month, but every time we have that conversation, he gets all upset. It's not much extra, and I know he can afford it." I rolled me eyes and inhaled silently. *Can we end this conversation already?*

"Umm hmm," I mumbled as I looked at my fingernails. *I need, scratch that, want a new manicure. Guess what? I can get it because I have a job with disposable income that I can use for little extras.*

"I know that Anthony would not want Arielle to have to do without. He tells her that all the time, but that's exactly what's happening. She has to do without," Alycia explained. Silence from me. I looked at the dust on the ceiling fan blades and decided that I would clean them as soon as this call ended.

"The last thing I want to do is take him to court to petition for more alimony and child support, but if it comes to that . . ." she suggested.

"Then do what you have to do," I finished her sentence. What I really wanted to tell her was to get off her lazy ass and get a job. That would certainly help her make ends meet, but that was not my place. Just as it was not her place to call me to solicit my help. I wanted to tell her to lose my number and never call me again, but I did not want to alienate Arielle's mother. I wanted to keep the lines of communication open with her for Arielle's sake. The conversation ended abruptly after I lied that someone was ringing my doorbell.

That sneaky bitch. She talked to Anthony later that night and told him that I encouraged her to take him to court for more child support. He believed her. He didn't even let me explain. He didn't even want to hear about the rest of the conversation. He just took her word for it! We argued, and then we didn't speak to each other for a week.

When she went to court, she lost on her request for more alimony, but she won more child support. Nevertheless, she continued manipulating her child to slyly ask for more money every month. Every time she asked, Anthony copped an attitude with me. I vowed to never let Alycia dupe me again.

—5—

Angry Alcoholic with Evidence

Afer a week of not talking, we finally started seeing each other again. I was leery of Anthony's behavior so much now that I was beginning to be more and more guarded when I spent time with him. It felt weird, and I didn't like it. I avoided him by working over a lot. It was easy to pull off because there was so much that needed to be done at the store.

One evening, Anthony called and told me that he needed to see me, and we needed to talk immediately. I could tell that he had been drinking, so I stalled for nearly two hours until he called me again and impatiently demanded, "Amina, get your ass over here right now, or I will come over there." I didn't want him driving in his condition and he knew this, so I dropped my book, quickly dressed, and rushed over to his apartment. He was sprawled on his couch with an empty vodka bottle on the coffee table. It was the first thing that I noticed when I walked in. I dropped my purse on the table, stood there and looked at him. He glared at me with red, irritated eyes.

"Seriously, Amina? Are you trying to provoke me with this bullshit?" he asked in an irritated tone. His voice sounded like his throat was raw.

I looked at him with wide, questioning eyes and quietly asked, "What bullshit Anthony?" He tried to get up; it was too much for him, so he collapsed back down on the sofa. I looked down at him, disguised my disgust and remained calm. Clearly drunk, he was ripe and ready to argue.

After composing himself, he stood up quickly, stumbled a bit, but he managed to stomp over to the dining room table. He grabbed a piece of paper and "stumble stomped" back into the living room. He stopped directly in front of me. I looked up at him and tried to keep my eyes neutral, but it was so difficult because I was 50% scared and 50% angry. He shook the paper at me. I had no idea what it was.

"What is that Anthony?" I asked with my eyebrows raised and forehead wrinkled to show that I was clearly baffled.

"You know damn well what it is!" he hissed. His eyes were like flames. I couldn't help but think about Tim and some of the things he put me through – things that Anthony knew great detail about! *Why was he doing this? Did he fall and bump his head? Does he have amnesia? Was he trying to traumatize me? Did he forget how much I suffered?*

"No, I don't. Let me see that!" He held the paper up high, out of my reach and continued to glare at me. Avoiding his angry gaze, I tried once again to grab it, hoping that his reflexes were off, but he snatched it out of my reach, so I gave up, put my hands on my hips, and glared at him.

"I'm not in the mood to play games with you," I stated with finality. He swayed a bit, but he continued his angry staring and holding the paper up high where I couldn't reach it. Hell, I couldn't even see it! It was such a challenge for me to remain calm with Anthony during alcoholic times like these. It would have been so much easier for me to say, "Fuck this! I'm out! I don't need this drama in my life!" because I've had my fill of this type of nonsense. Regardless, I continued to at least try to react with care and concern. He was angry with me, I didn't know why, but I intended to find out instead of taking the easy way out and just walk out on him. I kept looking in his eyes and trying to find my Anthony in there. I tried the loving route.

"What are we doing? Why are you angry? Let's talk this out. Sit down baby," I soothed as I gently nudged him toward the couch. He stood there like a statue at first, looking down at me with a stone face, and then he moved an inch.

"Don't try that shit with me," he grumbled, but I ignored him and continued urging him toward the couch. He wouldn't comply until I stopped pushing him toward it, and even then he would not sit until

I moved back an inch. *I was going to sit next to him, but damn! Fuck it! No thanks! Sit there by yourself. Drunk ass!*

"I don't want to argue, okay?" I whispered and looked down at him. His fiery gaze did not cool down, not even one degree.

"May I please see that paper? I asked calmly. Even though he was sitting, he was holding the folded letter out of my reach, so I could not grab it. He was staring deeply into my eyes as if he was trying to find the answer to a complicated question.

"Will you at least tell me what it is? I pleaded. *Damn! I'm not going to keep this nonsense going much longer!* My patience was wearing very thin, like a frayed rope with only one thread holding it together. His angry gaze made me uncomfortable, exposed, and dirty. I didn't have anything to hide, but he was staring at me as if trying to read my deepest, darkest secrets.

"What?!!" I screeched in an elevated tone as I shrugged my shoulders and threw my hands in the air. *I'm no damn criminal, so why the hell was he treating me like I had committed a terrible crime!*

"I'm just trying to figure out how you could tell me you love me and make me think that I'm the only one, and then turn around, in the blink of an eye, and cheat on me!" he boomed. Spit flew out of his mouth and the pure volume of his voice rattled my bones. My knees felt weak, and my heartbeat increased rapidly. He was seriously scaring me.

Is this the moment that I have unknowingly feared for so long? Is this the bothersome thing that I have never figured out? Is he about to snap? Would he hurt me? Why does he think I'm cheating? He's already made up his mind because of whatever is on that paper, so that means he has some type of proof. Or maybe, he's faking it with the hope of getting some type of confession from me? But I don't have anything to confess! He thinks that I cheated. Oh God! Do I need to leave now? Will he let me leave? Shit! I don't know what to do!!! What the hell is on that paper?

"Maybe I should leave," I suggested and wondered with a smidgen of terror if he would actually let me go.

"Oh! That's your damn answer to everything, isn't it?" he roared without moving. I looked at him with huge questioning eyes.

"When the going gets tough, Amina gets going!" *That's not true!*

I've stayed with his ass this long! There were many times that I wanted to throw up my hands in surrender, sprint away screaming, but I stayed. Unbelievably, I could probably count 99 reasons why I should break up with him, and only 1 real reason why I should stay. Love is a powerful force. I haven't given up on him . . . yet. If he keeps pushing . . .

I moved an inch away from the couch because I had no idea about the cheating that he was referring to. "Yeah, instead of facing the problem and working to solve it, Amina punks out and has to **escape**!" he accused with heavy emphasis on that last word.

Awww shit! Not again! He's talking about Clayton. I thought we had moved past all that. Obviously, he has not. So, he knows that I have been in contact with Clayton. I should have told Anthony about it, but since it was work related, I thought nothing of it.

I stood up, grabbed my purse from the coffee table, and took one step toward the door. He quickly and clumsily moved in front of me to block my path.

"No, you're not leaving until you explain this shit!" he hollered in my face. I squinted. Despite my impatience and innocence, a shiver snaked its way up my spine because I was slightly afraid of what he was about to show me. A tiny ball of fear mixed with anxiety was forming in the pit of my stomach. I refolded my arms in front of myself to try to coax it away as I braced myself for his angry revelation.

"Tell me why there are so many calls to Dayton, Texas from your cell phone?" he demanded loudly. *Really? This is what you are so upset about? You have drunk yourself to oblivion because of some damn phone calls? Sheesh! What the hell is wrong with him? If he has trust issues that are this damn bad, maybe I really don't need to be with him! Maybe it's time to surrender!*

"Seriously, you need to calm down," I warned. He unfolded the bill and showed me all the numbers he highlighted. *He fucking highlighted the numbers! In three different colors! He actually sat down and highlighted every call to Dayton! What the fuck? How long has he been doing this?*

I shook my head and rolled my eyes at him, "Those are all for work, Anthony, and you know it! Have you forgotten that the corporate headquarters for USDSI is located in Dayton?" I answered calmly.

Maybe he really does have alcoholic amnesia or something. Oh shit! Please tell me that I did not slip and call Clayton's cell phone on my - excuse me - Anthony's cell phone! Still, every call and conversation between us has been entirely work related.

"You think I'm stupid, don't you?" he sneered. He made an ugly face, and I looked away. This argument was starting to feel painfully familiar.

"Yeah, I figured out that those calls to Dayton were work related, but three calls stuck out like sore thumbs because they were to a different number, and they lasted 30 minutes or more each!" he yelled. *Wow! He's done some clever detective work on that phone bill! Well, it's time to get my own damn cell phone. It was nice while it lasted, but I can certainly afford my own phone. So, he can take his phone, his highlighters and his suspicions and shove them down his throat!* Desperately, I looked at the door because I needed to leave right at that minute. He stepped toward me and stood directly in my face. *Dammit Anthony! Can't you see that you're scaring me?*

"I called the number, and guess who answered?" he hissed in a raspy voice, "Clayton Burrell." I was too scared to say anything. Anxiety was rolling rapidly in my belly, and I feared that it would attack any second and leave me breathless and uncontrollably shaking.

"Hasn't he told you about our conversation?" he mocked, and I simply stared in disbelief. *No, he hasn't. I haven't talked to him in a while. Why hasn't Clayton mentioned that Anthony called him? Maybe Anthony is bluffing, and he just looked up the name and number in a directory or something? Maybe he's trying to get me to incriminate myself. Well, it's not working!*

"Why did you call to talk to him? What was so damn important that you had to call him one night at 9:30? You slipped didn't you? If it was business, why didn't you use your office phone?" he questioned as he looked down at the page.

"In fact, two calls were at night, outside of business hours. What do you have to say about that, huh?" he taunted in my face, making me flinch. I couldn't say anything because it seemed so ridiculous.

Actually, it was so obvious. The store closed at 9:00, and I often worked until closing and well beyond. If I wanted to hide any calls from him, I could have simply called him from my home or office phone as he suggested. The truth of the matter is that I did slip. I should have made all of those calls from my office phone, but using the cell phone made it so much easier to take care of business whenever and where ever I needed to get it done. I didn't think anything about it until right at this very moment. *Which is why I'm so glad that I finally submitted my application for a company cell phone. That should put a definite end to rampant bullshit like this!*

"I'm waiting. Tell me why you called him! Wait! Don't say anything! I think I know. It was time for an **escape**! Your life was too stressful at the moment. Your boyfriend was drinking too much, and you just needed to get away, so Clayton could fuck your cares away!" he yelled with wild eyes. I stared in disbelief and struggled to keep the disgust from exploding on my face. His breath smelled like a dead skunk, so I couldn't help but frown as he yelled at me, but I refused to lose my temper. *Yes, I need to escape all right. Escape this situation and never look back! This is some bullshit!*

"Will you please calm down? Yes, I called him, but it was not for what you are thinking. Yes, it was outside of business hours, but that's only because I had been trying to call him and missing his calls. I had to schedule a time to talk to him and these were the only free time slots when he could talk. Clayton is one of USDSI's new corporate attorneys and he was assigned the Southeastern Region's Safety and Security Project that I've been working on for months now," I explained.

Anthony popped his lips before growling like Tony the Tiger, "Grrrreat! That's just fucking great! Fuck me running! The one man who you would drop everything for is now working for the same company? And you have to talk to him? **Shit!**" he shouted as he paced about the room for a few seconds, and then he was right back in my face. The anger seemed to have cooled down a few degrees, but he was still livid.

"Why didn't you tell me about this last month when you made these calls?" he asked in a slightly softer tone. *Can I breathe now? Is he starting to calm down?* I shrugged my shoulders and looked down. My anxious stomach quivered violently. Tears threatened to surface, but I inhaled deeply and sucked them back in.

"For one, I didn't want to argue with you like this," my voice trembled, *Oh shit, here come the tears.* "Two, I didn't quite know how to bring it up. Not to mention that I didn't really think it was such a big deal. How was I to know that you were scouring my phone calls looking for incriminating evidence? Three, we haven't even been talking like we use to talk, so I just haven't had the opportunity to talk to you about anything really. Honestly, I was going to talk to you about this. It just slipped my mind," I tried to explain. *Lame excuses, but all true. Sounds feasible, but his drunken ass probably wouldn't buy it. He is not the least bit reasonable, understanding, or sensitive when he is drunk.*

"But what did you talk to him about?" he asked in still a softer tone, but it had an accusing edge to it, like he already knew what we talked about. *Why didn't you ask him this when you supposedly called him? See! I'm not getting caught up in your police tactics! He probably didn't even speak to Clayton!*

I looked him directly in the eyes. "Other than the information from the virtual tours, safety and security audits, video surveillance, numerous reports, and lawsuit implications, we didn't talk about anything else. I told him that I was surprised to see his name on the list of attorneys, and he congratulated me on my VMM promotion. We talked about the current case that he and his team were working on, we went over some specific numbers for several stores that are in trouble, read through some transcripts from interviews, and that was about it," I explained.

That's almost everything. Of course Clayton told me how much he missed me. Of course he tried to solicit a meeting between us. Of course the idea was tempting, but I did not accept it. I stuck to business and shut Clayton down quickly. Anthony has his number, so he can get a complete recap from him. Clayton's recall would probably match mine entirely because every time, he tried to drift into personal areas of conversation, I moved the conversation right back to business issues.

"Shit! Don't tell me that this means you are going to have to work with him directly?" *Yep Anthony. This is exactly what it means.* "Wait! Amina! Did you see him or talk to him when you went to Dayton a while back?" Anthony asked, with once again angry eyes, as he threw down the bill and plopped on the couch.

"No, I did not see or talk to him when I went to Dayton. He hadn't even been hired on, and I was working on something totally different back then. What if I do have to work with him directly? Dang, this is not a big deal! You really don't trust me, do you? Do you even believe the love that I have for you is real?" I asked, afraid of his answers. Gingerly, I sat beside him on the couch. I hoped that we could move past this tonight and try to get to a happy place.

"I do trust you, but I don't trust him," he scowled and let out an irritated sigh. *It sure doesn't feel like you trust me! I can't wait to call Clayton to see if Anthony called and interrogated him!* Anthony grumbled something under his breath, and then he gave me a disgusted glance. Once again, my patience was hanging on by a single frayed fiber, and I was afraid of what I would say or do if it broke.

"Will you continue to trust me when I have to work with him directly?" I ventured as I moved an inch closer to him. He turned abruptly, moved away, glared at me because he did not like my line of questioning, and glanced toward the door. "You can leave now," he dismissed me with a wave of his hand.

"Hold up! Wait a minute!" I yelled, a bit on the angry side now.

"You're judging this situation from the past. Back then, I had strong feelings for him and my feelings for you were just starting. Things have completely changed." He ignored me, rose from the couch, and strode into the kitchen. His boxers were terribly wrinkled like he had worn them for several days in a row. His unshaven face and scraggly hair were also signs that he was neglecting his personal hygiene and grooming. I hated seeing him this way. He pulled another large bottle of vodka from the refrigerator and grabbed what looked like a dirty glass.

"Baby, don't drink that right now, please! We need to finish talking about this," I begged.

He turned, he glared at me, his nostrils flared, and he hissed through his teeth, "Get out!" *Oh my gosh! Really? Okay. Fine! You don't have to ask me twice dragon breath!* I shot him an injured look, grabbed my purse, and left without hesitation and without looking back. I wanted to slam the door on my way out, but I didn't. I refused to stoop to his level of nonsense.

Once outside, I deeply inhaled the frigid night air, and immediately my stomach felt like it would collapse, and my chest felt like it would explode. I slowly walked down the stairs with hot tears bursting from my eyes. *Oh God! What just happened? Why did he react in such a volatile way? Alcohol. I know that's the reason why, but damn! Would things have been any better if he were sober? If I told him everything as it happened?* The tears rolled down my face and started to drench my sweater as I opened the car door. I got in, sat down, and glanced back up at his apartment. *Should I wait a few minutes, go back up, and try to talk to him? Hell no! He's too upset and too drunk right now. He needs to cool down and sober up. I need to take my ass home and try to forget about him. He's no good for me anymore.*

I drove home slowly and tried to think about things from his perspective. Several weeks ago, we discussed moving in together again. The original conversation started with the idea of getting married and having children. I shut down marriage and children almost immediately. Moving in together was not such a bad idea though. I would think about it like a trial run, so this time, I agreed because now it made sense to me, and I was tired of him just spending the night or vice versa.

He had asked about moving in several times before, but I wasn't ready. We both needed time and space after Vickie's death. I told him that once we were way past all that hurt and complication, I would be ready for anything he suggested: living together, then marriage, and then children in that order. *For the first time in a long time, I was open. I was down for whatever. But now look! Just because I wanted to avoid an argument and suspicion, he's angry. But wait! What about trust? Why does he feel the need to highlight my calls on a damn phone bill? Has he been doing that all along? Have I moved all the way back to square one? This is almost a damn repeat of my marriage to Tim! Maybe we are not ready to settle down after all? Maybe I need to totally rethink our relationship?*

This time, it took two weeks for Anthony to snap out of it. I was so tempted to go and purchase my own cell phone, but I worried that doing so would make it look like I had something to hide. Then I thought that I should get a phone and keep it a secret. That thought quickly left my mind because it was ridiculous. Secrecy was what started this whole quarrel. I realized that I should have been honest with him about everything. I also realized that I was scared to reveal the truth. *I was scared of Anthony. I was scared of how he might react if I told him the truth even though I had not done anything wrong. Wow! Is this how abusive relationships start?*

I felt dejected and lonely during the weeks that we did not speak, and I started blaming myself even though I knew in my heart that alcohol was the fuel behind that fiery fight. I wondered to myself if I had some type of "abused wife syndrome" or if I was simply a glutton for punishment, dysfunctional relationships or whatever.

Why was I hanging on to him? Clearly, our relationship was not going to make it past this obstacle. I don't want to be with another alcoholic, bad tempered, suspicious, jealous, mistrusting man. How long would it be before our verbal battles became physical melees? I shivered at the thought of Anthony hitting me.

—6—

Aftermath

Anthony called me at work and asked if he could take me out to lunch. Somberly, I accepted his invitation. He showed up with a bouquet of flowers and an embarrassed smile. I looked at him with the flowers and I felt awkward as well. The ride to Sally's Sandwich Shop was uncomfortable because we were completely silent. He jumped out of the vehicle to open the door for me, and I let him. It was a gentlemanly gesture, but it was only a drop in the bucket of nice things that he would have to do to make up for that terrible argument and his subsequent dismissal of me from his home.

Rashad noticed my sullen mood several times during those two weeks, but he kept our conversations strictly about business. I wanted to confide in him and ask him questions to get a male perspective, but I chickened out of each opportunity. I knew that if I initiated conversation with him, he would not walk away. Out of respect for my relationship with Anthony, he passed several opportunities to simply ask me, "What's wrong?" I shook my head sadly when I thought about Anthony's ultimatum. Because of it, I chose to give up on two very good friendships with excellent communication.

We ordered our sandwiches, and finally he apologized for going off the deep end. Everything came spilling out, and he admitted that alcohol intensified everything: suspicion, jealousy, anger. He moved closer and touched my bare arm. Absent was the usual attraction, the sexual sizzle, the breathless anticipation that I usually felt when he touched me. *Okay, that's my sign. My attraction to him is fizzling out, so we are getting closer to the end now. *Sigh* Never thought it would end like this. I never would have guessed it in a million years!*

"I am so very sorry for talking to you that way and treating you so terribly," he whispered. Sadly, I looked over at him, and I could see the sorrow and pain in his face. He looked like he was going to cry. I wanted to reach over and touch his soft, curly hair, kiss his smooth, soft lips, but I kept my hands to myself. We needed to end this debacle before the situation got out of control. *No sense in prolonging the inevitable.*

"Will you please forgive me baby, and give me another chance?" *Another chance to do what? Get incredibly drunk, mad at me, lose your temper, and possibly beat my ass to a bloody pulp? No thank you.*

"You admitted that alcohol is the catalyst, so what are we going to do about it?" I asked, smoothly ignoring his question. It was time for me to issue an ultimatum.

"What do you mean 'we'?" he asked with a grin, "I'm the one with the problem." *Thank you Jesus! He finally admitted that he has a problem!* I touched his shoulder, and words that I couldn't believe started spilling from my mouth.

"We're in this together baby. If you need my help, I'll be there for you," I assured him as I wondered to myself if I really meant that. *Where was all this coming from? I should be telling him that it's over, that I can't take this anymore, and that I refuse to put myself in the position to be terrorized by my husband again.* He moved closer and hugged me.

"That's exactly what I needed to hear baby," he whispered before covering my lips with a soft kiss. I let him kiss me for a few seconds, and then I pulled away. *No spark, no flame, nothing. Yes, it is time to end it.*

"What are you going to do about it? I demanded. He looked uncomfortable talking about it, but I needed to know that he was going to take prompt action. He looked down and put his hands on his neck.

"Well, first of all, I already admitted that I have a problem, right?"

"So. . .?"

"I don't think it's that bad, so I'm just going to quit drinking. Cold turkey," he explained and looked up at me. *That's it? That's your plan? Not enough buddy!*

"It is bad Anthony. In fact, it's terrible," I whispered angrily, "It's so terrible that when you get drunk, I am scared of you! I am terrified that you are going to completely lose control and physically hurt me." I glared at him with, I'm sure, an ugly face.

"No, baby! No!" he grabbed me and embraced me gently. He caressed my face, kissed me tenderly; I relaxed a bit, but I still needed to hear something better.

"Except to love you, I would never put my hands on you. Ever. You have to believe that!" he pleaded.

"I did believe that until you started drinking so much, and you transformed into the monster in my nightmares," I murmured in a shaky, tear threatening voice. He squeezed me tightly and continued gently kissing the side of my face.

"No baby. No. No. No. Not even if I was drunk and out of my mind, I could never be that," he whispered his assurances and continued holding and kissing me until we noticed that the waitress was standing there waiting to serve our sandwiches. We were so engrossed in each other that neither of us even heard her approach, so we didn't know how long she had stood there watching us, listening to us, and waiting for us to acknowledge her presence. We disentangled from each other and waited.

She giggled, "Valentine's Day is in a couple of days, you know?"

We both smiled and separated an inch more. After she arranged his Philly cheese steak sandwich and my Italian chicken sandwich on the table, we finished our conversation.

"Anthony, I don't think quitting cold turkey is going to be enough," I said and looked down at the piping hot sandwiches on either side of the table. The plates were colorfully decorated with a small salad and a pickle wedge. Melted mozzarella cheese oozed down the side of my sandwich, and pepper jack cheese bubbled from his.

"Well, what else do you think I need? What? Do you think I need to go to AA or something?" he asked in an elevated whisper. I gave him a surprised look. He softened his expression and shrugged his shoulders.

"Actually, a support group or counseling is exactly what I was thinking about. I could ask Dr. Branson for a referral for you," I offered.

"Dr. Branson? What? You think I'm cray . . .?" Our eyes locked, and he realized what he was about to say. He took a large bite of his sandwich, and I took a bite of my pickle. I took my time chewing, and I waited for him to finish, but it seemed like he was going to conveniently try to change the subject when he looked out the large picture window at the looming clouds, took another bite of his sandwich, and started talking about the possibility of ice storms later.

"No, I don't think that you are crazy. I still see Dr. Branson. Do you think I'm crazy?" I challenged with a direct look into his eyes.

He held my gaze and answered, "Of course not baby. I don't think you're crazy. It's just that I don't think I'm that far gone with drinking that I need professional intervention. I can handle this on my own."

I chewed slowly and listened to his reasoning, and then I told him how I felt the same way at first. I also pointed out that I have not had a single anxiety attack since Vickie died. I hated bringing up her name, but she was part of this alcoholic equation, and he knew it.

"You're right baby. There's a substance abuse program and a counselor at CPD that I will check into. Will that be enough baby?" he asked with an animated expression. *Get serious! This shit is not funny!*

"I sure hope so," I surmised.

"Am I forgiven?" he asked with raised eyebrows. I just looked at him and tried to keep my face relaxed. *You fucked up. Hell no you are not forgiven!*

"I am truly sorry baby. I was so wrong for the way that I acted. I'm sorry for scaring you, not trusting you, and kicking you out. I'm sorry for everything!"

I bit my sandwich and chewed it slowly. I looked out the window again and ate two chips and a bite of pickle. He waited breathlessly for my answer, and I wanted to keep stalling him, but finally I answered.

"I forgive you, but I can't keep going through this! You have to get better because I don't think I'm strong enough to deal with alcoholism again. In fact, to be honest, I just don't want to deal with it. Can't you understand that?"

"Yes baby, I do. I'm going to beat this and come out on top. I promise you that," he said as he caressed my hand. *There he was touching my bare skin again and still . . . nothing.*

The remainder of our lunch date was perfect because we kept the conversation light. We didn't talk about my job or Clayton, and I was glad because I'm sure that probably would have started an argument. *Drunk or sober, Anthony hated the idea of me and Clayton working together. It's about to happen. How was I going to handle that?* We talked about the weather, current city events, and remodeling plans for my house. He told several jokes to further lighten the mood.

I was laughing when he walked me back into the store after lunch. Rashad saw us, gave me a funny look, and continued with what he was doing. Now, I really wanted to talk to him, but I guess that would just open a can of worms with Anthony if he found out that I was talking to my coworker about something other than work. *Put yourself in his shoes Amina! You wouldn't like it if he had a female friend that he confided in! Shit!*

The next morning, we met at the city park. He was there to run, and I was there to walk. He ran four laps around and then he caught up with me. He was sweating profusely, and the sweat smelled like alcohol. He noticed my wrinkled nose and let out a half laugh, half snort. *I'm glad you think that your funky sweat is funny Anthony!*

"Yeah, I know that I stink," he stated, "because my body is sweating out all of the alcohol that I have been recklessly consuming. We stopped at a bench, so I could retie my shoelaces and stretch. He bent down and put his arms on his knees. It was difficult not to look at him with concern on my face, and he immediately noticed it.

"I can get past this. Don't worry about me," he continued. I tried to find a dry spot to touch on him, but that was an impossible feat, so I just encouraged him to keep working on it.

"I'll stand by you. I'm not going to give up that easily," I assured. He looked up and the sun grabbed a hold of the greenish flecks in his eyes. He smiled at me and the deep dimple sunk in his cheek. *Finally. Something happened! My knees quivered. My stomach did its usual flip flop. Yes, I meant it. I love this man. I'll stand by him. He can count on me. He's worth it.*

"Thank you for saying that baby," he replied.

"I mean it. I'm lucky to have you. I love you," I said softly. I laughed, blew him a kiss, and ran away. He easily caught up with me, grabbed me and covered me with fiery kisses and smothered me in his hot, sweaty embrace.

—7—

Arielle's Agony

"Why don't you just ask him?" Jade exhaled. "He's your dad. He loves you and my auntie is really cool; she loves you too." Arielle sighed heavily and a single tear rolled down her cheek.

"But what about my mom?" Arielle whispered.

"What about her?" Jade asked while rolling her eyes and moving her neck. From what Arielle had been telling her for months now, her mother wasn't really interested in what happened to Arielle.

"She'll be all alone. I'm all she has," Arielle explained.

"Well, I can't tell you what to do, and I don't mean to be rude, but you can't have your cake and eat it too," Jade said with a hint of attitude.

Arielle laughed then asked, "What the heck does that mean?"

Jade giggled and answered, "I don't know, but my dad says it all the time when I ask for a lot of stuff."

"Yum . . . cakes sounds good," Arielle remarked.

"So, your mom still hasn't gone to the grocery store?" Jade asked in a high pitched voice.

"She said that she would because she had some money, but she hasn't gone yet."

"You don't have anything in the house to eat?"

"There's some peanut butter and some crackers."

"Is that all?" Jade quizzed.

"Some ketchup, mustard, pickles," Arielle listed as she looked through the refrigerator and cabinets, "Some ramen noodles, potatoes, pork and beans, rice, and tuna."

"Dang!" Jade blurted and sat up to adjust the phone on her shoulder.

"A jug of water and some ice," Arielle continued sadly, "but other than that our cabinets and refrigerator are so empty. But um . . . it's not just that."

"What else is happening?" Jade asked with wide eyes and in an even higher pitched tone.

"My mom has a new boyfriend," Arielle exhaled.

"Wow! That's great news! If she has a new man now, then she won't be lonely when you come to live with your dad! What's this new guy like? I hope he is better than the last one. Eeewww! He was scary," Jade babbled.

"He's . . . uh . . . he's okay. He took us to Playground Pizza last week," Arielle informed.

"That sounds good, even though you're too old for Playground Pizza and Patty the Platypus!" Jade giggled.

"But I love Patty the Platypus!" Arielle giggled and did an imitation of the character's voice. Soon, both girls were laughing hilariously and imitating the cartoon character who was the star of the restaurant that boasted "food and fun for everyone".

Suddenly, Arielle was quiet as Jade continued giggling and imitating the voice of Patty the Platypus from Playground Pizza. When Jade realized that Arielle was quiet, she stopped and listened. Jade heard a sniffle, and she wondered if her friend was crying on the other end.

"He's not as bad as the other guy, but he's not a good guy either. Not like my dad anyway," Arielle whispered.

"Well, no one will be like your dad because your dad is . . . your dad! How do you know that's he's not a good guy? You haven't known him that long. How long has your mom been dating him?" Jade inquired.

"It hasn't been long. Like two months, but I can tell he is not a good guy," she sniffed.

"But how can you tell? What did he do?"

Arielle was quiet. Jade listened to the silence for as long as she could stand it. "Arielle! Tell me!" she screeched.

Tears welled up in Arielle's eyes as she explained that he smokes and drinks a lot, and her mom does too.

"That doesn't make him a bad guy Arielle. My mom and dad smoke and drink too!" Jade compared.

"It's not just the drinking and smoking," Arielle huffed as her frustration started to grow.

"What is it then?" Jade impatiently asked. She was growing increasingly concerned as they talked. Just as Arielle was about to tell Jade everything, Alycia stomped in, slammed the front door, and immediately started complaining. Jade could hear her in the background. Arielle's mom made everything seem like it was Arielle's fault.

"Gotta go! I'll text you later," Arielle rushed off the phone. Jade stared into space for a few minutes, and then she called her Aunt Amina.

"Who were you talking to?" Alycia asked as she plopped down on the sofa and lit a cigarette.

"Heather," Arielle lied without a flinch. For some reason, her mother disliked Jade and didn't want Arielle talking to her. Jade was the nicest friend that she had. She never made a big deal about silly stuff like brand name clothes or shoes, who had the latest phone, or other dumb things that thirteen year olds seemed so concerned about. Arielle could relax when she talked to Jade, and the one time they were together at Miss Amina's Thanksgiving dinner, they became instant friends. They had a blast! They were honest with each other, they talked about smart things, they told each other jokes, they talked about their hopes, dreams and fears and they relaxed, laughed and enjoyed being preteen girls.

Since then, Arielle has been telling Jade everything that happened in her life, and Jade listened like a good friend. She gave her advice and encouraged her. She didn't judge her because she made mistakes. Instead, she shared her own mistakes. She didn't laugh at her because Arielle didn't know what was cool and what was not. She didn't say stupid things like her friend Heather does, and Jade didn't go back and tell other girls who teased her at school. *Heather is a mean, selfish, spoiled, rich bitch.* Arielle thought with a smirk.

"Why don't you ask Heather if you can sleep over tonight?" Her mother sucked on the cigarette, rested her curly blonde head back on the sofa, and closed her eyes without exhaling.

"On a school night Mama?" Arielle reminded. *Maybe she forgot what day it is again?* Her mother exhaled the smoke, and then she looked at her through the haze. She raised one eyebrow and sighed.

"Yeah, so . . . you did it before," her mother replied and pressed her lips into an O and let the smoke flow out of her mouth.

"I have a lot of homework to do, and I'm hungry," Arielle replied.

Her mother sucked on the cigarette again and held it in her mouth. Unblinking, as if in a daze, her mother blew the smoke into the air.

"Are you going to cook Mama?" Arielle inquired.

"No, Jeff wants to take me out to eat tonight," she said through a blanket of smoke.

"Just you?" Arielle asked in a tiny voice.

"Yep, just me!" she giggled, oblivious to her daughter's eminent need.

"Well, will you bring me something back?" Arielle asked quietly.

"Probably, yeah, I'll get a "to go" box because I'm sure I won't be that hungry," she grinned.

Arielle twirled a strand of her light brown, curly hair around her index finger. "Is that why you want me to sleep over at Heather's?" Arielle challenged, "So you and Jeff can make out?" Her mother didn't say anything. Instead, she smiled a huge smile and continued smoking.

Arielle went to her bedroom, slammed the door, and fell face first on her bed. *Why couldn't she go with them? She would not cause any problems. She wouldn't eat too much, and she would stay out of the way. That was it. She was in the way! She was in the way of her dad's relationship with Miss Amina, and now she was in the way of her mom's relationship with Jeff.* She didn't want to go to Heather's house. Heather was only nice to Arielle because her mother made her.

Heather's mom and Alycia knew each other from high school, but it seemed like they didn't really like each other now. According to Alycia, she and Arielle were Heather's family's charity case. They gave away clothes and food, and attempted to include Arielle in normal things for a girl her age.

Heather's mother also knew Alycia's mother, Arielle's grandmother whom she has never met. This was even more of a reason for Arielle to want to stay away from Heather and her family. She felt very jealous when she thought about it. Heather and her family have seen and talked to her grandmother, and she has not! Not even a picture! They probably get to do fancy country club rich things that rich people do in the presence of her grandmother, and she has never done that! She has an uncle, her mom's brother – his name is Ayden, whom she has never seen, and what if he has children? That means that she has cousins! This terribly angered Arielle, but she kept it to herself.

Furthermore, Heather's twin brother Heath was a jerk. Once when she slept over at their house, Heath came in the bathroom and peeked at her while she was in the shower. She was going to tell on him, but he begged her not to. He swore that it was an accident and convinced her that his parents would kill him if they found out. He gave her his allowance for the week, $20, and promised he would give her the next week's allowance as well. He seemed sincere when he apologized; she actually felt sorry for him, and the $20 was irresistible.

He made good on his promise the next week and gave her the other $20 stuffed inside a library book. Arielle never got a regular allowance from her mom. When her dad sent money for her, she rarely got any of it. Sometimes, her mother would give her leftover change, but it never amounted to more than $2 or $3.

The thought of spending the night at Heather's house forced a huge sigh to escape, and Arielle contemplated running away. Where would she go? Grandma Jacinda's? Aunt Angie's? No, they would only let her stay a couple of days then they would bring her straight back.

"Call Heather back and ask if you can spend the weekend with her," Arielle's mother called through the door. Arielle could hear her mother excitedly talking to Jeff on the phone. Arielle rolled her eyes because she hated him. He was tall and skinny. He had a bushy mustache that looked like it belonged on a Halloween costume. He wore cowboy boots, a cowboy hat, plaid shirts and tight jeans all the time. He stared at her and smiled a weird smile that made Arielle's skin crawl.

He never really wanted to include Arielle in anything that he and her mother did, and they were always going out and doing things - except for that stupid day at Playground Pizza, *what a joke,* and a trip to Riverside park. The picnic in the park was not fun either. Jeff and her mom went exploring for over an hour, and when they came back, they were both acting extremely weird: stumbling, falling, laughing loudly, and they attacked the food.

Arielle was glad that she ate while they were gone because they ate the rest of the food, and then they collapsed on the blanket and fell asleep. For the rest of that afternoon, Arielle sat by the river and watched the ducks, children playing on the other side, and the traffic that passed over the bridge in the distance. Even though her mother was less than fifty feet away, Arielle's loneliness was multiplied times ten that day.

Arielle knew that Jeff and her mother smoked more than just cigarettes. They also smoked marijuana and something else that Jeff sometimes brought in a funny shaped glass bottle with a long handle. They both drank a lot of alcohol. Sometimes there was more alcohol in the refrigerator than there was food.

Additionally, Arielle observed Jeff and her mother taking funny little pills. He brought them to Alycia in tiny zip top plastic bags. Once, he dropped one, it rolled under the couch and later Arielle picked it up, wrapped it in tissue, and hid it in her sock drawer. She vowed that she would show it to her dad the next time she saw him. *If that ever happened.*

Jeff had some weird friends who came looking for him sometimes. Arielle thought it was weird because her mom never invited his friends inside, and he always went out to talk to them. Alycia also warned Arielle to never open the door for Jeff's friends if she and Jeff were not there, not even with the chain on the door. This warning scared Arielle, but she didn't tell her dad about it because she didn't want him to get mad at her mom. *They argued enough already.*

Finally, she could hear her mom and Jeff having sex whenever he spent the night. Her mom was loud and he was a dirty talker. *Disgusting!* She was so embarrassed to be there when they were doing that. Even with headphones on or loud music blasting, she could still hear them through the thin apartment walls.

Once in the middle of the day, they were doing it and they were extremely loud, so Arielle decided to go outside and sit on the swings at the playground. Her next door neighbor, an elderly black woman, who always sat and looked out her front window as if she was waiting for someone, was sitting in her usual spot. As Arielle walked past her window, she said, "Your mother and her boyfriend are at it again, aren't they?" Surprised, Arielle only shook her head up and down, and then she ran across the parking lot to the sandy lot that housed the playground. *She didn't want to talk about it! Gross! It made her sick thinking about it!*

Not only did she hate the way Jeff looked at her, she hated the way Jeff looked at her mother, like an animal looking at its next meal. She thought about her dad. *Oh how she missed her daddy!* When he looked at her, his eyes lit up and he smiled all the time, except when he was angry or disappointed, and then he frowned a little and his forehead crinkled up. He never stayed mad for long though. That was love. He looked at Miss Amina the same way. His eyes lit up and crinkled around the edges. Arielle wished with all her heart that her mother would look at her like that.

She thought about Jeff again. *Maybe she should lighten up and give him a chance? He's only been around for a little while. Maybe he excludes her because he needs time to get to know her mom, and then he will start treating her like a stepdad should treat his stepdaughter. But wait! They're only still dating! Maybe he doesn't know how to treat the child of his girlfriend because he's never been in this type of relationship?* Arielle contemplated these questions as she sent Heather a text:

Arielle – My mom wants u to ask ur mom if I can sleep over Friday and Saturday.

Arielle waited. Usually, Heather answered instantly. She hoped that Heather would reply that her family was going out of town or something since they did that often. Arielle just wasn't ready to be anywhere near Heath. She would much rather stay at home, read, watch TV, or just stay in her room staring out the window than go and hang out with Horrible Heather and her evil twin Hideous Heath lurking in the shadows. Arielle giggled as she thought about the comic that she drew in her notebook that featured the characters that she created, Horrible Heather and Hideous Heath. She couldn't wait to show them to Jade! Arielle's thoughts were interrupted when her phone beeped with Heather's response:

Heather – I'm sleeping over @ Tiffany's this wknd.
Arielle – O. Ok.
Heather – Britney is coming 2. Ask ur mom if u can come.
Arielle – Ok.

Britney was cool. She was like Jade, not judgmental, not mean, and her family was not rich. This might be fun. Arielle thought. *But why didn't Tiffany invite me in the first place? Because Tiffany is a mean, snobby, rich bitch, that's why! Just like Heather.*

Heather – We r going skating Friday night, 2 Pancake Palace Sat. morning & then 2 the mall, so bring $$$.
Arielle – Ok!

Arielle's heart dropped whenever she heard the word money. When she asked her mother for money, the answer was always "No." Her dad had already sent her mom money this month. For the first time this year, her mom gave her $20, which Arielle spent on a new pair of jeans and a bag full of junk food. Her mother found the bag and ate two bags of the chips and a candy bar! Arielle was mad at her mother because she always invaded her privacy. If Arielle stuck her toe inside her mother's bedroom, Alycia had a fit and said things like, "Only adults are allowed in this room little girl!" Maybe she could ask grandma or Aunt Angie for some money for the weekend? No, she wouldn't do that because somehow it always gets back to her dad and then to her mom even if she asks them not to say anything. She still had the $40 from Heath. It was hidden in an old sweatshirt in the back of her closet. In all, she had $55 dollars saved, and she planned to keep saving until she had enough for a plane ticket or bus fare. She decided to get $15 from her stash.

Heather – Have u finished ur math & history hw?

Arielle – No, Y?

Heather – I need help, & ur super smart. Want 2 come over 4 dinner tonight, so we can do our hw 2gether?

Arielle – Ok.

Arielle knew what she meant. Heather was smart, but she was lazy. She would simply copy Arielle's answers. Dinner sounded nice though. Heather's mom was a stay at home mom too, but she cooked all the time. Heather's dad was a computer programmer, and her little sister Hillary was adorable. They even had a little fluffy dog, Heinrich. Arielle wished she had a dog. She had a fish once, but it died because she fed it too much. *The opposite would happen if she had a dog.*

Heather's family lived in a new subdivision down the street from Arielle's apartment complex. It was hard not to notice the difference in the apartment complex neighborhood and the subdivision. Her dull, gray neighborhood was mostly buildings, concrete, cars, and parking lots. Heather's neighborhood consisted of lush green landscapes, shrubbery, and colorful flowers. Everyone parked their cars in their garages, so their concrete driveways and sidewalks looked white and clean.

Arielle often wished that she had a family like Heather's or Jade's, and they lived in a nice neighborhood with grassy green lawns instead of a dingy gray apartment complex with asphalt and concrete.

Arielle's mom smiled a little when she learned that Arielle could go to Heather's for dinner and then stay to do her homework. She smiled even more when Arielle told her that she was invited to stay for the weekend, but she frowned when she learned that Arielle wasn't sleeping over that night.

"It's a school night Ma!" Arielle whined. *Why didn't her mom want her around tonight?*

"How long will you be out?" Alycia asked.

"Well, their dinnertime isn't until 7, and we are doing our math and history homework. We have a lot of math homework," Arielle answered. Alycia lit another cigarette, sucked on it, closed her eyes, and held the smoke in her mouth.

"It will probably be dark when we finish," Arielle offered, hoping her mother would change her mind.

"Girl, it's just down the street! You can run fast. If it's dark, run your ass home!" Alycia opened her eyes, laughed as she blew smoke into the air, and got ready for another draw. Arielle glared at her mother.

"Seriously, your friend and her brother can walk you to the gate if you're too scared," she giggled, "Even better, ask Hannah to drive you home!" She burst into laughter, not even noticing her daughter's angry stare as she finished smoking her cigarette, and then she hopped up from the couch and walked quickly to the bathroom to take a shower.

Arielle followed her, stood at the door and said, "I'm going to need some money for this weekend."

"For what?" was her mother's muffled reply.

"For the skating rink and after the sleepover, we are going to eat breakfast at Pancake Palace then to the mall," Arielle said hopefully.

"You know we don't have money for shopping," her mother scorned, "but I will give you a little for breakfast. The Palace has some pretty good $5 or less value meals. Maybe Heather's mom will pay your way into the skating rink if you ask?" Arielle rolled her eyes.

Why don't we have money for shopping? Or food? Or clothes? Or soap, shampoo and conditioner? Or cable TV? Or a home phone and internet? Or anything? Why is that mom? Britney's mom is a single mom too and they have all those things! Oh wait! Britney's mom has a job. Do I have to get a job, so we can have stuff like that?

Arielle stood at the door for a few minutes as her mother prepared to get in the shower. She was humming. Humming! *What was she so damn happy about?* Fighting back tears, Arielle went to her room and slammed the door again. She sat in the middle of her bed staring at her closet door for what seemed like forever. *She was so mad that she wanted to scream!* Realizing that she left her cell phone in the living room, she went to get it, and she heard someone tapping on the front door. Quietly, she hooked the chain.

"Who is it?" Arielle asked cautiously.

"It's Jeff, sweetie pie," he crooned. She rolled her eyes. Why was he so early? Arielle opened the door with the chain still on, peeked out, and then let him in. He stood tall in the doorway with his cowboy boots and cowboy hat. He walked in and removed the hat revealing a shock of dirty blonde hair. He looked Arielle up and down and said, "Howdy, little lady. Where's your mom?"

"She's in the bathroom," Arielle said without emotion. He walked into the living room, his boots clicking on the cheap laminate floor. He stopped just before sitting down on the worn out couch. Arielle walked past him on her way toward the hallway to go to her bedroom.

"Why aren't you getting ready to go?" he asked.

"Because I'm not invited," Arielle said glumly. With a surprised look, Jeff stood, adjusted himself, and sat back down. Arielle frowned, but she didn't say anything. *Really? This is Heath all grown up.*

"Sure, you're invited!" he said with a huge smile and a penetrating look into Arielle's eyes.

"Uh, no, she was invited over to her friend's house for dinner, and then they are studying," Alycia interjected. She walked in wearing black high heels, and a tight, short red dress. She had straightened her hair and put on a lot of makeup. She looked like the daughter on the "Married with Children" show that Arielle sometimes watched.

"Mommy, you look beautiful," Arielle exclaimed in awe of her mother's speedy transformation. Less than an hour ago, she was wearing a t-shirt, leggings, flip flops, no makeup, and her hair was in a messy curly ponytail high on top of her head.

"Thank you baby," she kissed the top of Arielle's head, "when are you going to Heather's?" Alycia feigned affection and concern although she was looking directly at Jeff and they were mouthing dirty words to each other. Without a word, Arielle went to her room, grabbed her backpack, and walked past them.

"I'm leaving now," she stated glumly. Arielle wasn't sure why she felt this way, but she was ready to leave so her mother could enjoy her date with Jeff. They were already kissing and feeling all over each other before she even made it to the door. Arielle noticed that Jeff seemed surprised that Arielle was sad about not being invited. *Maybe she was wrong about him?* She thought about how he looked at her when he fixed his tight jeans. *Maybe not.*

She walked on the sidewalk until she made it to the street that led out of the apartment complex. She ignored the cat calls and rude remarks from the men and boys in her neighborhood. *Animals.* She kept her head down, eyes forward, and she walked with a brisk pace like Britney taught her two years ago when she lived in this apartment complex. She would definitely ask Heather and Heath to walk her home because she hated walking alone at night.

Once inside the subdivision, it only took Arielle a few minutes to get to Heather's house. Arielle admired the green, manicured lawns, which looked like emerald carpets, the identical sidewalks and pruned shrubbery as she walked to Heather's house.

A tall lanky boy with blonde hair and blue eyes named Heath answered the door. He was such a jerk, and Arielle didn't trust him. She tried to stay as far away from him as possible. She refused to walk in front of him. Heather thought that they would make a "cute couple." The idea made Arielle's stomach gurgle and her head hurt.

"Oh, hi Arielle. Come in," Heath invited, "Heather's in the den," he instructed cheerfully. He walked ahead of her and motioned for her to follow even though Arielle knew how to get there. Heather was sitting on the end of an L-shaped sectional sofa. She had a laptop computer balanced on her lap and a cell phone in her hand. It looked like she was using both devices simultaneously. Heath stopped walking suddenly, and distracted, Arielle bumped right into him.

"Stop touching my butt!" he accused loudly.

"I am not!" Arielle retorted, shocked that he would do and say such a thing.

"Leave her alone, shithead!" Heather called out then returned to typing out a text on her phone then typing on the laptop. Arielle looked around and wondered where their parents were. Hopefully, they were not home alone. Their house was huge though, so she couldn't tell if anyone else was home or not.

"What's up?" Heather asked without looking up.

"Why is he such a creep?" Arielle asked with a shake of her curly head.

"All guys his age are creeps. That's why I only talk to guys aged

16 or older," Heather advised. Arielle bucked her eyes and listened as Heather excitedly told her about a boy she's talking to in a chat room named Jason. "He's 16, totally hot, drives his own car and he is 100% into me," she gushed. Arielle listened with both interest and disgust. It seemed like every girl she knew was boy crazy. She wasn't ready to be in a relationship with a boy yet. They were just gross.

All Arielle wanted was to have fun with her family and friends. Jade understood exactly how she felt. Now, they both had celebrity crushes and they admired guys from afar, but neither girl was falling over herself in the quest to be some guy's girlfriend. Arielle continued listening and looking as Heather showed her pictures and texts from Jason. Arielle read through the conversations and was shocked by the way they were talking to each other.

"Sounds like he just wants to take your virginity," Arielle concluded.

"Too late!" Heather giggled. Arielle couldn't believe her ears! Heather was not a virgin? They were the same age: thirteen! Heather quietly told her the story of how she lost her virginity to a boy who lives in the town where they vacation every summer.

"He was sixteen!" Heather bubbled. Her braces glistened under the bright lights of the den. She never stopped texting or typing on the computer.

"And you're just thirteen!" Arielle reminded.

Heather giggled, "Not everyone wants to wait until they are thirty years old and married to do it Arielle!" She continued talking, telling intimate details of her first sexual experience, making no move whatsoever to get started on homework. Heather explained that the boys that she is talking to now think that she is a virgin and it really turns them on. Arielle had heard enough, so she took her history book and notebook out of her backpack and got started on her homework while Heather continued texting on her phone and typing on the laptop.

Every so often, she would giggle, stop, and share what Cody texted or Jason shared in the chat room. They both sent her shirtless pictures. She had to admit that they were both very handsome. Arielle smiled and giggled, but she could not believe that Heather was communicating with two different boys at the same time! She stared for a moment at

Heather. Her long straight blonde hair looked soft and shiny and Arielle could smell the faint scent of strawberries coming from either her hair or her body. Her skin was clear, cheeks were rosy and lips were shiny with pink lip gloss. *No wonder sixteen year old boys like talking to her. She's perfect!*

Thinking of her own appearance: light brown curly hair pulled back into a ponytail, sweatshirt, jeans, and gym shoes, no makeup, lip gloss or anything, and definitely no fruity smells coming from her hair or body, Arielle looked down abruptly. Out of necessity, she dressed like this all the time, but she wanted to straighten her hair and wear lip gloss, but her mom had a cussing fit when she asked. With a sigh, Arielle concentrated on her history homework, worked until she finished, and was glad that she finished before dinner. Heather stayed on her phone and computer the entire time even though she had her books and notebooks spread out beside her as if she was working. When her mother called out to them in the den, Heather switched from texting and typing to pretending that she was doing her homework.

"Hello Arielle, we're so happy that you could join us for dinner," Heather's mom greeted with a smile.

"Thank you Mrs. Harrison. I'm glad I could come," Arielle answered politely.

"Girls, are you ready for a homework break?"

Heather yawned and stretched before replying, "Just a few more minutes Mom, and we will be right there." Arielle had to look away to refrain from rolling her eyes. *Lying bitch. What a joke!*

"Ok, we won't start without you," her mother said cheerfully as she walked away. Heather pulled her phone from under her leg and quickly texted something to Cody, and then she grabbed the computer and typed something quickly to Jason. Arielle neatly placed her history book and notebook back inside her backpack, and the two girls went to the bathroom first to wash their hands and then to the dining room.

Dinner was delicious. Heather's mom, Hannah, was a pretty red-headed woman with freckles and green eyes, just like her youngest daughter Hillary. Heather, Heath and their father Harold had blonde hair and blue eyes. They were all beautiful and obsessed with the letter H.

"Our family crest," Heather explained to her one day at school when Arielle asked about the embroidery on her sweater, and engraved H on her lunch box, backpack . . . everything. Their house was decorated with the letter H in various forms. Arielle thought it was extreme, but her mother told her with a chuckle and a smirk, "When you're rich, you can do whatever the hell you want to do with your money, even get your name changed just to please your husband."

Arielle didn't know exactly what that meant, but she wondered if Heather's mom's real name was really Hannah or if it was a name that started with another letter of the alphabet. She looked past the spread on the table at Hannah and wondered if her name was really, Rebecca, Courtney, Ashley or Jennifer. She smiled to keep from laughing, and Hannah brightly smiled back, totally unaware.

Dinner was delicious: meatloaf, oven roasted potatoes, steamed green beans, buttered rolls, fruit punch, and chocolate cake for dessert. Arielle followed Heather's lead and ate slowly while engaging in conversation with the Harrison family. Heather didn't eat much, so Arielle did not eat much even though she was starving.

Hannah must have noticed Arielle copying Heather because she said, "Heather, eat your dinner, or no dessert! I made your favorite." Arielle was sure this was not the norm because Heather gave her mother a confused look and Hannah returned the look with a sternly raised eyebrow. Arielle stared again at Hannah and admired her beauty. Her eyes were an emerald green and her face was so pale white that her freckles looked really dark, but they matched her dark red hair and eyebrows. Heather looked like her dad. The blonde and blue combination was not as strikingly beautiful as the red and green.

Arielle thought about her dad, and smiled. Like Heather, she looked like her daddy too, with the skin color, same right cheek dimple and eye color. She really missed him. He called her pumpkin, and he always told her that he loved her every time they talked. Her mother was the exact opposite and was often cold and emotionless. Arielle was always much more affectionate and attentive to her mother than her mother was toward her. It hurt sometimes, but as she got older, Arielle reasoned that it was just part of her mother's personality. Arielle thought about the way her mother acted with her present and past boyfriends Jeff, Billy, Jack, and Alan. She hugged and kissed them! Why couldn't she hug her own daughter and say, "I love you," every once in a while? Arielle said it to her mom all the time with no response or "Umm hmm . . ."

Sitting there, surrounded by a loving family, Arielle looked around at the Harrisons, and she felt alone. She listened to their conversation which included joking, bickering, reprimands and praise. Then they started asking her questions, and she kept her answers brief and evasive.

Additionally, she started stuffing her mouth with food to avoid answering, and they finally stopped asking. She was glad because she did not want the Harrison family to know the boring details of her life. Really, she did not want anyone to know, except maybe Jade. Arielle left a little piece of meatloaf, two small potatoes and a few green beans on her plate, just like Heather did, before she declared that she was finished.

She wondered what her life would be like if she lived with her dad and Miss Amina. Well, her dad still had an apartment and Miss Amina had a house, so she was thinking ahead. Maybe she would just live with her dad? She was sure that they would get married because they always acted like they loved each other. Would they have dinners like this? Would her mother even care? If she went to live with her dad, would her mother feel sad and lonely, or would she feel free? Maybe she should ask? The thought frightened Arielle, and she wasn't really sure why. *Maybe it was because she didn't really want to hear her mother's honest answer?*

-8-

A Definitive Defeat

Arielle had only two friends whom she could confide in: Britney and Jade. Britney's life was similar to Arielle's, but her mother worked and was very affectionate toward her daughter and son, Miguel. Britney was two years older than Miguel, but they acted like they were twins. Britney's mom and dad were divorced too, but Britney and Miguel spent equal time with their mother and their father.

Dinner was over, so Heather and Arielle cleared the table, loaded the dishwasher, and cleaned the kitchen while Heath carried out the trash. Arielle admired the shiny granite countertops and ceramic tile floors because they were so easy to clean. Once Heather finished loading the dishwasher, she sprinted back to the den. Heather's mom and dad took Heinrich the dog out for a walk, Heather reabsorbed herself in her multiple technological communications, and Heath disappeared. Arielle returned to the den and diligently worked on her math homework. She liked math; it was like a game to her. She was almost finished, but she had to stop to go to the bathroom because her stomach felt funny.

Remembering the last incident in this bathroom, she made sure that she locked the door. Her mother always yelled at her when she locked the door of their bathroom because they only had one, and if one was the showering and the other needed to use the toilet, too bad, she had to wait. So, out of habit, Arielle left the door unlocked, and Heath did what he did. She trembled at the thought of him looking at her taking a shower. She finished, cleaned up, and washed her hands. Just as she was about to leave, she noticed the shower curtain moving, and Heath pulled it back and stepped out of the tub. Arielle was about to scream, but Heath put his hand over her mouth. He backed her up against the wall, and she struggled to break free.

"Shhh," he warned with a weird look in his eyes. Terrified, Arielle's eyes grew large and wide. Her heart thundered in her throat.

"I have a video of you pissing and farting that I will send to every guy in school if you don't shut up and do what I tell you!" he hissed.

He slowly moved his hand away from her mouth, but he quickly put it back when Arielle started to scream. He flushed the toilet and turned the faucet on before he fiercely pressed her against the wall and started humping against her repeatedly. He held her hands against the wall as she continued to struggle to break free. He overpowered her and continued humping and bumping against her and breathing strangely. After a few minutes of this weird behavior, he made a high pitched sound and stopped. Arielle broke free, slapped him hard across the face, pushed him away, and ran out of the bathroom.

"I have video!" Heath called after her. Arielle ran back to the den where Heather was now deeply engrossed in the chat room with Jason. She was typing quickly and smiling from ear to ear. Trembling and breathless, Arielle sat and thought about what just happened. *What exactly happened? What did he do? What should she do?* Soon, Heather's parents returned and went into the living room to relax. Arielle could hear Heath taking a shower, so she nervously finished her math homework.

When she finished, she tapped Heather on the shoulder and said, "I'm getting ready to go," in a weak, trembling voice. She was on the verge of tears, yet Heather didn't even notice. She stopped what she was doing long enough to copy homework answers then she went right back to her chat room conversation with Jason. Arielle's hands shook as she put her math book and notebook in her backpack and swung it over her shoulder. Her heart skipped several beats because she could no longer hear the water running in the bathroom. *She had to get out of there!*

Heath met her in the hallway wearing a white t-shirt and gym shorts. He was acting normal, like nothing weird had just happened.

"Your parents are back. I'll scream!" Arielle warned so he would move out of her way.

"Don't scream," he calmly instructed, I just want to thank you for helping me with my little problem," he continued with a weird grin and a brief grab of his crotch. He stepped toward her and she moved backward. She would surely scream if he touched her.

"Here's something for your trouble. Sorry if I scared you," he said as he dropped a wad of money on the floor between them. Confused, Arielle looked at it, and then she gave Heath an equally perplexed look.

"For this weekend . . . Tiffany's sleepover . . . the skating rink . . . Pancake Palace . . . Shopping at Riverside mall," he reminded before he sauntered away.

"Good night Mr. and Mrs. Harrison," Arielle called loudly, bent down and grabbed the money, crammed it in her pocket, and sprinted all the way home. The run home was a blur that she could barely remember because she ran like a lion was chasing her, never looked back, and only looked forward. Once there, she was winded, her chest hurt, her throat burned, and she wanted to cry. What just happened? What did Heath do to her? She wasn't hurt, just embarrassed and confused.

The apartment was dark, and she did not bother to turn on any lights. She secured the chain on the door. *Where's my mother?* She went to the kitchen and filled a glass with water from the faucet. She sipped it slowly to soothe her aching throat. She started to open the refrigerator, but she heard weird sounds coming from her mom's bedroom.

From late night television shows and the numerous times she heard her mother and her boyfriends before, Arielle knew what sex sounded like, and she sort of knew what it looked like. Is that what just happened between her and Heath? *No! We both had on clothes!* She thought about the weird breathing and weird sounds he made just before he stopped humping, bumping, and rubbing against her.

She could hear similar sounds coming from her mother's bedroom. Heavy breathing. "Uh, Ah, Oh, Umm, Yes . . ." A bump against the wall. Grunts and moans. The slap of sweaty bodies against each other. She closed her eyes in disgust. She tiptoed to her mother's bedroom door and listened for a moment to the hard heavy breathing, grunting, moaning, dirty talk, and squeaky bed springs. She tiptoed into her bedroom, closed the door quietly, put on her pajamas in the dark, and got into bed.

After about fifteen minutes, she received a text from Heather:

Heather – Why did you leave so fast?
Arielle – It was getting late. I had to go.
Heather – My mom wants 2 know if u made it home safely.
Arielle – Yes.
Heather – Ok. C u tmrw.
Arielle – Ok.
Heather – We will pick you up @ 6:00 b/c Tiffany wants 2 get 2 the skating rink before it gets 2 full.
Arielle – Ok.
Heather – It costs $10 for all night skate.
Arielle – Ok. My mom gave me money 4 the wknd.
Heather – Ok. Kewl!

Through the thin walls that separated them, Arielle heard some noise in her mother's bedroom. Hysterical laughter. A crash. Bumping, stumbling, more hysterical laughter. Then they were in the bathroom laughing and talking loudly. Arielle could hear them peeing, the water running in the sink, and the toilet flush. Arielle grabbed her two favorite teddy bears, Berry and Cherry, hugged them tightly, pulled the cover up over her head, shivered, and wished for a thicker comforter or more blankets on her bed.

She hated the pink, threadbare, once frilly, ruffles and bows, bedspread. It was a remnant of some little girl's happy childhood; it really had nothing to do with her except that it was her mother's futile attempt to decorate her young daughter's bedroom with pieces that she purchased from a thrift store. Arielle sighed heavily and sent a text to the one person she knew she could talk to without judgment and without getting in trouble.

Arielle – Wyd cuz?

Jade – NM cuz. Wyd?

Arielle – lying in bed. Trying 2 figure out wth just happened.

Jade – Gurl! What happened???

Arielle – Ugh! IDEK, and if I did I wouldn't even want 2 say.

Jade – what?

Arielle – SMH ☹

Jade – tell me!

Arielle – went 2 Heather's 4 dinner b/c my mom didn't want me 2 tag along w/ her and her bf.

Jade – *sigh* Sorry cuz. Try not 2 feel 2 bad about it. She just wanted 2 be alone w/ him. That's all. R u still @ Heather's?

Arielle – No. Home. Mom and Jeff are in her bedroom. They just finished doing it. ☹

Jade – Eeeeww! while u were there?

Arielle – they were finishing when I got home.

Jade – double eeewww! U didn't c them, did u?

Arielle – Eeeewww!!! No! Yuck! I heard them. Gross! They sound like nasty animals. But wait til I tell u what happened 2 me.

Jade – Wait! There's more? More than hearing them doing it?

Arielle – Yes. ☹☹☹

Jade – OMG!!!!!!! I better sit down.

Arielle - ok

Jade – well??? TELL ME!!!

Arielle – when I was @ Heather's house, something weird happened.

Jade – tell me everything!

Arielle – remember I told u that her brother is a creep? Well, he is a pervert 2!

Jade – what did he do?

Arielle – Heather was super distracted b/c she was chatting on her phone and computer w/ 2 different guys while she was pretending 2 do her homework.

Jade – really? Wow! She sounds like a creep 2!

Arielle – she is. But she's not that bad, but guess what!

Jade – gurl what???

Arielle – she's not a virgin anymore!

Jade – Noooooo!!! Did that happen 2night? Please don't tell me u lost your v card 2???

Arielle – No. She did this summer. Me . . . I'm not sure.

Jade – Wait!!!!!!! What???????

Arielle – something happened w/ her brother.

Jade – what happened? did he force u? tell me Ari! R U hurt? should I call ur dad?

Arielle – Noooooo!!! Please don't tell my dad!

Jade – what happened cuz?

Arielle – I'm not hurt. I'm just shocked.

Jade – Ari! Please tell me what happened!!!

Arielle - After dinner, Heather and I were in the den, her parents went out 2 take the dog 4 a walk, and Heath was somewhere in the house. My stomach felt funny, so I went 2 the bathroom. I made sure that I locked the door this time. Remember what he did before?

Jade – Yes! If I were u, I would carry a pocket knife around him @ all times. Horny Toad! ☹ they don't call me Jade the Blade for nothing!

Arielle – LOL! Jade the Blade! I wish you were with me tonight.

Jade – me too cuz. Now, what did he do?

Arielle - after I finished using the bathroom, Heath pulled back the shower curtain and told me that he had recorded me using the bathroom and he was going 2 show everyone @ school.

Jade – He is a nasty jerk! Did u scream 4 Heather 2 save u?

Arielle – she wouldna heard me if I screamed. I was 2 shocked 2 do anything anyway.

Jade – whats his effin problem? He needs his @ss kicked!

Arielle – he put his hand over my mouth & pushed me against the wall. He pressed up against me and I couldn't move.

Jade – Ari! you should tell on him!!!!!

Arielle – he started humping on me. He was rubbing against me & bumping me against the wall. He was grabbing my butt and pressing himself against me. He was grunting and breathing hard like we were having sex. It was COMPLETELY GROSS, but I just stood there like a statue. I was so shocked and scared and IDEK what to do!

Jade – OMG!!!! Were u scared out of ur mind?

Arielle – YES! I didn't even understand what was happening until he finished. ☹

Jade – Finished? Ugh!!!!!! EEEWWWW! Ari, please tell me that he didn't . . .

Arielle – Yuck!!!!! Yes! He did. He grunted & whimpered like a dog. He wet the front of his pants. That's when I snapped out of it broke free & I slapped the hell out of him & then he backed away from me kinda humped over. Like he was embarrassed. Him? Embarrassed? Can u believe that? I ran out of there and wondered if I had just been raped.

Jade – yes you kinda were. I think. IDEK! It's awful. This is terrible! He dry humped you. That's what it's called. Girls let boys do it to them all the time here. But rape is when a guy puts his thing inside u and forces u 2 have sex. I don't think u had sex, but Ari, he did force u. Rape is forced. He made u do something that u did not want 2 do.

Arielle – but it is not rape cuz we both had all of our clothes on!

Jade – but he masturbated on u w/o ur permission! He forced u!

Arielle – but is that rape?

Jade – y don't u ask ur dad? He's a cop, remember?

Arielle – NO! Jade u promised! U can't tell my dad!

Jade – I won't tell ur dad, but u should. He will know what 2 do! IDEK what 2 do, but I know that something should be done!

Arielle – Yes, I know. I don't want my dad 2 get mad. And OMG I don't want my mom 2 know. She would probably blame me and she would hate me.

Jade – ur mom would never hate u. No matter what. She'll always love u. Even though she shows it in a weird way, all mothers love their children.

Arielle - but that's not all. Something else happened.

Jade – Oh noooo Arielle!!! I don't think I can take anymore of this!

Arielle – before I left, he apologized 4 scaring me, thanked me 4 helping him w/ his problem and gave me a wad of money.

Jade – problem? He has an effin problem all right! He should be in jail! He should get punished for doing this 2 u. A wad of money? Ari, that's suspicious! He apologized and gave u money. I think that's a bribe.

He knew that what he did was wrong. I saw this on a movie once. What he gave u is called hush money. Wow! Arielle this is really serious! Did u keep the money? U should definitely tell ur dad about this.

Arielle – He dropped it on the floor and said that it was 2 help me this weekend.

Jade – He dropped it on the floor? That's weird. Maybe he wants to deny that he gave it to u? This guy is a total weirdo! What's happening this weekend?

Arielle – Sleep over at Tiffany's. Skating, breakfast, shopping & probably dinner, cake and ice cream for Tiffany's birthday.

Jade – Yes, all that sounds expensive, but if he really wanted 2 help, he would have just given u the money not spied on u in the bathroom and then forced you to help him masturbate! He's a stalker. He's a sexual predator! I bet he has done something like this 2 someone else b4! He took advantage of u Arielle, but u can turn this around and make it work in ur favor.

Arielle – How?

Jade – How much money did he give u?

Arielle – IDK! I put it in my pocket and ran all the way home!

Jade – where is it?

Arielle – still in my pocket. I didn't even look at it. I was so upset disgusted and scared. Wait.

Jade – well . . . how much?

Arielle - It's $65 dollars. A twenty, 2 tens, 2 fives and 15 ones. Wow that's a lot of money! This is hush money! He gave me this so I wouldn't tell on him? How can I use it 2 my advantage tho?

Jade – Will u c him tmrw?

Arielle – UGH! Yes probably.

Jade – Make sure u c him tmrw. He will probably try 2 avoid u.

Arielle – but why Jade? I don't want 2 c him. If I never c him again, that will be ok. I will probably blow chunks when I c him again.

Jade – that will make what u have 2 say 2 him even better. Do it! Blow chunks in his face!

Arielle – I don't want to get close enough 2 throw up on him.

Jade – u should! U can't let him know that ur scared of him. He thinks he has the upper hand, but u have 2 show him that u have the upper hand. U are in control of this situation. When u c him u need 2 stare him down with the meanest look that u have.

Arielle – I don't have a mean look.

Jade – Think about what he did to u & u will have a mean look. Practice it in the mirror!

Arielle - Ok ok, I can look mean, but what am I supposed 2 say?

Jade – Tell him that u told ur mother everything & showed her the money.

Arielle – WHAT??????

Jade – Do it! Tell him that u begged ur mother not 2 tell his mother, & she agreed but only if he gives u his allowance every week.

Arielle – What if he doesn't believe me?

Jade – He'll be 2 scared not 2. What's he gonna do? Ask ur mom? And if his family is as rich as u describe them 2 be, the money won't be a big deal. He'll just hand it over. He'll think that he got away with it, but later on, u can tell on him.

Arielle – and how long am I supposed 2 make him give me hush money?

Jade – just long enough 4 u 2 buy a bus ticket out of there. You need to get as far away from him as possible! And when u do u should tell on him!

Arielle – I have been saving 4 a plane ticket. My aunt says it costs $239 one way. It will take 2 and ½ hours to get there with one stop along the way. An adult will have 2 buy the ticket though. I don't know if my aunt will do that for me w/o telling my mother. I think she will though because I can tell that she can't stand my mom, and my mom doesn't really like her.

Jade – Oh wow! Did they argue?

Arielle – No, but I can tell by the way they talk about each other that they don't like each other. I haven't looked up the price of a bus ticket. It's gotta be cheaper though and maybe I can buy it myself.

Jade – It is! I looked it up and wrote it down.

Arielle - how much is it?

Jade - $155 and it will take 12 hours to get here on the bus.

Arielle – damn Jade! I thought we were just joking about me running away, but we have it all figured out. I was just curious about the plane ticket. I saved $55, but this sounds crazy! I'm supposed to turn it around on him 2 keep him quiet and paying me? Save the money until I get enough 2 buy a bus ticket? Run away from home and come there on a bus? What am I supposed 2 do when I get there?

Jade – Yes! Brilliant, don't you think? U can live with me until u get the courage to tell ur dad and my auntie.

Arielle – My dad would kill me. Ur dad would kill you!

Jade – Ur dad would kill Heath.

Arielle – yes, he would. And ur right. I do need to get away from here, but I can't run away from home. It would kill my mother.

Jade – You think so? She seems like she is enjoying life w/ her bf right now. I think she would be ok. Don't u think?

Arielle – IDK what to think anymore.

Jade – She would probably be mad at first. She would miss you, but then she would be ok with it.

Arielle – I'm not going 2 tell her, but if I did she would b so mad at me.

Jade - Well, u didn't do anything wrong. U have to do what is right for u.

Arielle – I just don't want 2 b here anymore. I'm in the way. My mom doesn't want me here because she can't do all the things she wants 2 do with her bf.

Jade – It doesn't sound like u are stopping her from doing anything that she wants 2 do! Ari, I don't want u there anymore either. It's not safe. U should call ur grandma or aunt and tell them what happened. They would let u stay w/ them until your dad figures something out.

Arielle – NO! If I tell my grandma or aunt, the first thing they will do is tell my dad.

Jade – but that is what needs to happen!!! U have 2 talk to your dad! He loves u! he wants u 2 be safe. Ur not safe! And I'm not just talking about Heath and what happened 2night.

Arielle – But I did something wrong 2! I'll get in trouble.

Jade – Please tell me what u did wrong because I don't understand.

Arielle – I took his hush money, and the more I think about it, the more I think I will follow ur plan and get more because he should pay 4 what he did 2 me. That's the wrong part. I shouldn't take his money.

Jade – yeah, it is wrong Ari. Maybe u shouldn't do it. I don't want u 2 get in trouble. U are using his hush money against him 2 get more. That's not right. I'm sorry that I suggested it.

Arielle – No! I'm gonna do it! U R brilliant Jade.

Jade – I am?

Arielle – U R! U r a good friend and ur idea is brilliant.

Jade – it is isn't it! I just wish you had a pocket knife.

Arielle – Why? You want me 2 cut him?

Jade – No just scare him. That's how I got my nickname. If a boy touches me the wrong way, I'll slice him. The boys here know that I don't play! If I was there with u, I would cut Heath's funky balls off! Evil bastard.

Arielle – He is evil. I hate his guts. U are brave. I need 2 be there with u. Soon I will have enough to come live there and get away from all this mess. That is what is right for me.

Jade – I agree.

Arielle and Jade continued texting late into the night. Alycia and Jeff continued their loud escapades in her bedroom. She never came out to check on her daughter.

Alycia and Jeff slept late the next morning. Arielle woke up a bit late because she forgot to set the alarm. She ran into the bathroom and took a shower. There were only small broken bits of soap left, so she used them to wash her body and her hair. She cringed at the thought of having to go to the school clinic again and getting the travel sized samples of soap, deodorant, shampoo, conditioner, toothpaste and lotion, but she would have to do it. Her mother rarely bought these items at the store, and when Arielle asked her grandmother or aunt to buy them for her, they would, but they would tell her dad and he would argue with her mom about it. It was a vicious circle, and she hated being in the center of it.

She thought many times about buying these items for herself, and once she did, but her mother used her stuff up faster than she could! Her mom kept her own stash of personal hygiene items, and she rarely shared them with Arielle. It bothered Arielle to think about this situation, but this is exactly what she thought about as she rushed to get ready for school. She did not have time to blow dry her hair, so she towel dried it and pulled it up into a damp tangled bun at the top of her head.

She ran to the kitchen and anxiously opened the refrigerator to see what her mom brought back. She didn't get a chance to look last night because she was too upset. There was a tall bottle of wine and some beers, but no take home box from a restaurant.

Crestfallen, she had peanut butter, crackers, and a glass of water for breakfast. She looked at the clock on her phone. Her bus would be there in less than ten minutes, so she had to hurry.

Before she left, she tiptoed to her mother's bedroom, opened the door a crack and peeked in. Her mother and Jeff were snuggled together under the covers in bed. His head was tilted back, and he was snoring. Her mother's face was buried in his chest. Their clothes littered the room, and there was a plate from the kitchen on the bedside table with a rolled up dollar bill in the middle of it. Arielle thought that it was strange, and she decided to ask Jade about it the next time they talked.

—9—

One Step Forward

Months passed and Anthony and I went back to what we were doing – working nonstop and barely spending time together. We talked a lot, and we had a few date nights, but it was hard to snap out of our workaholic tendencies. He still had his apartment, and my house was still waiting for him to move in. I didn't really know how his alcohol treatment and counseling was going because I felt kind of weird asking him about it, and it was an easy subject to avoid. Our comfort level was just not what it used to be, and I desperately wanted it back.

Additionally, my niece kept telling me alarming stories about Arielle and Alycia and what they were up to, and the fact that I had not disclosed this information to Anthony made me feel like an accomplice in a felonious crime. I was keeping a secret again, and this time it involved his daughter.

Actually, I felt scared and uncomfortable talking to him about it. I didn't want to give him information that might actually set him back in kicking his alcoholism. I relied on the fact that he talked to Arielle on a regular basis, and I hoped she was telling him some of the stuff that she told Jade. *Yeah right. That's not the case. If Anthony knew some of this stuff, he would hit the roof. He would definitely take a few drinks.*

I was in Crockett, Arkansas working on an assignment for corporate headquarters. In some ways, I enjoyed going out of town to take care of business, and in other ways, I simply hated it. It didn't take long for me to get tired of living out of a suitcase, eating fast food, and spending lonely nights in a hotel room. This was exactly the case, but I was deep into my assignments, and there was nothing that I could do but continue to do a good job and follow through.

I sat at the desk in my room, closed my eyes, and thought about Anthony. I missed my honey. The thing that I missed the most was his flattery. He was always full of compliments, and I loved that about him.

Whenever we talked and whenever we spent time together, he always said and did things to make me feel special, beautiful, and highly desired.

"It's how I saw my dad treat my mom," he said with a dazzling smile and a reveal of the deep dimple in his right cheek. During the awkward time that we were both trying to accept Vickie's death and our role in it, Anthony and I became workaholics. Work was the perfect excuse, distraction, and method of ultimate avoidance. We worked to hide our pain. We worked to keep our brains productively functioning. We worked to keep our feelings in check. We still had strong feelings for each other, but it just hurt to see each other face to face sometimes. We felt guilty about being happy. After all, a pregnant woman was dead simply because we insisted on being together.

I accepted the out of town assignments a lot, every chance the opportunity arose, and Anthony worked nonstop; sometimes he even worked double shifts to avoid facing the guilt. We both used the "advancing our careers" excuse, which was partially true, because we both wanted promotions at our jobs.

That evening, we were on the phone and undeniable truths just started spilling out of our mouths.

"You know, going out of town all the time isn't really an effective way to deal with what you're feeling," he announced out of the blue. We had been talking about what to do for Arielle's upcoming summer break. We both had some good ideas, and I was about to check my calendar to see when would be a feasible time for me to take off for a few weeks.

Somehow, I ignored his statement and managed to change the subject to home improvement projects that we could do together. We easily transitioned into a discussion about removing the wallpaper in the dining room and replacing the flooring in the bathrooms. Soon, our superficial conversation drifted back to what we really needed to be talking about.

"You know, working 24 hours a day isn't helping you deal with your feelings either, is it? I asked after a moment of silence. I expected him to revert back to the home improvement discussion, but he softly replied, "I do miss you baby; however, keeping busy seemed like a good way to deal."

"Yeah, you're right," I agreed.

"But what exactly are you trying to deal with? Vickie's curse?" I asked without thinking. I rolled my eyes because I knew that I should not speak ill of the dead. *Forgive me Lord.*

"Really Amina?" You're joking? He exhaled what sounded like an irritated breath then remained silent.

"I'm not joking! That was just a slip. I'm trying to figure out why we are both feeling so bad about being happy?" Silence.

"Every time we are together enjoying ourselves, something happens to both of us and we abruptly change the course of our time together," I whined. He exhaled another agitated breath, but he remained silent.

"Why are you doing that?" I asked as I tried to keep my tears inside my eyeballs and my volume below screaming.

"I've been thinking about this a lot too baby, and I have concluded that we just feel bad that she did what she did because of us. We are not to blame. I know that you understand that. We both hate that she did it because she could not accept us as a couple and just move on. Deep down, I guess we both wonder if we are really any good as a couple." *Wow! You just said exactly what I have been thinking for the past few months.*

"Is that how you feel? Deep down?" I asked with raised eyebrows. *Because I'm not the problem here! You are! We are not a good couple because you are a drunk!*

"No, I think we are a great couple. We are wonderful together. We love each other, we support each other, and we make each other happy. That's all that really matters," he stated in a resigned tone. *Ok, now I feel bad about what I was thinking.*

"But why do we feel so bad about that?" I inquired, sounding a bit like Dr. Branson.

"Because we are good people who can't fathom the thought of our happiness causing someone to do what she did," he exposited.

"But we can't keep letting this get in the way of us proceeding on with our lives," I said sadly, afraid of how he might respond.

"Our lives together," he corrected.

I smiled, "So we are not having this conversation as a means of getting to goodbye?" I asked with uncertainty. *Maybe we should be?*

"Hell no!" he laughed, "We are finally talking it out because it has been eating us alive." *What about your excessive drinking? Are you controlling that? Or are we purposefully avoiding all mention of this issue because it's still . . . an issue?* I thought and exhaled a relieved sigh when I realized that I didn't actually say it aloud. That has to be a discussion for another day. Since our last upset, I haven't noticed any of his drunken attitudes, and I was extremely grateful for that. However, that did not equate to him having the situation under control.

"I wish you were here, so I could come over and make love to you right now baby," he murmured.

"Yes, that would be nice," I sighed in a defeated manner as I thought about the badly merchandised, terribly organized, lawsuit waiting to happen store here in Crockett with its lackluster, incompetent employees. I went in yesterday posing as a customer and took video footage with both my phone and a digital flip camera of several areas that were grossly out of safety and security compliance.

I didn't even have to hide the fact that I was recording because none of the sales associates greeted me, paid a speck of attention to me, or offered any assistance. I spent two hours in the store wandering from department to department, reaching in and out of my large purse and pants pockets, and I was not once greeted by a sales associate! Even the assistant store manager scurried by without acknowledging me!

The store was not busy, but the associates on duty were not following established protocols for slack time duties. Instead, I saw sales associates talking, shopping, sitting, chatting on their phones and ignoring the few customers who were in the store. It was hard for me to hide my disbelief. As slow as business was that day, the store should have been neat, clean, and well organized rather than looking like a tornado blew through it.

After I gathered enough information, I casually strolled out of the store. My oversized purse could have been filled with items that did not have security tags, but no one bothered to acknowledge my departure.

I drove slowly back to the hotel wondering how I could handle this situation in the most appropriate and professional manner. Justin Dean, the Crockett store manager would not like what I would be forced to include in my reports especially since I had to send a copy of it and the recordings to the compliance manager at corporate headquarters in Dayton.

The Crockett store would never have been on the radar for a safety and security audit if there was not a pending lawsuit filed by a woman whose son was allegedly injured after a mannequin toppled over onto him. While in the store, I recorded 3 display violations, and several safety violations. I mentioned this while I talked to Anthony.

"Wow! I didn't realize what you did was so . . . important," he said.

"Really Anthony?" I smirked. *What did he think I did? Shop all day?*

"Well, your job title is a bit deceiving," he countered. When you hear the term Visual Merchandising Manager, you think that is the person who is in charge of keeping the merchandise neat, pretty and nice to look at, so people will see it and want to buy the stuff," he continued.

"Wow! Really Anthony?" I shook my head and giggled.

"Think about it – visual has to do with being seen; merchandise is the stuff for sale in the store, manager is the person in charge; so the Visual Merchandise Manager is the person who is in charge of keeping things looking neat, pretty and nice so people will buy it!" he extrapolated as he withheld laughter.

"Okay, you are partially correct," I accepted, "I am in charge of a lot of displays and beautification, but my job is a lot like yours in that I make sure everyone is doing what needs to be done, following the rules, and keeping the store safe and secure."

"That's my baby! Beautiful lady in charge! Miss VMM," he teased. I laughed, and then there was an awkward silence.

"I love to hear you laugh, and I love your smile," he whispered.

"Why are you whispering?" I whispered back.

"Because I wanted it to be quiet when you laugh again," he whispered in response. I laughed, and this time, it sounded unusually loud. I couldn't stop, so I moved the phone away from my mouth.

"Umm hmm," he was moaning when I repositioned the phone.

"What is it now?" I asked with a giggle.

"I'm envisioning your beautiful smile, and I'm melting right here in this chair. I giggled a bit more and my smile would not stop beaming from my face.

"When are you coming home baby?" he inquired softly.

"Day after tomorrow," I purred equally as soft. I could feel my body heat rising.

"I don't think I can wait that long," he proclaimed in a regular but somber tone of voice.

"Well, I'm only 77 miles away!" I hinted.

"That's right!" he perked up, "I could be there in about an hour and fifteen minutes!"

"But you have to work tomorrow," I reminded with a suddenly racing heart and flutter in my belly. The possibility that he could be with me tonight was causing definite physical reactions.

"After all the extra shifts that I worked for people, somebody owes me," he explained with delight and a sudden realization that we were wasting time talking.

"But you're tired honey," I condescended.

"Just the thought of your love gives me an abundance of energy baby," he announced. It was 6:40 p.m. He quickly got off the phone with me and started making plans to join me. By 7:30, he had found someone to work in his place, packed a bag and was on the road. I was extremely flattered, but at a loss for what I should do while I waited for him to arrive.

I fluttered around the hotel room, picking up things here and there, straightening this and that, wondering if I would even still be awake and alert when he arrived. I had been waking up early to work, and I haven't stayed up past 9 since I have been in Crockett. I looked at my suitcase with a sudden horrifying thought: I didn't bring any sexy lingerie or underwear which he loved. I threw the case on the bed and rambled through all of my comfortable underwear. I considered running back out to UpStage to buy something, but I quickly decided against it. I called him and asked if he was hungry.

"I'm hungry for your love baby," he sort of growled in a deep voice. I giggled. He explained that he had bought a foot long submarine sandwich that he would share with me after our "love fest."

"Sounds great baby," I answered carefully and slowly, afraid that my enthusiasm would seep out of my pores. I glanced around the somewhat messy room.

"I can't wait to see you," he said in that same deep voice. I wiggled my toes as a chill raced up my spine.

"Same here baby. Drive safely though. I need to get ready for you," I explained as I snapped out of my temporary love trance. I grabbed a clean white t-shirt.

"Ummmm hmmmm," he moaned. I gave him the hotel name, address and my room number as I looked out the window. The last little bits of daylight were starting to disappear. I quickly tidied the room, ran out to the grocery store across the street, and bought his favorite chips, soda, chocolate chip cookies, and some scented candles.

I hurried back to the hotel, filled the ice bucket, lit the candles and turned the TV on an all music channel. I ran to the bathroom to take a shower, and when I finished, sprayed perfume all over and smoothed lotion in every nook and cranny before slipping into my favorite sleeping attire: an oversized plain white v-neck t-shirt and panties. I thought twice about the panties and took them off, scooted my feet into flip flops, and laughed as I thought, "I can't get much sexier than this." He knew that I was a bit on the modest side, so not wearing panties would definitely turn him all the way on. For some reason, I started feeling nervous and restless; I couldn't sit still, and the room suddenly felt cold. I jumped up and adjusted the air from 67 to 70, and scurried to the bathroom to look at myself again. The mirror had fogged back up, so I wiped it with my towel and looked at myself.

My big brown eyes were sparkling, my forehead was shining, and my hair was frizzy in several places; so I blotted my face with a dry section of the towel, and brushed through my hair a few times. Still frizzy. I sprayed my brush with oil sheen and brushed through it again. Finally, the frizzy strands laid down and behaved.

Smiling, I turned my head back and forth a few times to make my hair move. I love the fact that he loves my hair, just as it is – not long, not short, exactly medium and perfect for the shape of my face. He always touches it, smells it and compliments my hairstyle even when I'm having a "bad hair day" and even though it is usually the same style day in and day out. I definitely missed his compliments. He genuinely admired me, and this was the best part of his love.

I couldn't help but frown when I thought about how we haven't had time for each other lately, and what little time we did manage to spend together seemed to always somehow erupt into an argument usually because I ask about his alcohol consumption or he asks about who I have been working with or talking to on the phone. While I was worried about his health and well being, he was jealous and letting his suspicions get the best of him.

I couldn't blame him though. My liaisons with Clayton back then were intense, and just when Anthony and I were getting to know each other, I went running back to Clayton one last time. It was a mistake; I apologized profusely, but obviously, Anthony hasn't forgiven me. *I wish I could zap his brain and make him forget about it!* I caught a glimpse of myself in the large mirror and noticed my frown. *Fix your face Amina! Your man is coming to see you, and he loves to see you smile.*

Nearly a month had passed since we made love. I missed him terribly, and I could tell from the yearning in his voice and his selfless gesture of jumping in his car and driving for nearly 80 miles to see me that he missed me too. I glanced in the mirror again and forced a smile. A wrinkle of worry was still on my face as I promised myself that I would not say anything about his drinking.

Damn! I hope he doesn't bring any alcohol! Shit! I hope he hasn't been drinking tonight! I didn't hear any indication of his tell tale signs of drinking when we talked tonight, but then again, his voice, mood, and attitude really only changes when he gets to the hard liquor phase of his drinking routine.

I glanced again at the worried crease on my forehead and tried to relax and make it disappear. *Why are you worrying? Tonight is going to be great!* I walked back into the bathroom, blotted the shine from my face again, breathed deeply to relax, looked in the mirror, and smiled a big bright smile before walking back out into the room. The burning candles and the music made the room appear romantic, but I still wished that I had something sexy to wear. *Maybe I'll run and jump into his arms, wrap my legs around him, and cover his face with kisses? Yes! That will definitely show him how much I miss him and how happy I am to see him!*

I walked over to the bedside table, picked up my phone, and sent him a text message: Leaving the room key in the glove compartment for you! Can't wait to see you baby! He responded immediately: Ummm . . . you have a surprise for me? My response: Don't text and drive! Keep your eyes on the road! His response: Yes dear. 12 miles away. My heart started thumping erratically and joy washed over me. *Finally, my body was reacting like it was supposed to!*

Quickly, I pulled on a pair of shorts and ran out to my car. Glad that no one was parked beside me, I opened the passenger side door and the glove compartment and dropped the card inside. I looked around the somewhat empty parking lot and wondered if I should lock my door since Anthony has a set of my car keys. I closed the door without locking it and ran back into the room. My heart continued its crazy rhythm, and I had to sit on the edge of the bed and breathe for a few minutes. Inhale. Exhale. I closed my eyes and giggled at the funny feeling in the pit of my stomach. I wiggled my toes and smiled.

After all that has threatened to break us up, he still makes me feel this way. *Wow! I really love this man!* I laughed out loud and gripped my chest for fear that my rapidly beating heart would break through. For fifteen minutes, I meditated: eyes closed, head down, clutching my heart, breathing deeply, and thinking about him until I heard his vehicle pull up beside mine.

Expecting to be dizzy, I stood up quickly and got ready to run into his arms. With my feet planted slightly apart, I was steady as I heard my car door open and shut. I was ready as I heard him whistling as he walked to the door. Whistling! I heard the card click in the door, and he walked in slowly as if he expected me to shout "Surprise!" Looking straight at me, he dropped his duffle bag on the floor, put a brown paper bag on the table, and stood there waiting.

My eyes scanned the full length of his body. He was wearing a gray t-shirt, black athletic shorts, ankle socks and Nike slippers. He smelled fresh and clean, and I could no longer resist. I ran over to him and tried to jump into his arms, but he was definitely not expecting this, so he stumbled backward into the door.

"Baby! Whoa!" he started to talk and regain his stance, but I smothered his mouth and his face with kisses. He beamed as I continued kissing him and gripped my bare butt as my legs wrapped around him.

He returned my kisses, and in between he murmured, "Ummm baby! No underwear? Now, that's a damn surprise!" I would not stop kissing him. We started kissing frantically in this manner until we could not take it anymore. He made me stop, placed me on my feet, and looked down at me as he was about to speak.

"Oh my God! I love you Amina. I have missed you so much. Every time we talk and start arguing, I get really worried that you are going to break up with me. I don't want that baby," he seriously pronounced. I didn't know what to say, and I sensed that he was not finished talking, so I kept quiet. He pushed me back a few inches, so he could get to the bag that he dropped on the floor. He unzipped the side pocket and grabbed a brown velvet looking pouch. It looked like a bag for a liquor flask or at least a bag that once contained a bottle of liquor. For a split second, my eyes turned to angry slits and I gritted my teeth. *We don't have to toast! We don't need alcohol tonight at all!*

He nervously smiled at me, so I tried to keep my anger at bay and my face relaxed. *Why is he nervous? Was he feeling the same giddiness that*

I was feeling while ago? He bent down on one knee. *Wait a minute! Wait! What is he doing? Wait a minute!*

"Amina, will you marry me?" he asked before I could even make the full connection in my brain to figure out what was about to happen. Dumbfounded, I stood there staring down at him. Perplexed, I tried to open my mouth to say something, but I didn't know what to say. *Now, this is a surprise! Your timing is totally off! This is not where you should be asking me to marry you! Oh my gosh! What am I going to say?*

I looked at the painting on the wall above the table; it was an abstract swirl of colors. I could see bold swirls of navy blue, baby blue, and royal blue. It made me think of the ocean. I shook my head and smiled at the distraction. I certainly was not expecting this tonight! My little surprise was nothing compared to this surprise! I looked back down at him, and he was holding a ring up for me to accept. I remember seeing this ring long ago when he showed me pictures of his grandmother. It was her custom made engagement ring.

A single tear slid down my cheek during this moment of temporary paralysis and thankfully snapped me out of it. A worried frown started to form on his forehead and I could see a desperate plea taking shape in his beautiful eyes.

"Yes, Anthony, I will marry you," I whispered. More tears fell. Between us, there was a lot to think about, there was a lot to fix, there was a lot that needed to happen, but above all, there was a lot of love and understanding. I was not quite ready to marry him, but we had time. We could be officially engaged while we worked on getting ourselves ready to get married. He stood up and started kissing my tears which were abundantly falling by now.

He hugged me and said, "Don't cry baby! You're going to make me cry too!" I sniffled, brushed the tears away, and looked down at my trembling hand as he slid the ring on my finger. It fit perfectly.

"How?" I wondered aloud as I looked at the dazzling creation.

"The last time we were together, while you were sleeping, I measured your finger with a piece of string. I took the string and the rings to a jeweler to have them sized. I also had them engraved," he explained as he gently slid the ring off so I could see. *-Anthony loves Amina- Forever -*

was written around the entire space inside the ring. The words were cut in half, partially on the engagement ring and partially on the wedding band, but I could still read them. The tears started again, and I asked, "Do you still have the string?"

"The what?" he chuckled.

"The string that you measured my finger with," I sniffled and blotted at tears that seemed to just keep falling. He picked up the brown velvety bag and looked inside. Sure enough, the string was inside. It was a piece of red satin ribbon, probably from a gift bow. He had tied a tiny knot in the area that marked my ring size. It was nothing special about it, but I looked at it with great fascination.

"You sneaky thing you! I giggled and reached up to kiss him. He grabbed me and covered me with kisses, picked me up, pretended that he might fall, and this made me laugh uncontrollably.

"What are you doing?" I giggled.

"Practicing for our wedding night!" he boasted, and then he pretended to struggle again.

"I'm going to have to pump some iron baby!" he joked. I playfully punched him on the arm before he put me down.

"You are going to be my wife," he said softly before kissing me deeply and taking my breath away. Our kissing intensified quickly and led to our undressing.

"I'm about to make love to my future wife," he breathed between kisses. He started calling me his fiancée a long time ago. He actually introduced me as his fiancée to his mother, his father's friend, his sister, Alycia and Arielle. I thought it was cute, so I didn't object. In fact, I had been looking forward to this day until Vickie's suicide polarized our relationship with guilt and sadness.

"I think we should wait until after we get married, I teased as I clawed at the muscles in his chest and kissed him passionately. He grabbed my breasts, kissed them both, and murmured, "Well, we better get married right now baby because you're about to get this thang in a few minutes!"

He picked me up again, this time with ease, and slowly walked over to the bed. I closed my eyes, inhaled deeply, buried my head in his chest, and whispered, "Ummm . . . talk dirty to me baby."

He put me down and responded instantly, "You want this dick baby?" he asked against my head. I smiled, and he pressed his erection against me. He kissed my forehead and my temples and continued, "You got this thang throbbing baby. Look at it." I rested my head on his chest and looked down. He flexed his chest and ab muscles before making his manhood jump from side to side. He grabbed my face in both hands, kissed me hard and continued his dirty talk, "He's ready for a long, vigorous swim, baby."

"Oh yeah?" I whispered.

"Yesssss. He's ready to dive all the way in that wet pussy! My face flushed hot, and I could feel the fine, tiny hairs on my arms stand at attention. He pressed his hardness against me once more. Because he was light skinned, it looked red and ready to pop with swollen veins running down the length of it. The intense look on his face told me that he was beyond ready, so I eased back on the bed, but he pulled me back to a standing position. He turned me around, kissed my neck and shoulders, and pushed me gently to bend over.

"You want to do me like an animal?" He growled in response. Of course, we had done this before, but I was hoping that after his proposal that we would be more romantic – face to face. I guessed that I opened up this can of worms by encouraging the dirty talk.

Nevertheless, I let him take charge, and once he pressed his hot, swollen member inside my fiery wetness, there was not much more that I could do besides throw my hair back, brace myself, scream, and moan. "You feel so good. It's so hot. It's so wet," he moaned behind me. I don't know why, but his words took me back.

~+~+~+~+~+~+~+~

"We need to talk about this baby," Anthony said and pointed to the condom hanging on his now limp lifeless soldier.

"What is there to talk about?" I smiled and rolled over, quite satisfied. We had spent much of the night making love, and now we were lying in the semi- darkness talking.

"We're together, we're committed to each other, we trust each other and we love each other, right?"

"Right," I agreed and turned around so I could face him for the rest of our pillow talk.

"So, why do I have to keep using these?"

"You want to stop using them?" I smiled at him because I knew that this conversation would come sooner or later.

"Hell yes! I want to feel you without any restrictions!"

"Okay."

"Okay? That simple? Okay?"

"Sure baby, I'll make an appointment to see my gynecologist as soon as possible," I informed him. He got up, removed the condom, and walked to the bathroom. I rolled out of bed and followed him.

"Damn! I should have asked sooner! So, are you going to get a prescription for birth control pills?"

"No," I answered bluntly, "I have no desire to take a hormone pill every day. I'm terrible with pills."

"So are we going to take our chances? That's not such a bad thing, you know, since we are planning to get married and have children anyway," he eagerly replied. I grabbed a washcloth, wet it, squeezed the water out and started wiping. We finished in the bathroom and walked slowly back into the bedroom.

"No, I'm not going to take any chances. There are other forms of birth control, you know? I'm not ready for babies right now!" He looked crushed.

"Why not? I thought you loved children!" he exclaimed with a look of confusion splattered all over his face. I noticed this, but I blew it off as no big deal. He seemed genuinely crushed when I told him that I wasn't ready for children. I explained that I wanted to get things straight with my career before I could even fathom the thought of children. Again, he looked at me with a confused frown when I told him this, but we didn't talk about it any further.

⌐+⌐+⌐+⌐+⌐+⌐+⌐+⌐

At that moment, I was extremely pleased with my decision to start getting the quarterly birth control shot because I totally agreed with him about how good it felt without a condom between us. We both kept looking at ourselves in the mirror and feeling more turned on with each glance. "We look good together!" he moaned as he thrust with intensity. Every muscle in his body flexed.

"We fit together perfectly!" I hoarsely replied.

"Yes baby, this dick was made for your pussy," he stated, grabbed my hips tightly, and plunged deeper. This caused the mattress to slide against the headboard and a loud scream from me. He reached around and started fondling my clitoris and sent shock waves all through me. He knew exactly what to do and exactly when to do it. Just a few minutes of this turned my legs to mush, and I struggled to remain standing. He never missed a beat and continued on with the deep thrusting until a loud moan escaped from deep within him, from his belly, and then several smaller thrusts later, he was squirting the evidence of his satisfaction into me. My arms felt weak and threatened to collapse from under me. My legs were trembling, almost violently, and chills were racing up and down my back. Finally, he made a move, and we both collapsed on the bed: sweating, breathing deep ragged breaths, smiling, and muscles contracting.

After a few minutes, he scooted up to the pillows and reached out to me. "Come here baby. I want to hold my future wife," he softly invited. I raised my head from its face down position, looked up at him and smiled before repositioning myself so I could snuggle beside him. He smoothed down my hair, which I surmised must be a complete mess, and kissed my temple.

"Oh God! I love this woman so much!" he shouted loudly as he looked up toward the ceiling. I snuggled deeper into his side.

"I love you too, but," I blurted without thinking. He turned quickly to look at me.

"But what sweetheart?" I exhaled loudly. *I didn't mean to say "but."* *Where the hell did that come from?* I sure didn't want to ruin this perfect evening with an argument. *Was now a good time to bring up our issues?* I nuzzled the side of his chest with my nose. "But what sweetheart?" he repeated and raised my face to look at him. I exhaled again. *Might as well put it all out there. Now is as good a time as any.* "We have some issues to resolve before we get married," I stated in a matter of fact manner.

"Yes, we do," he agreed quickly which surprised me. *Well, okay then. Shall I pull out my numbered list?*

"Let's start with your unusually close relationship with Rashad," he began. I giggled because I knew that he would bring up another man.

"We're just friends. In fact, he is a lot more distant since you said whatever you said to him on New Year's Day. If we are not talking about work, he barely even wants to talk to me at all. By the way, what did you say to him?

"We had a man to man conversation. Rashad is cool. I have no beef with him whatsoever, but I had to lay it all out on the table. I just told him the truth about how I feel about you, and I asked him some questions that probably made him rethink his relationship with you. I gave him a scenario and asked him to look at it from my perspective," he answered.

"We're just friends and co-workers. There's no relationship between us!" I insisted.

"Yes, but I see how he looks at you. Not only is he attracted to you, but he also cares about you. That's fine, I understand why. You and Rashad have been friends and coworkers for a long time, but you're my lady, so I asked him to respect our relationship, and I'm happy to hear that he was a man about it and did what I asked," Anthony explained. I frowned, but I could not deny Anthony's accurate observations.

"Okay, you might be right about that, but he does respect my relationship with you baby," I countered. Anthony raised his eyebrows. *Oh shit! He knows more than he's saying. I better leave this alone.*

"You should get to know him better. Hang out and do some guy stuff," I suggested.

"That's not a bad idea sweetheart. Then I will introduce him to some single ladies, so he can stop looking at my woman like he wants to devour her!" he joked. I giggled and nudged him in his side.

"Men can't help looking at me like that because I'm so tantalizing," I joked and tickled him. He flinched, bent and kissed me, stuck his tongue in my mouth and teased me.

"Yes, you are Mrs. Wallace!" he kissed my temple again and squeezed me.

"Amina Wallace. Anthony and Amina Wallace. Mr. and Mrs. Wallace. Mrs. Amina Wallace. Amina Rechelle Wallace. Mrs. Wallace," I recited slowly, "Hmm . . . it has a nice ring to it."

"I'm ready baby!" he said and squeezed me again. "When are we going to do this?"

"Hold on! Wait! I didn't talk about my issues, actually your issues!"

"Baby, I already know, and believe me when I tell you that I'm getting my drinking under control. In fact, I'm almost on track completely," he explained.

"What do you mean by that?" I asked and moved to completely face him.

"I mean that my taste for it, my desire to drink, has diminished almost completely," he confessed seriously.

"What needs to happen to make it disappear completely?" I asked as my heart started beating erratically. *Why was I getting nervous?*

"A few things need to happen baby," he evaded.

"Like?" I coaxed. He exhaled what seemed like an agitated breath, sat up slowly, and excused himself to the bathroom. This move frightened me for a few seconds, and I wanted to follow him, but I didn't want to hover over him like I was overly concerned . . . or suspicious? I could hear him peeing, so I calmed down. He came back, and I went to the bathroom. I could feel his eyes on me as I walked away from the bed. Suddenly self-conscious, I said softly, "Don't look!" He heard those same words many times from me, so he was used to it.

"I can't help it baby! I love your body," he chuckled in his deep mellow voice.

"Ummm . . . hmmm . . ." I giggled as I attempted to cover my bare butt with both hands. After I finished cleaning up a bit, I grabbed my robe, put it on, brushed my hair down, and swiped on some lip gloss. He was waiting to cradle me in his arms when I came out.

"We can talk about your other concerns in a few, okay?" he asked after kissing me on my nose and tugging on my robe's belt until it came untied. I let the robe slide off and fall onto the floor.

"I want to talk about this right now!"

"Ok," he quickly agreed.

"Well, I don't want it to seem like it's a problem, but it is definitely something that you need to get straight before we get married," I began.

"Go ahead. I'm listening baby," he said and kissed my forehead.

I inhaled and just blurted, "It's Arielle."

His eyebrows shot straight up, his forehead covered with wrinkles, and suddenly his face transformed from relaxed and peaceful to completely concerned.

"What about Arielle baby?"

"She's in a bad situation, and you know it. She needs you to help her get out of it," I stated definitively. He sat up and pulled me up along with him. He had a look of distress, and it seemed like he didn't really want to talk to me about this.

"The only way that I can help Arielle is to sue for full custody and move her here with me," he replied.

"With us," I corrected. He turned abruptly to face me. His face was covered with confusion.

"You would be okay with that?!!!" he enthusiastically asked. Light was beaming from his beautiful eyes. He jumped up and walked over to my side of the bed to sit beside me.

"But the last time we talked about it, you said that you didn't want to have kids any time soon!"

"Yes, but I meant that I don't want to get pregnant and have a screaming, dependent infant just yet! Arielle is 13," I started explaining, but he wouldn't let me finish. He grabbed me and hugged me tightly. He squeezed me hard, and I could feel a shake or a tremble rise from him.

"I love Arielle. I would love for her to come and live with us. We've already talked about this!" I explained in a muffled voice against his chest. *Maybe he was too drunk to remember? We did argue about it a lot.*

"We just didn't agree on a timeline. I was tired of you dragging your feet," I continued, "I was ready for you to take immediate action. Baby, you have to know that I want her here with us," I finished. Silence. I waited patiently for him to say something or let me go because this was getting weird.

Something hot and wet landed on my shoulder, and I heard Anthony sniffle. I tried to push him away, but he wouldn't let me. He was crying. I could hear it in his voice. Tears dropped on my shoulders and rolled down my back. I was quiet, closed my eyes, and tried not to cry along with him. *I'm convinced that crying is contagious. What do you think?*

"That is what would make my taste for alcohol leave me completely. If I could have my daughter here with me . . . with us," he said in a raspy voice straight into my hair. A few more tears fell on me, and he kept me wrapped in his tight grip for a while, and then finally, he let me go.

Immediately, I looked at him. He had wiped his tears, and he was smiling wide, his dimple sinking deeply into his cheek. His eyes were red, and he seemed a bit embarrassed that he cried in front of me, but it only made me love him even more. We shared a brief kiss before he got up, put on his boxers, and grabbed his phone.

He called Arielle to tell her the good news. He braced himself because he believed that Arielle would be adamantly against leaving her mother and coming here to live. I told him several times that Arielle's talks with Jade indicated otherwise. However, he relied on what Arielle said when he talked to her. I surmised that he still talked to her like she was a little kid not a teenager, and she was just not emotionally mature enough to get into a serious discussion with her father if he was not the one to initiate it.

I looked at his animated expressions and giant smile while he talked to her, and my heart raced for him. The little bit of time that he has spent with her occurred mostly when she was a child, so he only knows how to relate to her as a child. He asked her to be quiet about his good news and plans to bring her here to live with us. He put her on speaker so she could talk to me.

"Congratulations Miss Amina!" she giggled, "Can I call you step mommy?" she asked in a high pitched squeal. Sunlight exploded from Anthony's eyes, and I tried to stifle my laughter. I told her that she could, but she should wait until after the wedding. When I told her that she and Jade would definitely be in our wedding, her giggly squeals intensified to an ear shattering level.

With a huge smile, Anthony shook his head and took the phone off speaker mode. He continued talking to her as I set up our dinner on the small, round table, turned off the music, and flipped to the news.

When he finally got off the phone, his smile was replaced with a huge frown. "She is not going to be able to keep this information to herself. She is too sweet and naïve, and her mother is quite devious when she is trying to get information," he worried aloud.

"Maybe her new boyfriend is keeping her so busy that she won't have time to pick up on Arielle's happiness?" I ventured.

"Yeah, you're right. She has been paying way more attention to him than she has been paying to our daughter. She's with him now, and Arielle is home alone. Can you believe that crap?"

"Yes, I can. Jade has told me a lot about what's going on there. It worries me a lot since we've been working so much and not talking like we used to," I sighed heavily before continuing.

"I haven't told you everything," I confessed. He sat down and scooted his chair up to the table. I grabbed my phone and let him read all the text messages that Jade sent me. Many of the texts were forwarded straight from Arielle. Jade begged me not to get Arielle in trouble, but instead do something to help her get out of her situation. Anthony lost his appetite. He glared at me, and I was terrified that he would be angry with me for keeping this information from him. He wasn't. He said that he knew about some of this stuff because Arielle told him bits and pieces, but clearly, he didn't know everything.

—10—

Two Steps back

A nthony called Arielle back and they talked for a long time. I ate ¼ of his sandwich, some chips, and drank about 16 ounces of my soda while he talked. I watched a sitcom on television, and I was surprised when it went off that he was still on the phone with her.

"Why didn't you tell me about all this pumpkin?" I heard him ask softly. I smiled. *Because you still call her that!* Daddy's little girl. Sweet, but she's a teenager now.

Yawning, I grabbed my briefcase and laptop and started working on my reports. I worked for a long time and only caught small snatches of their conversation because he was pacing back and forth between the bedroom and the bathroom of the small hotel room. Finally, I finished my reports, double checked them, and shut down the computer. He was still on the phone.

"You know better!" I heard him chastise in a firm voice. I went to the bathroom and prepared to take a shower, prolonging my preparation in hopes that he might join me. He didn't. I took my time in the steamy bathroom, reapplying lotion and perfume, brushing my hair for the millionth time, brushing my teeth, flossing, and rinsing with mouthwash. Still, no Anthony. When I walked back out into the room, he was still pacing back and forth.

An exasperated look covered his face and he was apologizing, "I'm so sorry Ari Poo. I feel like coming there right now and strangling that kid. Why would he do that to you?" He was near tears, and the look on his face had transformed from frustration to anguish.

"Ari, is that all that happened?" *Are you telling me everything? Did he do anything else? Why didn't you tell his parents? Or his sister? Did you tell your mom? A teacher? Anyone?* Jade, yes. Jade is a good friend Arielle. Jade cares about you very much. You can trust her. You can tell her anything. You did the right thing by telling her. She wants to help you get out of that situation," he continued on his end of the conversation.

I continued listening because there was nothing else for me to do. I considered ironing my clothes for tomorrow, but I remembered that I had already taken my clothes to the dry cleaners, so they were already pressed and ready to wear.

"I want to kill that kid!" He punched the air several times. I stood and watched in shocked silence. *Damn! What kid? I wonder what the kid did. I'll have to ask Jade about this!*

"I'm going to talk to a lawyer tomorrow, okay. Don't worry pumpkin. I'm not going to get your mom in any trouble, but it sounds like she is going to get herself into trouble. Yes, stay in your room when she has her boyfriend over. Always sleep with your bedroom door locked. Even better, call grandma or auntie when he's over to stay for the weekend, so they can come and get you. I'll talk to them about this, okay?"

"There's nothing you can do that stop that. She's an adult, and she has to make good decisions. She's not making good decisions pumpkin. Above all, she should make you her number one priority sweetheart; nothing or no one else should be number one on her list, but she's just not doing that."

"No, she's not a bad mom. She is just mixed up right now and probably very sad because her mom, dad and brother won't talk to her anymore," he soothed.

"Yes, I have met them before."

"No, they were not very nice to me. They did not like me at all," Anthony continued his end of the conversation. She talked for a long time, and he shook his head in frustration.

"That's not for you to worry about Arielle. Right or wrong, you can't make someone want you or love you. I'm so sorry that it is this way. I never wanted you to know about that. You should concentrate on the people who love you unconditionally like me, Amina, Jade, Grandma Jacinda and Aunt Angie. Don't give them a second thought. They are the ones losing out, not you sweetheart," he persuaded.

"Of course!"

"I promise you that if they ever want to meet you, while you are living here with us, I will make it happen."

"Yes, sweetheart, I'm going to do what it takes to get you here to live with us," he promised. He listened to her for a long time, and then he looked up at the ceiling as if trying to hold back tears.

"Arielle, whatever happens, you have to remember that I love you, and the end result is that you'll be here with me. You won't have to deal with that stuff anymore, okay? Your mother is an adult. She can take care of herself. Try not to worry about her so much." He listened to her for a long time with a pained expression on his face.

"From this point forward, you must tell me everything, okay? No matter how uncomfortable it is, okay? You can call me, text me, send me an email, call Amina, use Jade as your messenger – I don't care how you tell me what's happening – just make sure you tell me everything, okay?" He listened again for a long time. Observing him in this conversation was entertaining, like watching one of my soap operas, but I felt a sliver of guilt for enjoying it.

"Don't cry baby. No! You don't have to give him any of the money back. Yes, that would be the honest thing to do, but he's evil and I want you to stay as far away from him as possible. Don't take any more money from him. Just stop talking to him. If you see him coming, turn around and go the other way. Don't even say anything about it! Definitely don't tell your mother! Listen Arielle. Listen baby! I need you to calm down and stop crying," he instructed sternly.

The intensity of the conversation had elevated quickly. The mention of money made my eyebrows rise. *What the hell was going on? What the hell happened with her?* I would definitely have to talk to Jade about all this because I knew that Anthony would be too exhausted to tell me all about it tonight. *Hell, this conversation was exhausting the hell out of me!* I settled into bed before looking at the clock – after midnight.

"Stop crying pumpkin. Everything is going to work out just fine, okay. Don't worry about your mother. She is going to be fine. She has always been able to take care of herself, so don't worry about her. She's doing what she wants to do, and guess what? She's an adult, so she can do whatever she wants. I just don't want you there to have to deal with the consequences. I wish you had told me all this sooner, and you probably would already be here with us. Calm down okay?" She talked for a few minutes more, and then it seemed like their conversation came to an abrupt end.

"I love you pumpkin. Amina loves you, and Jade loves you. We can't wait for you to be here with us. We are all going to be very happy together. Daddy is going to make that happen very soon, okay?"

Finally, he hung up the phone, ate quickly, took a shower, and joined me in bed. I was falling asleep, but he wanted to talk. He got up and turned the television off, so it was completely dark in the room. *I'll surely fall asleep now . . . but I guess he won't know unless he asks me a question.*

"Alycia and her boyfriend are doing drugs," he started before he even got back into the bed. That definitely woke me up.

"What? How are you sure?" I looked up at him and wondered why he was just standing there.

"From what Arielle described, they are drinking, smoking pot, smoking crack cocaine or meth, snorting cocaine, popping pills, and who knows what else," he explained with his hand on his hips. He looked like he wanted to start pacing again.

"Who knows what else they are doing? They are doing this shit in the apartment while my baby is there!" he roared, throwing up his hands and pacing back and forth.

"Not only that, they have their pusher coming to the apartment to deliver the shit!" he yelled. I sat up, pulled the cover back, patted the area beside me, and softly urged, "Calm down baby. Come here and let me hold you." He was quite upset: breathing rapidly, shaking slightly, full of nervous energy, like a firework after being lit and just before the explosion. I propped the pillows up on the headboard, sat back on them and pulled him between my legs. I rubbed his back and shoulders, massaged his temples, massaged his scalp, and rubbed through his hair until some of the tension subsided.

"Breathe baby," I soothed. Eventually, his breathing returned to normal, and he relaxed.

"You haven't been talking to her every night, have you?" I asked as I massaged his back and shoulders.

"No, since I've been working so much, I only talk to her a couple times a week," he sighed.

"I'm so sorry that I have not shared all the stuff that Jade told me," I apologized. He leaned back and I put my arms around his chest. "It's okay baby. It's not your fault. I've been slacking. Honestly, I've been avoiding her because it seemed like all she wanted was money. Our conversations were getting shorter and shorter, and I knew that she was keeping information from me. I know everything now, and I have to do something about it immediately," he replied.

"Let me know what I can do to help baby," I offered. We continued talking. He told me everything that Arielle told him, and I listened intently. When he paused to yawn, we finally decided to get some sleep.

He tossed and turned, while I slept like a baby. He woke me up at one point when he turned abruptly and socked the pillow a few times to try to soften it up a bit. A few minutes later, he went to the bathroom. He came back, got into bed, and scooted toward me. I wasn't asleep, but I pretended that I was. He kissed my nose softly and whispered, "Thank you Jesus for bringing her into my life. I love her with all my heart." *I love you too Anthony!*

–11–

Work in Progress

June 2000

"So according to this report, Amina, 32 of the stores in the southern region failed the safety and security specifications for visual merchandising?"

"Yes sir, unfortunately, that is correct," I affirmed. I was talking to Andrew Wiggins, one of the big shots at the corporate headquarters of USDSI in Dayton, Texas. We were going over a report that I sent him a week ago, but I guessed that he just now had a chance to read over it and ask me a million questions.

"Amina, that number is staggering and quite disconcerting," he breathed, "it looks like you visited twelve stores and did a virtual tour of the other 20. Is that correct?"

"Yes," I answered and wondered why I was confirming all of the information that was contained in the report. *Maybe the information was so unbelievable that he needed to hear it from a real person!*

"We are going to have to meet, discuss this, create an action plan to make corrections, and do whatever it takes to get those stores up to compliance," he directed.

"Absolutely," I agreed.

"Amina, clear your calendar again. Choose an assistant or two to accompany you to Dayton this time, bring all of the virtual tour footage, transcripts of your conversations with store managers, VMMs, reports, research, anything you have showing the stores that were in compliance – hell your store always exceeds standards – and bring your ideas for the action plans for the ones that did not meet standards. If you can put together a detailed plan to get the Crockett store and others up to code, that would be great a great model, or if you already have plans ready for another store, that would work fine. We will have to get someone from legal to provide all of the lawsuit implications and protections. I could go on and on, but you understand that we have a lot to do!" he rambled. I finished taking notes. *Sounds like a big raise, promotion or both to me!*

"When do you want me there?" I inquired.

"Is Monday too soon?"

I looked at the calendar and frowned.

"Regional Planning Committee meeting in Breckinridge on Monday. I'm supposed to attend and answer questions about this audit," I answered. He exhaled loudly and was silent for a few minutes. He moved the phone away, but I could hear him flipping through papers in the background, and then he asked someone a question that I could not hear.

"Send someone in your place Amina; this is way too important to put on hold. We need to get this in motion immediately," he huffed.

"Okay, no problem," I responded. I started thinking for a few seconds - *Damn, who would I send in my place? This last minute change of plans was not cool at all. Perhaps if he read through the report last week, this would not have happened!* – and missed part of Andrew's rambling.

". . . but we can discuss that Monday," he finished. *Damn! What did he just say?*

"My assistant, Connie, will contact you promptly to get you set up with travel and accommodations. Do you have any questions so far?" *Yes, what the hell did you just say?*

"None at the moment, but may I call you if I do?" I asked sweetly.

"Oh most definitely! Connie will provide you with some contact numbers for not only me, but also other members of my staff and people you may need to speak with in other corporate offices, okay? If nothing else, we will see you soon." I hung up because he had already rushed off the phone before I could even answer.

I bolted into action. Suddenly, I had a million things to do between Thursday and Monday. First, I would have to decide who I wanted to go in my place to Breckinridge and who would go with me to Dayton. It needed to be someone who seriously took pride in his/her job.

My first thoughts were Rashad, Michelle, Whitney and Katy, so I moved to my computer and pulled up the work schedule. Rashad's regular time off was Sunday, Monday and Tuesday, so he would be perfect for the trip to Breckinridge. He would also represent me well because he helped me call and interview store managers when the stores were audited and determined to be out of compliance.

Michelle was my first choice for accompanying me to Dayton, but she had requested the weekend and Monday off. *I hope she doesn't have anything special planned for those days because I really need her help.* I paged the junior department to get her to come and talk to me.

"Michelle?" I spoke into the phone's intercom system. No answer. I waited a few minute before I said her name again, and Serena picked up the phone.

"Michelle is helping a customer. How may I help you?" she answered nicely. Serena, one of my least favorite coworkers, hated me for two reasons: 1- Rashad didn't want her. 2- She thinks Rashad wants me because we spend a lot of time together at work, and we enjoy each other's company.

"Hi Serena. This is Amina. Will you send Michelle to my office when she finishes? Please?" *Be nice to the silly heifer and maybe she will do it.*

"Yeah," she answered and pressed the button to hang up. *Bitch.*

I got to work gathering file boxes and filling them with materials. I talked to Connie and decided to drive instead of fly, which meant that I would have to leave Sunday afternoon. She gave me the hotel information, and I was pleased to learn that it was within walking distance to USDSI's corporate headquarters. I called Rashad in the men's department and talked to him about covering for me at the regional meeting in Breckinridge, and he was happy to do it.

"Hell yeah I'll do it! I've been waiting for my chance to break into the big league!" I envisioned him smiling and the fluorescent light catching the shine from his gold crown. We talked details for a few minutes, and he cracked a few jokes and made me laugh. It felt like old times, but I remembered what Anthony said about how he felt about my friendship with Rashad, so I cut it short. He wouldn't have noticed anyway because his department was busy with customers at the time.

I glanced at the clock and wondered why Michelle hadn't called or came to talk to me. I decided to go to her. Rashad had just escorted a customer to the customer service desk, so he walked with me to the junior department. I told him about the situation, and invited him to come to my office later so we could hammer out the final details for the meeting in Breckinridge.

"She probably didn't even tell her," he said as he nodded at a surly-faced Serena. She looked at Rashad and smiled, but she looked at me and rolled her eyes. I strode into the department and found Michelle hanging a pile of clothing.

I looked back at Serena, who was just standing at the register, and calmly commanded, "Serena, please go and clean out the dressing rooms while I talk to Michelle. We'll handle any customers until you finish." She turned, looked at me with distaste, and walked slowly to the dressing rooms. I walked over to Michelle and started helping her.

"Good morning sunshine!" I beamed at her. She forced a smile, but she seemed genuinely frustrated.

"Good morning!" she brightened at my sentiment and perhaps the fact that I was helping her. I already knew part of what was bothering her: Serena was no help in the department that Michelle worked tirelessly to keep clean, organized and operating at top sales. I hoped my invitation would cheer her up.

"I guess you didn't get my message?" I asked as I hung up three blouses.

"What message?" she asked with a confused crease on her forehead.

"I called down here and asked Serena to tell you to call me. She said that you were busy with a customer," I informed.

Michelle dropped a hanger, looked up into the sky, and said, "Lord, give me strength!" I just looked at her. I wanted to laugh, but this seemed serious.

"Let's go to my office and finish talking," I instructed. She looked around hopelessly at the disheveled department.

"Don't worry about it right now," I coaxed, "I'll talk to Dottie about what is going on here.

"But . . ." she started and looked at the dressing room. I walked over to the entrance and called, "Serena, Michelle and I are going to the office, so you are on your own for a while. Do you need someone to come and help you get the department back in order? I looked at Michelle and winked.

"No," Serena answered rudely.

"Well, it's pretty messy right now. It must have been a busy night and a busy morning. I'll see if Dottie can come and help you since Michelle is about to be tied up for a while," I smirked. That got her attention. She came out with a hand full of clothing and hangers and looked at us as if trying to figure out what was going on.

The only thing ugly about Serena was her attitude. She was tall and thin with a smooth light skinned complexion and her hair hung down in small, neat braids. She wore colored contacts, sometimes to actually match the outfit she was wearing. Tacky, but today she was wearing grayish blue contacts and they were kind of cute. Since she started working at UpStage, she had drastically improved her wardrobe, hair and makeup. Her attitude and work ethic were the only things that needed an upgrade. I looked at her and a sudden, strange idea struck me.

"Tied up doing what?" she asked with a frown.

"We need to go over some department manager business, but when I finish talking to her, I need to talk to you," I stated, watched, and waited for an ugly reaction that I was sure to get from her.

"Talk to me about what?" she frowned.

"Well, get busy, and when I am finished with Michelle, I'll talk to you," I said as Michelle and I started walking away leaving Serena with a pile of clothes to hang. She rolled her eyes at me as we walked away, and I shook my head and smiled. *So simple and predictable.*

In my office, Michelle sat down and sighed, "It feels good to get off my feet! It's only 11:45? Wow! It feels like I've been here all day!"

"Your hard work is definitely appreciated Michelle. That is exactly what I wanted to talk to you about," I explained. She sat up straight in the chair with her eyes wide open and keenly interested in what I was about to say.

"I see that you requested this weekend off," I started.

"Yes, I need to rest and I have a project due in one of my classes, she answered.

"So, how's your senior year in college going?" I continued. I could see her getting antsy, but I enjoyed this stall tactic.

"Classes are great! I'll be so glad when it's time to graduate!" she bubbled. I looked at her and smiled. She fidgeted.

"Amina! I know that's not what you brought me up here to talk about!" she whisper screamed. I giggled.

"As a result of all the safety and security audits that I've been doing for the past few months, I've been invited to some very important meetings in Dayton at corporate headquarters. I can bring an assistant or two with me, and I was hoping that you would be willing to go?" Her smile beamed at me and she clapped a little.

"But wait! There are a few conditions," I continued, "We'd have to leave Sunday and probably not return until Wednesday maybe even Thursday."

"That's not a problem, is it? We can get my department covered," she interrupted. I shook my head to indicate yes.

"Will I have time to work on my project while I'm there?"

"Yes, that should not be a problem. We should be able to work out some personal time."

"There's an even bigger catch," I said and raised my eyebrows.

"In fact, I just made the decision on this one," I explained.

"What?" Michelle asked with huge eyes and an open, smiling mouth.

"I would also like to bring Serena as a manager trainee," I said. Michelle's smile darkened. She frowned and her forehead transformed from smooth milk chocolate to a wrinkled candy wrapper.

"Are you serious?!! She's not management material! She's not even sales associate material! I don't even know why she works here! No! She is the last person you should take!" she screeched. It was totally out of character for Michelle who was unusually tolerant, welcoming, and open minded. *Wow! Religious girl really knows how to speak her mind! Obviously, Serena has gotten on Michelle's last nerve. Damn!*

"And that's exactly why I want to take her. She claims to want to be a manager, she claims to want promotions and raises, but she doesn't show it at all. I want to take her so she can see why visual merchandising is so important and why she has to be serious about it, so your department can remain the most successful department in the store," I expounded.

"I guess. She's not going to make manager by standing around stealing customers and popping gum all day!" Michelle said with a roll of her eyes.

"Is that what just happened?" I asked with a shake of my head. *That bitch! Gosh! I can't stand her!*

"Yes! I spent close to an hour helping a lady and her three teenage daughters. I left them for a few seconds and looked up to see Serena ringing up the sale! She does it all the time. She thinks that because I'm a department manager now that I don't care about my sales because they are no longer commissioned, but I do. It's one thing if I ask her to close a sale, but it's another if she just sneaks and takes the sale like she does every chance she gets!" Michelle vented.

Dottie walked in at that moment and said, "You must be talking about 'Sales Stealing Serena' and her sneaky antics in the junior department!" We quickly filled Dottie in on the day's developments.

"Congratulations!" she smiled at me as she manipulated her sandy blonde hair behind her ear and over her shoulder.

"So, Michelle, will you be able to go?" Dottie asked as she gave her a congratulatory pat on the shoulder.

"Yes, but I'm not sure about the Serena deal. Why don't you just take her" she questioned, "or leave her?" We laughed in unison.

"I see what you are trying to do Amina. It's a good idea for someone who is willing to accept the training. I'm not sure if Serena is that person but good luck my friend! I hope it works!" Dottie left the office with a chuckle.

"Well, I don't see what you are trying to do! Explain it to me, please!" Michelle complained as she pretended to choke herself and pull her hair out. I laughed at her and explained that Serena did not fully understand the importance of a neat, clean, organized, USDSI's basic standards of visually merchandised, department and how it connects to safety and security.

Since the entirety of the meetings at corporate headquarters is focused on the visual merchandising audits that I did for the past few months, we will be discussing these standards at length and in great detail. Serena would get to see up close and personal why we make such a big deal out of certain things.

"They want to create action plans which I'm sure will include employee training to get all of our stores up to and exceeding standard. The big thing is money. They want to avoid lawsuits and increase profits. Basically, Andrew Wiggins told me to drop everything and bring an assistant, prepare to present all of my findings, and be ready to assist in creation of actions plans to improve all stores in general, but mainly to assist the 32 stores in the southern region that did not meet compliance standards," I explained and took a small breath. I smiled at her. She looked overwhelmed.

"Sounds like a lot of work!" she said and fell back into a slumping position in the chair.

"It will be, but it's not that bad. You'll see. You will get to see a whole new side of things. Well? Will you go with me? Please?"

"Yes, I'll go, but Lord help me if that girl doesn't act right!" Michelle said while rolling her eyes and punching the palm of her left hand. *Damn! She sure can snap out of religion fast when she's angry!*

"I'll keep her so busy with the virtual tours, transcribing, and filling in reports that she won't have time to misbehave," I informed.

"I'll pray for us all," she giggled. We talked for a few minutes more before Michelle left and sent Serena back.

When I told Serena about the plans, she gave me a strange look and asked, "Why me?"

"Why not you? You've been waiting for an advancement opportunity to open at this store; here it is."

"Yeah, right. Why did you choose me when you could have chosen another one of your friends? Is this some type of set up to get me fired?" She narrowed her eyes and pressed her red lips together in a snarl.

I rolled my eyes to the ceiling, shook my head and tried not to laugh. *Damn! Bitch! Why are you so simple?*

"No offense Serena, but you need this trip more than anyone else who works here," I explained calmly.

"What is that supposed to mean?" she asked defensively. She stood up and moved toward the door.

"Serena, would you just calm down? Sit down. Can't you see that I'm trying to help you?" I asked and attempted to look her in the eyes. She avoided my gaze.

"I don't need your help!" she answered in an elevated volume that caused Mike, the store manager to stop and look at her funny as he passed by. She gave him an embarrassed smile. *Busted!*

"Hello Mike," she greeted nicely.

"Hey Serena! Is everything okay?" he looked at her, and then he looked at me. I smiled at him, raised my eyebrows, and looked him directly in the eye.

"Everything is just fine," she lied as she sat back down and told him all about the "honor" of being chosen to go on this very important trip with me as an assistant and "manager trainee."

"Well, congratulations!" he smiled at her then raised his eyebrows at me. This was probably his first time hearing about this.

"I just talked to Andrew Wiggins about an hour ago. Dottie will fill you in on all the details," I explained to Mike; he shook his head in understanding, and left just as quickly as he came after congratulating me and Serena. I turned and looked at her. She was sitting there with a confused look on her face.

"So, you are good with it now?" I asked and continued my quest to make eye contact with her. She continued to avoid my eyes.

"Yeah, I'm good," she said and gave me a strange look. *Hard to believe just last year, I was ready to strangle the life from this chick. I* opened my desk drawer, gave her a pen and a notepad, instructed her to take notes of every detail, and slowly told her everything that I could think of that we needed to do to get ready. She wrote everything that I told her and double checked to make sure she got it all right.

When I told her that I was finished for now, she left without another word. I moved my chair back so that I was positioned in front of the computer, and Serena ran back in, looked me in the eye, and quickly said, "Thank you," and she left before I could respond. *Just get your surly ass ready to work and prove yourself.*

Mike must have been watching and waiting for her to leave because once she bounded down the stairs, he came into my office and closed the door. For a man, he was of medium stature: about 5'9 slight shoulders, dark brown hair that stood up in little tufts in some places, bushy eyebrows, and a clean shaven face. He had two big white front teeth and when he was nervous or upset, some of his words were spoken with a lisp.

Frowning, he waltzed in. It was not an angry frown as much as it was a worried one.

"Are you sure Serena is a good choice to take with you to corporate? I understand Michelle, but Serena?" he screeched. However, when he said Serena, it sounded like "Tha-rena."

"I think she is the perfect choice because her department is a high risk area for compliance issues, and she doesn't seem to fully grasp the link between visual merchandising, safety and security," I explained.

"Yes, you are correct on that, but we need professional representatives from our store in front of those corporate guys," he said while wringing his hands.

"Don't worry! I plan to keep her busy with a lot of behind the scenes work, but even if she comes into contact with them, she will be a professional representative of this store. I'll make sure of it," I assured. He snort laughed and gave me a wild look.

"Are we talking about the same Serena? What are you going to do? Give her a miraculous instant personality changing drug?"

I looked at his wild expression and, I giggled; then I doubled over with laughter. He laughed for a few minutes too, and then he stopped and gave me that wild look again: eyebrows raised, eyes wide open, mouth hanging open with a slack jaw. I regained my composure and continued with my explanation. As store manager, Mike could override my decision if he wanted, so I had to make sure he understood my reasons.

"Seriously Mike, Serena doesn't seem to be going anywhere. She's sticking around, so I think it's time for someone to mentor her. She's shown interest several times in management positions, but she just hasn't backed up her interest with the hard work to show that she's serious. I can tell that she wants to do a good job, but she seems stuck or confused about how to go about doing it. I want to help her by showing her some important retail concepts, loss prevention, for example," I provided. He stared at me for a minute, relaxed his face, and closed his mouth. He moved like he was going to say something, but he changed his mind.

"Good luck on your trip. You definitely can see something that I cannot, but that's a wonderful thing. We need innovative ideas and great vision around here, so we can stay on top. I just hope that you are right. I'm going to stress to Serena how important this meeting is though because I don't want any mistakes. Mentoring and training are very important parts of the success of UpStage Department Store. Amina, I knew that I was making a smart choice when I hired you!" he beamed. His face had totally transformed as if he had an epiphany.

"Thanks Mike," I said and stood up to walk with him out of the office.

"I'll keep you updated on everything that happens," I assured. He gave me a thumb up sign and hurried back to his office down the hall.

I went to the lounge for a late lunch. Katie, Rashad and Whitney were there eating lunch and having a loud, animated conversation. When I walked in, they instantly stopped talking and pretended they had been silently eating all along.

I sat down, laughed, and said, "Obviously, you were talking about me! Carry on! Has the gossip hound already filled you all in on the latest developments?"

"No," Katy giggled, "Vanessa is off today!" We all burst into a chorus of laughter. They informed me that Serena was excitedly telling everyone the news. Katy came over and felt my forehead.

"Nope, she feels like she has a normal temperature, so maybe she isn't delirious after all!" More hysterical laughter. I looked around at the group, shook my head, and giggled.

"Somebody needs to go and check Serena's temperature," Rashad instructed, "because she's out in the junior department actually working and helping Michelle!"

Silence. Whitney's mouth dropped. I choked on my sandwich. Katy giggled. Rashad vigorously shook his head up and down to indicate yes.

"I don't believe you!" Katy finally said with a shake of her fiery red hair.

I displayed a humongous smile and said, "See my plan is working already!"

"Take me next time," Rashad chuckled, "You won't have to trick me to work! I'll do it voluntarily." I smiled at him and looked around at my co-workers. They were all managers or somewhat in charge of a section of the store. They all worked hard and valued their jobs, but none of them were upset with me for choosing Serena to go on the trip. They were all smiling and laughing about the whole thing.

"Thanks for the Breckinridge gig. I really appreciate the chance to get away, the opportunity to network, and the type of exposure that I might get there," Rashad exclaimed.

"You are so welcome," I acknowledged with a huge smile. It was so nice to be talking and joking with him again. Finally, I had my friend back.

"When you really think about it," Katy surmised, "she's taken all of us with her on auditing trips, training seminars, visual design trips, and other business trips in this region. She's taken everybody but the slackers, Serena and Vanessa!" *Oh shit! Was it that obvious? Mike doesn't care though. If he did, he would have said something by now. He always lets me choose who to take with me. Would he say something if he had a problem with my choices? Yes, yes he would. He said something about Serena today!*

"Oh yeah! That's right! That doesn't look too good Amina! You should stop playing favorites!" Whitney laughed. Even though her statement wasn't that funny, everyone laughed with her.

"Well, we all know why, don't we?" I asked and everyone shook their heads.

"I can really see what you are up to!" Whitney squealed, "You have given this entire store great exposure! We all work hard to achieve top sales, and we have the best compliance record in our region. We can't have a couple of weak links working alongside us. Either we have to train them up or figure out how to get rid of them!"

"Shhhhh!!!!!" Rashad and Katy cautioned at the same time. I shook my head and giggled. She was right, but I would never say it aloud.

"It's true!" Whitney continued, "I get so many calls from other department managers giving me compliments, asking for advice, and asking questions about our visual merchandising design models, but when you think about it, that's crazy since we all use the same designs! The difference is how our sales associates, department managers, and store managers execute the service behind the designs!"

"Preach sista!" Rashad waved his hands like he was catching the Holy Ghost on a hot Sunday afternoon in a Southern Baptist Church. Another chorus of laughter exploded from us. Katy giggled before adding her two cents.

"Yep, our Amina is a go-getter, a trend-setter, and an innovator!" Katy added.

"Welllllllllllll . . ." Rashad hummed.

"Amen!" Whitney added.

"Hallelujah!" Katy giggled. Their laughter erupted and rang out like a volcanic chorus.

"Okay, I said blushing, "y'all can stop now!" The compliments were great, but they were also very humbling. I saw some things that needed to be done, so I did them. Serena's attitude and work ethic need improvement, so I'm going to try my best to help.

If that goes well, I will add Vanessa to the mix. She is much more likeable than Serena. In fact, Vanessa and I were friends until Serena came along and poisoned her with negativity. Now, they are like two peas in a pod; their attitudes stink and their work habits are pathetic. Like Whitney said, we can't have two weak links in our store.

We ate, talked, and joked until our lunch break was over. I tried not to worry about Serena because I had a feeling that she would eventually see that I was trying to help her. If not, surely Mike would see that she has been given every chance that she could possibly get, and he will finally understand that our store needs to eliminate all of its weak links.

–12–

The Dayton Dilemma

*W*hen I got back to my office, I called Anthony.

"Hello my sweetheart," he greeted.

"Hi baby," I answered, "How are you?

"I'm great now that I'm talking to my baby!" *How would I tell him this news? He won't like it, especially the fact that I may very well come into close contact with Clayton. I might even have to work beside him. Hmm . . .*

"I need to see you," I said softly.

"Umm . . . I need to see you too baby" he grumbled and adjusted the phone.

"Well, since you worked over a couple of times, I lost track of your schedule for the rest of this week.

"I'm at work now until 6, tomorrow 6 – 6, off Saturday, then back to my normal schedule," he informed, and I took mental notes. The weekend could prove to be calamitous if he didn't have anything to keep him busy all day, but I had something in mind, and I hoped that things would not take such a turn.

"So, were you planning to come over?"

"Yes ma'am," he chuckled.

"Good. I need to see you," I continued my air of mystery.

"Okay, baby," he spoke with a sexy voice that matched my teasing, "Six o'clock can't get here soon enough!" he blurted.

"Actually, I need you to come at 8:00," I instructed, "Because I need time to get some things ready," I teased.

"Why are you doing this to me girl?"

I envisioned his cute dimpled grin, and I smiled.

"Because I miss you!" *I need to make sure you are happy and busy, and I need a huge distraction before I go away to Dayton where I will possibly come face to face with Clayton.*

"I miss you too baby," he concurred.

"We need to make up for all this time that we've been missing each other," I asserted.

"Yes, that sounds great to me!"

"Okay, I'll see you at 8:00, not 7:30, not 7:45, 8:00. Don't come early!" I warned. He chuckled.

"I'm serious!" I cautioned him again, and he agreed with a titter of laughter. We hung up and I got busy planning my seduction/distraction of Anthony.

I tried to think it through in my head: so, tonight – seduction and distraction; Friday – I work 9 to 6, and he works 6 p.m. to 6 a.m.; Saturday – Breakfast in bed and more seduction and distraction all day until Sunday morning when I tell him about the trip. I will have to leave sometime Sunday afternoon and he has to go in to work Sunday evening at 6, so that won't give him much time to be angry. *Hell, he'll be so happy and in love that he won't even fathom the thought of being mad.* Should I just tell him tonight? So he can do what he needs to do Saturday? Is all this trickery really necessary? Yes, it is. He will not like the news of this upcoming trip to Dayton. He will not absorb it with happiness and joy. *I hope it doesn't drive him to drinking! Shit!* It is going to irritate the hell out of him, and just the fact that it bothers him will annoy him even more! He puts up a good front for me by pretending that he is okay with me working with Clayton, when the reality is that he does not want me anywhere near Clayton (and with good reason).

～+～+～+～+～+～+～

"So you never told me what caused you and Clayton to break up," Anthony inquired. We were in my bed after a breath taking round of love making. Why he wanted to talk about Clayton is beyond my realm of understanding.

"And I never will. Can't we just leave the past in the past? It's over and done with. Stop looking back at it," I mumbled and turned over so that my back was facing him. He snuggled up behind me.

"I thought you said that we could talk about anything," he said and kissed my neck. I rolled my eyes and exhaled loudly. *Okay. Damn!*

"We can talk about it baby, but once we have this discussion, let's not talk about our exes anymore, okay?" He continued kissing my neck, shoulders and back in an attempt to break me down.

"Ummm hmmm," he murmured. I bumped him with my butt and said, "Seriously!"

"Okay baby! Don't get violent! Bumping me with that deadly booty!" he joked as he continued kissing me. I started laughing, appreciative of his ability to lighten the mood and make me laugh.

"So, why did he break up with you?" he continued with his joking.

"It was the other way around silly rabbit!" I giggled. I inhaled and started the recap, "Well, you know that I went to Chicago to escape the mess that was going on here at the time," I started.

"Did he ask you to come, or did you ask him?" he asked quickly, as if that question was burning a hole in his mouth. I turned to face him because I needed to see his eyes and facial expressions when we talked about this. His beautiful brownish green eyes were shining in the semi-darkness. I inched closer and touched his muscled chest.

"He asked me, and I impulsively jumped at the chance. We were still talking sporadically, but you knew this much. Remember I told you that he was a workaholic? We didn't get to see each other that much at all. During the entire 6 months or so that we were supposedly seeing each other, I probably only saw him 6 or 7 times," I explained as I looked into his eyes and tried to detect a change in his demeanor. Nothing. He was calm, patient, and seriously waiting for me to continue.

"We talked a lot at first, but it eventually trickled down to nothing, and that was right about the time that I met you. Months passed before I spoke to him again, so it was just a coincidence that he called me when we were going through the chaos with Vickie," I explained with another look into his eyes. No change. Not even a flicker of variation.

"When I went to Chicago, I felt terribly guilty about being with him because you and I had become close. But, you have to remember that I was up front and honest with you about the fact that I didn't really know where my relationship with Clayton stood, right?" I asked and looked at him. He did not respond. His expression did not change at all. My own expression darkened. *Well damn! Can't I get something? A frown, a glare, half of a damn frown? All I get is stone face!*

"Oh yes, I remember the way you had me hanging on a string, twitching, wriggling, waiting for you to take me off the hook and put me in your "keeper" bucket," he explained metaphorically but still no change in his countenance. *Hmm . . . that was a hint of sarcasm though, so at least now I'm getting some emotion.*

"Wow! What an analogy!" I giggled. This caused him to frown a little. *Okay! Now we are really getting somewhere! Let me see your true feelings!*

"Anyway, I decided long before I met you that I didn't want to just be his weekend fling, so we were headed for a breakup anyway. Like I said, when I went to Chicago, I felt terribly guilty about being with him, but he didn't even notice because he was working the entire time that I was there!" I paused. He was forcing himself to keep a straight, calm face. I wanted to continue, but I was quite unsure of how I should proceed. I inhaled deeply. Calm face. I exhaled deeply. He frowned. *What the hell? Did he want a blow by blow explanation of what we did while I was there?*

"Tell me everything baby," he insisted with the frown set firmly in his forehead. I inhaled and exhaled again and looked down at this chest. It was hairy in the middle and his pecs were shiny with sweat. I looked back up at him. He was still frowning.

"Well, of course we did that," I whispered softly, "but I wasn't thinking straight! I was a mess! I was all over the place! Honestly, I let him take advantage of my vulnerability. I wanted something to make sense, and at that time and place, he made a lot of sense. Nothing made sense in my life here except my relationship with you, and Vickie was steadily turning that into nonsense!" I quickly and loudly spilled. Afraid to look at him, I closed my eyes. Except for my breathing, the room was silent for a few moments.

"So basically, you let her get to you," he proclaimed as he sat up and balanced his chin on his hand.

"Everything got to me," I confessed, "I had to get away from it all because I couldn't take it anymore!" My volume had increased, my stomach was flip flopping, and my pulse was racing, but I continued, "She pushed me past my limit!"

"Okay, calm down baby. Turn back around, so I can hold you," he instructed as he kissed me gently. My heart was beating erratically, but as soon as he put his arms around me, it slowed down considerably.

"The anxiety attacks were getting to me. My urge to hurt her was getting to me. It was just too much Anthony. I'm so sorry that I reacted the way I did. I'm so sorry that I hurt you like that, but the time that I spent with him meant absolutely nothing," I explained on the verge of tears. "That time away was just a distraction and a useless waste of time because when I returned, nothing had changed. Everything was worse than I left it, and I made the situation between you and I turn into a terrible one," I confessed. He squeezed me and listened. He waited patiently.

"I'm so sorry baby. I wish I could take it back." I couldn't say anything else. I didn't know what else to say after spilling my guts.

"Is that it?" he whispered.

"No, the fucker was married and his marriage was annulled – some silly mess that I didn't care to get caught in the middle of," I huffed.

"Are you serious?"

"Yes, but I had already decided when he picked me up at the airport that I was going to break up with him. I couldn't get you off my mind. When I saw him, I didn't feel anything but guilt," I informed him.

"Go on," he prodded.

"Really, I had already decided that it was over on that first day before I even found out about his marriage and pregnant wife."

"Pregnant wife? What?" he shouted, startling me.

"Calm down baby!" I giggled.

"The pregnant wife is the reason his marriage was annulled. It wasn't his baby. Like I said, it was a bunch of nonsense that I wanted no involvement in. Much later, not during this trip to Chicago, he told me that the only reason he married her was because she was pregnant and she was going to somehow use that information to ruin him professionally if he did not marry her. I don't know all the details, and I don't really care. During that trip, a man that he worked with told me all about the fact that Clayton was married and that his wife was pregnant," I described, "I think she was very young or from a prominent family – some bullshit that I didn't even press to get the full story."

"John, the man he worked with, gave me his card and told me to call him, if I wanted the truth. After I left the hotel, I called him and he told me everything that I needed to know. Clayton was married, had been married the entire time that he was involved with me, and his wife was pregnant," I narrated.

"So Clayton never told you that he was married? Not once did he mention that he had a wife who was pregnant?"

"No. Not once," I said in a forced neutral tone. *But just talking about it and thinking about it was making me feel . . . sad. Why?*

"Now, that's some crazy shit!" he exhaled and loosened the pressure of his hug.

"Yeah, I seem to attract crazy," I giggled.

"Yes, you're a crazy magnet!" he announced aloud and pulled me closer to his hard, naked body.

"And guess what?" he continued, "I'm certifiable, cuckoo, delirious, insane in the membrane!" he joked. We laughed, and we snuggled back into our comfortable positions.

"So, after you broke up with him, and I forgave you for going to be with him, you said that you talked to him again and he confessed everything?" *Oh shit! Did I say that? Open mouth, insert foot. Shit!*

"Yes, I guess I did talk to him after that trip to Chicago," I answered.

"When was this?"

"Probably after Christmas or around New Year's. I know it was after . . . you know. I can't remember the date exactly, but I just talked to him on the phone. I told him what John told me, and gave him a chance to explain. I told him about my relationship with you and made it clear that it was over between me and him," I explained.

"So, you haven't talked to him since then?"

"Am I being interrogated?"

"Just answer the question," he instructed impatiently.

"No, I haven't talked to him since then. Now, we talked about my indiscretions, so let's talk about yours," I challenged.

"Okay baby, shoot!" he said excitedly.

"Not a good choice of words honey bun," I reminded, "especially since I am about to ask about Vickie."

"Yeah, I guess you're right," he agreed. We shifted positions: he lay on his back, and I lay on my side so that I could put my head on his chest. This was my favorite way to rest with him, with his strong arm around me, and my head resting near his heart.

"Did you sleep with her that day that I saw you two at Boudreaux's?" I fired at him.

"Damn baby! Get straight to the point!" he laughed. I waited. He didn't say anything, but he laughed again, as if to stall his answer.

"Did you?" I demanded seriously.

"Okay, hold up. You were with your boyfriend, Clayton, that day, and you were worried about me and Vickie having sex?"

"Yes!" I answered and thumped his hard abdomen. He didn't move. My finger throbbed from the impact.

"Hmmm . . . that's very peculiar!" he joked.

"Well, did you?" I demanded again.

"No baby. I did not sleep with Vickie that day," he answered calmly. His answer seemed like he chose his words very carefully. *He didn't sleep with her that day. Does that answer mean that he slept with her that night? Did he sleep with her the next day? I'm not stupid Anthony! Just as I was feeling hurt and vulnerable, you must have been feeling the same way. What man is going to turn down a woman who is ready, willing and able to give herself to him?* My eyes narrowed for a few seconds, but I doubt he noticed.

"Well, how did you get her to go out with you when you claimed that it was over? Remember you told me that you and Vickie had ended your relationship."

"That was a huge mistake that I really regret," he answered. *Oh shit, here it comes. Brace yourself Amina. Do you really want to know this?*

"I called her and sweet talked her when I asked her out. I was even affectionate with her, and I did it all just to make you jealous," he admitted. He exhaled and waited for me to say something.

"Did you make her any promises?"

"No. I owed her a nice lunch because she had brought me lunch to work once or twice without me reciprocating," he answered.

"I saw you hugging and kissing on her," I said sadly, "it seemed like you meant it, and it made me extremely jealous, so your scheme worked."

"Why are you torturing me with this?" he asked softly as he caressed my arm and shoulder.

"Well it happened, and it looked like you were enjoying yourself. She definitely enjoyed it," I continued glumly as I felt my tear ducts try to open up and allow a tear or two to escape. Instead, I willed them shut.

"No, I was putting on an act for you. I hated every second of the time that I spent with her. I should never have done that because it sent her all the wrong messages. It was a terrible thing to do, because from that point on, she was convinced that I wanted her. Even when I set her straight and told her the truth, that I was trying to make you jealous, I had to fight her off of me," he detailed.

"You are such a liar!" I almost screamed. I didn't move, but I wanted to get up, run into the bathroom, and slam the door.

"I'm telling you the truth baby! I was so into you that I was ready to walk over a bed of hot coals for you. I felt invincible, like no man could defeat my efforts to get you. I had my guns blazing and ready!" he shouted and shook the bed.

"There you go with the shooting metaphors again," I smirked, "you used her Anthony, and you actually told her that?"

"Yes, I did. You would have to understand her personality to know that normally, something like that would not have bothered her; she would have been all for it, and she would have put on quite a show," he explained.

"Obviously, you were confused about her feelings," I suggested, "because knowing that she had been used cut her deeply."

"Yes, I guess I was confused. I apologized though, and I told her the truth about everything. There should not have been any confusion about how I felt about you because I told her!"

"I believe you baby. Do you understand how difficult it is for a woman to learn that she's been used as bait to catch another woman? That's a hard pill to swallow. It's just sad to think that her refusal to accept it resulted in her death." He exhaled slowly. *Was he about to cry?*

"Weird question: do you think her spirit is hanging on to me or something?" he whispered.

"No, but sometimes it feels weird, like someone is watching us. Have you ever felt that way? Especially in your apartment?"

"Yes! Which is exactly why you should let me move in here!" he chuckled and hugged me tightly. I giggled and hugged him back.

"Stay away from the TV when there is static or snow, and you shouldn't have anything to worry about!"

We continued our pillow talk until all of our questions were answered, and we finally fell asleep. Our conversation lifted a heavy weight of unanswered questions, residual quiet and unnecessary jealousy off of our shoulders. That burden had worn out its welcome in our lives. *So, why was he still hitting the bottle on a regular basis, why was he hiding his drinking from me, why was he having mood swings when he did not drink regularly, and why was he working nonstop and using work to avoid . . . What was he avoiding?*

Of course, I learned later that he was avoiding the situation with his daughter. He was avoiding talking to me about her because of a simple miscommunication. I just wish I could get him to trust me and believe that I am so through with Clayton. *Maybe he'll believe it if I actually believe it my damn self!*

~+~+~+~+~+~+~+~

It took 6:00 forever to arrive. I zoomed out of the office and buzzed through the store to get out to the parking lot. I drove quickly to Johnny's Bar & Grill and picked up the grilled steak and grilled chicken dinners that I ordered earlier. I went to Blooms and Blessings Flower Shop and picked up two bags of fresh rose petals, and the cashier winked at me as I left.

My last stop was Traylor's Medical Equipment & Supply Company to pick up the item that I rented. I was dismayed to learn that it would not fit in my car, not even with the back seat folded flat. I paid extra to have it delivered just as someone called in to cancel a delivery. *Thank you God!* I slowed down my driving just a bit to accommodate the following delivery driver because he did not know my address. He agreed on the spot to simply follow me to my house. We arrived; he unloaded it and set it up in my living room. I gave him a generous tip and led him out. I glanced at the time, 7:20, and jumped into action. Anthony was extremely punctual, often to a point of irritation, but I appreciated him for his promptness as it started rubbing off on me.

I undressed and took a quick shower, put on a royal blue silk chemise with spaghetti straps with a matching robe. I combed my hair and fluffed it out, refreshed my makeup, and spritzed perfume all over. I looked at myself in the mirror and smiled. I was "glowing," my smile was genuine, my heart was beating happily, and I felt 100% good and confident about what I was about to do tonight.

I strolled to the kitchen and took the food out of the carryout packages and put it on plates, set the table, lit candles everywhere, and put the plates into the oven which I turned on to warm at 150 degrees. I ran and grabbed the rose petals and sprinkled them from the front door to the massage table in the living room to the dining room and finally to the bedroom. I sprinkled an abundance of rose petals on and around the bed.

My haphazard efforts at romance would hardly be noticed with the dim lights and soft music, I thought as I ran back to the kitchen, took the plates out of the oven, sprayed a light mist of water over them, covered them with foil and popped them back into the oven.

I grabbed the bottle of sparkling apple cider from the refrigerator, two wine glasses from the cabinet and my ice bucket from the pantry. With a bit of trepidation, I placed the wine glasses on the table, *maybe we should just drink iced tea or water out of regular glasses?* along with the rest of the place settings. I sprinted back to the kitchen, plopped the sparkling juice in the ice bucket and partially filled it with ice. *This is for looks only. It's for ambiance. I hope it doesn't make him thirsty for some alcohol!* I raced back to the dining room and placed the bucket and juice on the far end of the table.

The table was not gorgeous, so I trotted back to my bedroom, grabbed some rose petals then back to the dining room to scatter them on the table. I found more candles to place in the dining room and on the table, lit them and stepped back to look at the room. It looked much better.

I loved my new house compared to the duplex that I lived in when I met Anthony. It was very spacious with 3 bedrooms, 2 ½ bathrooms, 2 living areas, 2 dining areas and a 2 car garage. My favorite spot was the bonus sunroom that was adjacent to the patio in back of the house. It had a wall of windows and then three walls of nothing. Of course, I turned it into my study. It was absolutely perfect. It even had a nook for a window seat which I reupholstered immediately, and it quickly became my favorite spot to unwind. The house was expensive too, but I sacrificed as needed so I could pay the rent. It wasn't too difficult once I got my spending habits under control. Once you have rent to pay and other bills that leave you with very little to spend on frivolous items, then that nips the excess spending right in the bud. The house was very spacious, yes, but it was too much for just me all by myself. Tonight, I would do something to definitely change that!

Anthony arrived at 8:02 and rang the doorbell. I counted to 10, mainly to catch my breath, before I opened the door to look at him. He looked tired, but he tried to hide it with a huge dimpled grin.

"Hello sweetheart," he greeted and presented me with a large bouquet of fresh, colorful, fragrant flowers. I was shocked mainly because I was just there at the same shop where he bought these flowers! We could have run smack into each other! I took the flowers, thanked him, and then just stood there examining him.

He was an extremely good looking guy who was oblivious to this fact. Tall, about 6'2, hazel eyes with tiny green flecks in them, light caramel brown skin, dark wavy hair – curly when it grows out- well groomed, neat mustache and goatee. Anthony was physically fit with muscles in all the right places. I stood there admiring him way longer than I should have.

Finally he stated, "You look very beautiful Amina.

I love that color on you." I smiled and looked down.

"Thank you." My nipples were hard.

"Well, can I come in?" he asked with a chuckle, and I smiled even bigger and ushered him inside. He was wearing his usual casual yet sexy outfit: white polo shirt, khaki pants, black belt, and black shoes. I deeply inhaled his masculine scent and smiled at the instant turn on. He immediately noticed the rose petals and the massage table. "What's all this?" he asked with a huge white smile. I let him look around while I found a vase to put the flowers in. The flowers were the perfect touch for the table. "What's going on?" he asked.

"Shhh . . ." I whispered, led him closer to the massage table, and started undressing him. He started to say something, but I kissed him quiet and whispered, "Just go with it baby, ok?" He obediently shook his head up and down which made me giggle. His eyes rested on my cleavage which my robe allowed to peep out perfectly. I undressed him down to his boxer briefs, admiring his arms, shoulders, back, abs, butt, thighs, and calves along the way. I smoothly folded his clothes and placed them in a chair.

"Take off your socks and your underwear," I instructed. He covered his chest and asked in a feminine voice, I guess to imitate me, "Can't I have a robe to cover up?" I untied the sash on my robe, took it off and gave it to him. He gave me a hot sexy stare, looked down at me, and saw that my nipples were on high red alert under the silky top.

"Umm . . . blue . . . my favorite color," he murmured as he took the robe from me, held it up to his nose to sniff it, and then let it fall into a soundless heap on the floor. He bent down, removed his socks, straightened up, looked me in the eye, and removed his underwear to reveal a full, rock solid, hard erection.

I tried not to look with little success, but I remained focused on accomplishing my goal. I led him to the table which I had covered with soft blankets and I told him to relax, get comfortable, and ready for a full body massage. At first, I wanted him to lie face down, but that was impossible with his buddy poking out so noticeably. Instead, he laid on his back and I covered him with a light blanket and whispered, "Relax."

I sauntered to the kitchen to get cucumber slices. Hoping that he relaxed a bit, I returned and placed the dish of cucumber slices by his head. He sat up just a bit and grabbed a few slices and popped them into his mouth. I giggled. "Relax baby! Those are not for eating! They are for your eyes!"

"Oh! I thought those were appetizers! I'm sorry!" he chuckled as he relaxed back on the table and closed his eyes. As I placed cucumbers on his eyes, I noticed his slowly subsiding erection. Good. I went back to the kitchen and turned the oven down to 100 degrees and closed the blinds. I went into the sun room and closed the blinds in there as well. I was stalling, but he didn't need to know that. I tiptoed to the bathroom and grabbed the baby oil and massage cream and moved stealthily back to the living room. I peeked at his exposed body. He was definitely trying to relax, but I could tell that the massage would help. I snuck up to him, rubbed the lightly scented massage cream on my hands, waved it in front of his face so he could smell it.

"Umm . . ." he moaned softly.

Starting with his fingers, I started rubbing. His fingers were rough, tight and dense in some areas. I continued rubbing, and he started relaxing. I moved to his hands and his wrists and rubbed the concoction in vigorously. He moaned faintly, and I moved to his arms.

Admiring their muscled smoothness, I spent a considerable amount of time rubbing his arms and shoulders. I moved to his neck and chest and continued in my admiration of the smoothness of his skin, the definition of his muscles and the small hairy spots. As I worked on his neck, chest, shoulders and sides, his erection started lifting the blanket up off of his body. I stifled my laughter and massaged his temples and his head. Again, a faint moan escaped from his throat. I wondered if I could massage his lower body without being incredibly distracted and tempted to please him before moving any further. *Stay focused Amina! You have a job to do!*

After refreshing my oil and massage cream and rubbing my hands together, I rubbed down his chest to his incredibly tight abs. I thumped him. "Relax!" I giggled when I noticed his muscles flexing. His abs were not so tight and sexy when they are relaxed. I smiled. He was still fine as hell even though he had let himself go a little bit lately. Keeping his soldier covered with the blanket, I began massaging his hips and thighs. This part of the massage took a lot of muscle from me because his legs are quite muscular. It's much easier to massage areas that are not that muscled. His thigh muscles were large, defined and beautiful, but they were not easy to massage. I had to crack my knuckles several times while massaging him. His shins were not that difficult and his feet were quite easy to massage.

His feet were damn near perfect, I thought for a second, nothing like someone else I knew whose feet were somewhat monstrous. *Focus Amina! Think of no one else!!!* I moved back up the length of his body, and he started squirming because I conspicuously skipped his middleman who was standing straight and tall again, beckoning for me to notice him from underneath the light blanket. "I'll rub him later," I teased.

"No, rub him now, please!" he pleaded.

"No later," I continued with my rubbing.

"Come on baby! Touch him! He's begging you to touch him!" Anthony pleaded. I touched it with the tip of my finger. He trembled dramatically. Stifling my laughter again, I began a thorough massage of his rock hard erection for about three minutes. He was getting too excited, so I stopped abruptly and refreshed my massage cream and baby oil. I went back down to his ankles and feet. He whimpered like a puppy that lost its mother. "Later baby," I assured him.

"I need you to relax, so you can turn over and get your back side massaged," I instructed him as I rubbed his feet. I moved up to his knees and massaged them for a few minutes as his erection subsided. "Turn over," I hurried him.

"Okay, give me a minute," he agreed. I went to the kitchen, washed my hands, turned the oven off, and took the salad out of the refrigerator and small salad plates out of the cabinet. The salad which consisted of lettuce, grape tomatoes, shredded cheese, black olives, green peppers, and bacon pieces was left over from my dinner last night, but since Anthony was not a huge fan of salad, it would do fine because he would only eat a few bites. I pulled out dressing and croutons and placed them on the counter top. I scurried back to the living room.

"I'm ready baby," Anthony called out in his deep mellow voice just as I walked into the room.

"In addition to the hole for my face, there should be a hole for my . . ."

"Shhh!" I giggled, and bumped the table to shut him up.

"Relax baby. Breathe deeply. Erase your mind of everything except us," I soothed.

"Yeah, that's why I need that second hole!" he mumbled. I shushed him again and massaged him from head to toe, admiring how illustrious and beautiful his body looked after the rubdown. The massage only lasted about 40 minutes from start to finish, but I was exhausted afterward.

When I finally heard deep heavy breathing emanating from underneath the table, I knew that I had finally accomplished my goal of relaxing him completely. I let him snooze for a bit while I set up dinner on the dining room table. I set the table with the salad fixings and placed a pitcher of iced water on the table and two nice glasses. I contemplated finding a robe for him, decided against it, grabbed his boxers and undershirt to place near him when he got up, and went back to the living room to wake him up.

"Umm, baby that was wonderful," he moaned as he sat up.

"My hands hurt," I giggled and passed him his underwear. He sat up, pulled me to him, grabbed my hands and covered them in kisses. My heart fluttered. *Oh, how I love this man!* I would have to tread carefully in my actions tonight. I slipped on my robe as he slipped on his boxers and undershirt. We strolled into the dining room where I insisted that he sit first. He wanted to be a gentleman and pull out my chair for me.

"Tonight is your night honey," I insisted. He sat, cracked his fingers, looked around at the candles, rose petals and table setting and said, "I'm very impressed. Are you going to propose a toast?" I smiled and poured the glasses of the sparkling cider.

"Yes, I propose a toast," I said as I sat and lifted my glass to his. He lifted his glass and waited. I didn't actually know what I would say, so I improvised.

"To the man I love. I appreciate you. I'm extremely turned on by you, and I can't imagine my life without you. I want you with me here, now, and forever." *Boy that was loaded.* We touched glasses. I was about to sip, but stopped when I realized that he was about to toast me back.

"To the woman I love. Thank you for a wonderful massage and whatever else you have planned for me tonight!" We touched glasses again. "Cheers!" He sipped the sparkling apple cider, frowned and immediately put it down. I sipped it and looked at him with a smirk. *Surely you didn't think that I would serve you wine darling!*

We enjoyed light conversation and abundant laughter. Work was going well for him. He would be taking the detective exam soon, and he was excited about the possibilities that passing the test would bring. He wanted to move into the private sector.

"You want to be a private eye?" I asked, puzzled. *This was a different career choice than what he told me last year. Why didn't I know this?* The past year had been a particularly rough one, rougher than I truly knew and we had grown apart while working our fingers to the bone. The last I knew, Anthony wanted to work up the ranks of police and end with becoming the chief just like his late father. The route he chose did not initially include becoming a detective. *Hell, Vickie was a damn detective!*

"Yes, as well as do some other things with security and what not," he provided as he pushed lettuce around on his plate. It was time to clear the salad dishes and bring out the main course, but the mention of security provided the perfect segue into what I needed to talk to him about.

"Speaking of security . . ." I lost my nerve when I realized that I couldn't talk about this upcoming trip to Dayton without mentioning Clayton.

"Hold that thought!" I giggled and hurried off to the kitchen to get our entrees. I removed the foil from Anthony's steak, potato, and steamed broccoli and my plate which contained grilled chicken and steamed mixed vegetables. The luscious aroma and warm steam hit me in the face. I put the plates, steak sauce, butter, sour cream, and shredded cheese on a tray and walked carefully into the dining room.

He looked at the spread, smiled and asked, "Why do I feel like you are buttering me up for something?" I grabbed the butter and joked, "Take your clothes back off and I'll butter you up all right!" He got serious and looked at me with a pained expression. "Are you about to drop some bad news in my lap?" I opened my mouth to answer, but he interrupted me.

"What you were about to tell me about security earlier . . . did that have anything to do with it?" I sat down and looked into his serious eyes.

"I have to go to Dayton on Monday to head a presentation on the VMM Safety and Security Audit that I've been working on for the past few months," I started. I cut a piece of chicken and put it in my mouth. It was juicy, delicious, and I chewed it slowly to stall this discussion.

"Tell me the rest baby," he coaxed as he cut a large chunk off of his steak. I looked at the huge grilled chicken breast on my plate, thought about how much he loved breasts, and I giggled. The hurt on his face seemed to double.

"Relax baby," I soothed, "I was just laughing at the huge breast on my plate," I explained, "and how much you love breasts," my laughter bubbled out of me uncontrolled. Expressionless, he looked at the chicken breast, cut another large chunk of his steak, popped it in his mouth and chewed slowly, waiting for me to continue. I forked a steamed carrot, put it in my mouth and chewed slowly. He continued eating and waiting.

"I'm pretty sure that I am going to have to work beside Clayton during the time that I'm there," I blurted and stabbed a steamed cauliflower and put it in my mouth, chewing it rapidly. He finished chewing and, he let the information sink in slowly.

"Is he the only attorney there who can work on this? Isn't there someone else you can work with?" he asked as he cut another piece of steak, moved it around in the sauce on his plate, sipped the cider, and made a face. *Yes I would prefer wine too, but one of us can't handle it, can we?*

"Well, there's a team of attorneys working on this case because it can potentially affect all 225 of Upstage's department stores and its affiliates. I don't even know for sure that I will have to work with him, but I do know that we are going to cross paths quite a bit next week since the main reason that I'm going is because of the Southern Regions Safety and Security audits that I headed this year. Legal is getting involved to prevent further lawsuits and he is the attorney in charge of store safety lawsuits," I explained. He listened and ate calmly. There was a long awkward silence.

"Why is the universe conspiring against me?" he mumbled under his breath.

"What?"

"Never mind," he replied. He noticed my discomfort, so he asked me with a mouth full of baked potato, "So can you handle seeing him again?"

"Of course I can! I have zero feelings for him," I answered a bit too quickly, sure in my voice and mannerisms, but unsure in my erratically beating heart. He tried to hide his uncertainty by looking deeply into my eyes, searching, exploring the depths for as far as he could muster in hopes of finding the truth.

I had no trouble holding his gaze. I wanted him to be the only one. I don't know how I will react to seeing Clayton again. Talking to him did make my pulse race, but it returned to normal when I insisted that we stick to business talk only. *The attraction, lust, and desire that I felt for him is completely gone, at least I think it is.* One thing I'm sure about is that I want Anthony to be the only one. No doubts about that. I can't fathom throwing it all away for a roll in the sack with Clayton.

"I'm totally committed to you now baby. I would never make the same decisions that I made back then," I announced and grabbed the royal blue velvet gift box and plain white envelope from the chair beside me.

"To prove it, here, this is for you," I stated excitedly. He took the box and envelope from me and placed the envelope on the table, shook the box, and smiled at me, revealing the dimple in his right cheek that I loved so much.

"Go ahead. Open it!" I urged. He opened it and looked at the key inside.

"Key to your heart?" He teased.

"Key to our home," I revealed and pointed to the envelope. He put down the key and opened the envelope to read the lease papers that needed his signature. He kept reading and discovered that I added Arielle as an occupant.

"Damn! My baby is for real!" he exclaimed.

"Yes, I am. I know it took a long time, but I'm ready now," I stated definitively.

"When can I move in?" he asked rubbing his hands together. I laughed.

"Anytime. Whenever you are ready."

"Is tonight too soon?" he inquired.

"I think you will be too tired tonight! But this can be your last night just spending the night. You're off Saturday. Wouldn't that be a good day?" I bargained.

"No, I'm full of energy right now baby!" he beamed.

"Well, save it for dessert!" I purred and gave him a sultry look.

"Yes ma'am!" he shouted.

We finished a bit more of our dinner, and then followed the rose petals into the bedroom where we christened it as ours instead of mine.

~+~+~+~+~+~+~+~

Making love, having sex, the horizontal mambo, or whatever you wish to call it is actually a really dirty act. Think about it! Your body temperature rises, your heart rate increases, your blood pressure increases, bodily fluid secretes at elevated levels, you exchange: saliva, sweat, vaginal secretions, semen, possibly blood, all while humping and pumping, clawing and grabbing, squeezing and teasing, opening and inserting your body part(s) into another's from all different angles and positions. It's exercise. It's wild, raw, brutal and animalistic. It's uninhibited, unrehearsed and uncontrolled. Really? This is how we express our love for each other? I snuggled on Anthony's chest thinking about this after our lovemaking and smiled then giggled uncontrollably.

"Thinking about chicken breasts again?" he mumbled into my hair.

"No, I'm thinking about how much I love you!" I chuckled. He rolled over and moved on top of me, so we could repeat that ridiculously wonderful deed.

–13–

Fail to Plan . . . Plan to Fail

I was elated that Anthony took the news so well, but I tried not to think about it. Thinking on it too long unnerved me, and I really needed to keep it together so I could face all of the upcoming challenges that this trip would surely present.

Challenge #1 – getting all the plans, ideas, materials, and my two assistants together. I must have called Connie at the corporate office at least 15 times, but she did not seem to mind at all. She worked extensively with the rental company to get exactly the type of car that I wanted to drive, a midsize SUV, because I would be transporting several file boxes which are quite difficult to unload from a car. I have experienced that difficulty first hand from several trips in the past, and I wanted to avoid it this time around. It was so much easier to not have to bend and lift; I learned this from unloading items from Anthony's vehicle, a full size SUV.

Finally, Connie had tied all loose ends on the travel arrangements. She booked the hotel that was close to corporate headquarters, the type of rental car that I wanted and even made a list of suggestions for meals during our stay. The corporate building had a full service cafeteria that was open from 6 a.m. to 9 p.m., so we could enjoy our meals there on the company's dime, or we could spend from a budget that included gas, meals, and entertainment.

"Connie, what do you mean by entertainment?" I asked her with a smile. She rattled off a list of acceptable entertainment expenses.

"What if we wanted to visit a strip club?"

"Pay for it yourselves," she answered directly after gasping for air. *There it is. I'm about to break her streak of seriousness.*

"Can you recommend any good ones?" I asked with a giggle, and finally she burst into laughter.

"I was just joking!" I assured her.

"I know. I know. I needed that little break," she answered. She gave me an itinerary of expected meetings and the room numbers where we would work each day. We would be extremely busy the entire time that we were there, and she even mentioned staying an additional day to tie up loose ends before we left.

"I look forward to meeting you Amina. Please let me know if you need anything else. Have a nice day," Connie closed.

Immediately, I went to Mike's office and discussed staying an additional day. He was fine with it as long as the sales floor was covered. I bounded down the stairs and moved quickly across departments to get to Michelle and Serena. I talked to them about the additional day; we would be in Dayton from Monday – Thursday and return on Friday. Michelle smiled and immediately started calling sales associates to cover her shifts on Thursday and Friday. Serena frowned.

"That wasn't part of the plan!" she objected. When I calmly asked her if she would be unable to make it because of this change of plans, she rolled her eyes.

With an irritated expression, she said, "I'll have to make some personal arrangements as well as find someone to cover me, that's all." I didn't have time to question her about her vague response.

"Just let me know if you can't make it," I snapped and trotted back to my office without waiting for her reply. I had file boxes lined up in order on my floor. They were labeled and ready for me to pull materials to present to everyone in attendance at the meetings.

There was still a stack of reports that I needed to examine, so I unpacked them and started. I hated to admit it, but I needed Serena! I planned out our time, work duties, and materials according to Connie's itinerary to give each of us what I felt were somewhat equal amounts to deal with. Of course, I would have to deal with the bulk of materials and responsibilities, but without a third person, Michelle and I would be swamped!

Challenge #2 - The thought made me queasy. My stomach gurgled, and I swallowed what seemed like a sour after taste. I made a face and tried to remember what I ate for breakfast that day because I surely hadn't stopped for a lunch break. My brain was in a fog. My memory completely escaped me. *I can't be getting sick right now, can I?* I shook it off. No big deal. I felt fine. It's just this Dayton business. I wanted everything to be perfect, and I was letting the reality that there would be problems stress me out.

For hours, I combed through reports and looked for discrepancies, called the store managers, asked an abundance of questions, watched store surveillance videos, and looked for answers to two questions that bothered me regarding the Crockett store.

Despite my careful scrutiny, I couldn't find the answers. I gave up, surmising that a fresh set of eyes may be able to help me figure out why a mannequin would topple over onto a child. I stared at the wall and decided that I should go out into the store and find the answers for myself. I bolted down the stairs and sprinted directly to the children's department first since it contained the smaller sized mannequins. I checked the forms, wiggled them, jiggled them, and played with them the way a child might fidget with them. As she should have, Liz, the sales associate in the children's department, came over to see what I was doing.

"Trying to figure out how a kid could get something like this to fall on him!"

"Not easily! Even those little suckers are hard to deal with. You'd think they would be easier to knock over than the adult ones, but they aren't. The foundation weights are heavier on the child forms than the adult ones," she explained.

I gave the mannequin a strong shove. It didn't budge. I shook my head. I knew how a kid could get one to topple onto himself and Liz knew too: if the department was not being properly monitored. The Crockett store was toast. Most of my observation videos showed neglectful employees ignoring customers and not taking care of their departments. My videos would help the lawsuit complainants win! I released a huge, exasperated sigh.

This was not good, but it had to be shared at the meeting. I snapped out of my worry; I'll leave the legal matters for the attorneys to deal with. I had to gather as much information as possible to share with the corporate team. My action plan suggestions should be practical and easy to implement. Dottie walked past me, and an immediate idea formed in my brain.

"Dottie, how old is your daughter?"

"Eight. Why?"

"How soon can you get her into the store today?" "She's coming in after school to sit around and do her homework until I finish my shift. Why? You have me intrigued! What are you working on?"

"I'd like to use her in an experiment with the mannequins," I started and continued my explanation of the need to gather more information before I went to Dayton.

"I'm sure she'll love to participate, but I don't want her to get injured!" Dottie worried.

"Oh no! Of course not!" I assured. I went on to explain that we would be watching closely. When her daughter came, I conducted my experiment with Dottie recording and Alan, the custodian, waiting on standby to grab the mannequin or help save Dottie's daughter.

Since no video evidence existed to actually show employee negligence that day or even the actual footage of the event in question, I figured that this would be an integral part of my presentation. Dottie's daughter found it difficult to behave like a "wild child" but even when she did, she was not able to topple the mannequin because the base was too heavy. Even I had a hard time trying to knock it over. *This damn thing feels like it's bolted to the floor!* I called Rashad over to give it a try, and it was easy for him to knock it over. I pointed out that Rashad was muscular, and this prompted Alan to give it a try. He was a short chubby guy, but he could turn it over as well.

"It's heavy! You have to be strong to turn it over. You also have to know from which side to push it because of the way that it's weighted. It is easier to push it over from the front to the back than it is from the back to the front. Usually one of us guys has to help the sales associates when it's time to change clothes on these things," Alan explained. Rashad shook his head in affirmation.

I knew that it was easier for two sales associates to redress the adult and junior mannequins because I dealt with them all the time, but I never touched the children's mannequins. I incorrectly assumed that they would be easier to deal with, so this information was all new to me. *Glad I asked! This is something that a VMM is supposed to know! This could have made me look incompetent. Damn! I haven't even had the job that long and I'm dealing with this serious shit!*

I concluded the experiment by introducing all participants on camera thanking them for participating. I finished my video notes by explaining that it usually required two strong adults to dismantle the child size mannequins for redress. Unless the base was unusually light, it was close to impossible for a child to knock one over. That gave me another base to cover.

I raced back to my office, taking two steps at a time, sat down quickly, and found the number to the Crockett store. I asked to speak to a manager. Whoever answered the phone did not even answer with the usual friendly line, "UpStage Department Store. This is _____. How may I help you?" She just answered, "UpStage." *Damn! The whole store needs massive retraining!* After waiting for a few minutes, someone else picked up the phone and asked, "Who are you holding for?"

"A manager," I answered bluntly.

"Who may I say is calling?"

"Amina Jefferson."

"What is the nature of your call?"

"I need to speak to a manager please," I answered as I quickly grew impatient with this employee.

"Why?" came the rude reply. I wrinkled my nose and copped an attitude.

"Because I need to ask some questions that only a manager can answer," I replied and wondered why it was so difficult to page a manager to take my call. She put me on hold again. After waiting five minutes, Daniel, the men's department manager answered.

"Hi Daniel, this is Amina Jefferson at the Coronado store," I started. I could hear whispering in the background.

"Oh hi Amina from the Coronado store," he announced facetiously. The whispering stopped and giggling ensued. He put me on hold, and I waited impatiently. *What the hell is going on in that store?*

He returned to the call and asked how he could help me.

"I'm sorry if I caught you at a bad time," I offered as I rolled my eyes. I thought about it. Rashad was the men's department manager at my store. He would never allow a caller to form the judgment that I had formed based on my few minutes on the phone with Daniel.

"Yes, we are swamped. Fridays are quite busy here, and at this moment there are a lot of customers in the store. It's okay though. How can I help you," he asked. His statements seemed false and his offer pretentious, but I asked for what I needed.

"Could you fax me a copy of your children's department fixture inventory report?

"Sure, what's it called?"

"Fixture inventory control report #505QS772CH and then your store number will be listed," I supplied.

"Umm, where might I find this?" *He was a manager, really?* Again, I rolled my eyes.

"It should be in the office in a file called 'Fixture Inventory,' I explained, "the reports are in numerical order in binders which are separated by department. I'm looking for one that will be in the children's department binder."

"Maybe I should get you the children's department manager?"

"That's fine. It really doesn't matter who sends me the report. I just need it ASAP to take with me to corporate headquarters on Monday," I discoursed.

"What's the number again?" he asked quickly. Obviously my last statement lit a fire underneath him. I repeated it and told him that I would call to confirm when I received the fax. Without waiting for a reply, I hung up. *Sheesh! Why was the Crockett store full of incompetent employees? Perhaps Serena and Vanessa should apply there? They would fit in perfectly!*

I made a note to research the town of Crockett: its educational level, average income, and other demographic information. I also wanted to know the turnover rate at the store. Maybe this research already exists? Surely it does! I called the main office and told Katy to be on the lookout for a fax from Crockett. She told me that she would call or page me when it came.

I raced down the hall to Mike's office to ask him about store demographic reports. I knew they existed, but they never interested me in the least before. He was more than happy to direct me to the answers that I needed.

"Well, it certainly seems like you are getting your ducks in a row!" he beamed.

"I want this meeting to go off without any bumps or stumbles. I don't want to be asked a question that I cannot answer. Can you think of anything else that I may need to cover?" He named off a long list of general information that I needed to be on top of. I scribbled down a checklist, and I was pleased that I could check off every item.

In the past, Mike and Dottie took care of all visual merchandising manager concerns because the position didn't even exist. Dottie had already filled me in on everything that she thought that I needed to know.

"Amina, I'm going to be honest with you. You've taken this Visual Merchandising Safety and Security Project and ran with it. We didn't expect our VMM at this store to take charge of the entire region, but your hard work paid off and caught the eye of the corporate compliance team. You are on top of everything, and I believe that you've left nothing to chance. In addition to taking charge, you've even worked in a way to mentor and develop an employee. That speaks volumes, and you better believe that I'm going to let my boss know about it," he bubbled. I smiled slightly and nodded.

"You're making quite name for yourself at USDSI," he continued, "all I can say is to keep up the good work! If you need anything, just ask." *A raise would be nice!*

"Thanks Mike! I appreciate your support," I said. With that, I walked out with the small stack of information that he extracted from a humongous binder: demographic information for the three lowest performing stores in our region. I would study them and look for commonalities, and this information would help me formulate customized action plans to get the stores back into compliance. Crockett and Stratton were located in South Arkansas and Hollins was located in Northeast Louisiana. All three stores failed miserably on the VM Safety and Security audit, have low sales, and have registered multiple complaints from customers. Each store would be represented in Dayton by the store manager, assistant manager, visual merchandising manager or a combination of the three. They would all learn that I walked through their stores as a "Secret Shopper" and took meticulous notes no how well the store's employees complied with USDSI's standards of safety and security. I couldn't hold back. There was bound to be some hostility and hurt feelings.

"Just be honest and tell it like it is! The truth hurts, but it is also a powerful motivator," Mike advised when I talked to him about this after completing the audits. The thought of angering people with my information only made my stomach gurgle with anxious energy. *Or maybe it was the fact that my stomach was bubbling with nauseous juices? That's the second time today that my stomach has noticeably bothered me.*

Slowly, I walked down the steps and into the main office to tell Katy that I would be in the break room. I looked at the empty fax machine and shook my head. I needed that information before I left for the day.

"Don't worry. He'll send it," Katy assured.

"I hope so. I'm trying to do everything that I know to help that store avoid a lawsuit. Those fixture inventory reports have important specifications, measurements, and weights that I can supply to the attorneys," I explained.

"Well, do they know that you're trying to help? Maybe they think you are trying to add fuel to the fire," Katy wondered. I shook my head. *I'm almost convinced that the employees at that store don't think at all!*

"I'll be back in a few," I responded without feeling.

"Hey! Are you okay?" she asked with raised eyebrows, wrinkled forehead and bucked eyes.

"I'm fine. Last minute questions and stress are trying to get to me.

I haven't had anything to eat either, so I'm feeling kind of sick to my stomach. I'll be okay after I eat," I explained and continued my trek to the lounge. I brought a ham and cheese sandwich for lunch, but I left it in the refrigerator. Instead, I purchased a package of salt and vinegar chips and a lemon lime soda from the vending machines. The room was empty, so I stretched out in one of the cushy chairs, kicked my shoes off, closed my eyes, and ate in silence. The salty chips and the soda did the trick almost immediately. My stomach felt better, so I opened my eyes. Serena was standing in the doorway staring at me.

"Hmmph," she mumbled as she walked past. *Hi, hello, hey . . . any of those greetings would be nice! Silly bitch. She has a lot to learn, and I have volunteered myself to teach her. Ugh! What was I thinking?*

"So, do you have everything ready to go?" I managed to ask in a lively tone.

"I guess so," she answered bluntly.

"Do you need help getting anything together or reading any of the reports that I gave you?"

"No," she answered with an attitude.

"Then what's the problem Serena?" I asked.

"No one cares about my problems, so there's not a problem," she answered with the same rough attitude.

"Why don't you tell me what's wrong, and if I can help, I will," I offered.

"Why? Why, all of a sudden, are you so hell bent on helping me? You don't even like me! And I don't like you! So, everything was just fine with you in your office and me in my department," she huffed. I could definitely understand where she was coming from. I didn't like her, but my feelings stemmed from the way she felt about me. She was heating a cup of chicken flavored noodles in the microwave. The smell made me want to vomit, but I shook my head and sipped my drink to make the nausea go away. When she sat at a table, I got up and joined her.

"Serena, we got off to a bad start. The only reason that I don't like you is because you showed me that you didn't like me first. That line sounds like I stole it straight from kids on a playground, but it's the truth." She rolled her eyes at me and stirred her noodles. *Bitch! You better straighten up, or your ass will be here while Michelle and I are in Dayton!*

"Look, I have never tried this hard to develop a working relationship with anyone. I never had to! My coworkers just automatically liked me, and we became friends. Serena, you and I don't have to be friends, okay? We do need to try to be cordial at work," I explained. She rolled her eyes at me again, and I wanted to snatch her up from her seat by her braids and sling her across the room.

"My grandmother raised me, my brothers and sisters," she began as she stirred the noodles. She looked down into the cup intently to avoid eye contact with me. I sipped my soda, waited for her to continue and listened intently because I knew nothing about this woman. We have worked together for almost two years now, and I knew absolutely nothing about her except for the fact that she hates me because Rashad likes me. She hates me because I got the office manager job that she applied for, and then I got the VMM job that she also applied for. She hates me because I keep getting things that she wants. First, I was really childish about this and rubbed her face in it, but I realized how petty that was and I was honestly trying to make up for it. She seemed determined not to let me.

"My grandmother is in a nursing home. She has seven grandchildren all together, and we each pick a day to go and visit her for a few hours or sit with her the entire day. My day was Thursday. Now that I am not going to be here Thursday, I'm going to miss out on that time. My cousin could switch with me if I can go tomorrow, but I have to work until close. Visiting hours are over at 7:00. You want to meet with us in the morning before our shift begins, so I can't go in the morning either!" she explained sadly.

"No one will work for you tomorrow?" I inquired even though I knew the answer. Serena was hard pressed to get anyone, except Vanessa, to work in her place, because so many of the other associates did not like her. Dottie had to schedule a replacement for her on Thursday. *See what happens when you steal sales and don't do your part to keep the store in good shape?*

"No. Everyone has excuses," Serena frowned.

"I could cover your department for a few hours while you go and visit your grandmother," I offered. She looked up from her noodles.

"You could?" She grabbed a saltine cracker and crumbled it into the noodles.

"Yes, I could. After we meet in the morning, just let me know what time you are leaving and when you will return. Take your lunch break while you're gone, and everything should be fine," I instructed. She couldn't hide her smile. It lit up her entire face. I smiled back for a split second.

"Why are you doing this for me?"

"Because I don't believe in holding grudges," I responded, "I'm over the mess that happened with us last year. I don't even know why it happened, and I don't care anymore. Everyone in this store has had a chance to contribute to the store's growth and actually grow with it, except you and Vanessa. I want you and her to have the same opportunities."

"So it's all because I work here?"

"Yes. You deserve to be more than just a sales associate. You wanted to be more, but you didn't show the work to back up that desire. Here's your chance Serena. Are you going to take it, and are you going to leave the past behind?" She smiled again, and I was happy that I was finally breaking through her cold, hard shell.

"I'm going to take it!" she giggled. I gave her a high five and told her that I would see her tomorrow during our meeting.

"The meeting will be in the conference room upstairs at 8," I informed her, "come a few minutes early, bring your notes. Mike is going to provide breakfast."

"I didn't know Mike was going to be there," she replied with raised eyebrows.

"Yes, all management will be there. We are just going to add an agenda item to our biweekly manager's meeting," I told her. Her smile turned into a satisfied smirk. I waved goodbye to her as I walked out and wondered if she was thinking, "Finally, I get to hang with the managers!"

When I walked through the main office, Katy surprised me with the fax that I needed from the Crockett store. She had called the store, dealt with the same frustrations that I did, but this time insisted on talking to the store manager or assistant manager.

Indeed, Daniel explained to them that I was looking for more evidence to use against their store at the corporate meeting. They were both confused about it, but neither of them chose to call and check on it. They both chose to ignore it until Katy revealed everything that I told her. This is not exactly what I wanted her to do, but it got results and it would not change the course of the corporate meeting. *Unless I divulged the fact that the top managers did not want to cooperate with my compilation of information . . .*

The next morning, the managers showed up 30 minutes early and discovered Serena waiting at the front door. *Good move Serena. I didn't even tell her how early to get here, but she figured it out.* We proceeded through the store and up the stairs to the conference room.

Dottie arranged breakfast on the side credenza: love spuds, bacon egg and cheese croissants, yogurt, and fresh fruit. People started helping themselves. We all knew to bring our own drinks, but Serena didn't know that. Rashad, sweet and thoughtful as ever, volunteered to go and buy her the drink of her choice. She wanted coffee, so he dashed out to the coffee shop across the street. Michelle and Serena sat by Whitney. I put my notepad and coffee down beside Michelle and told them that I had to get something from my office.

Instead, I went to the bathroom. My stomach felt like it was going to explode. I went to the sink, washed my face, patted it dry, and fanned it. That didn't help at all. A sudden, debilitating warmth engulfed me, and soon I was vomiting in the toilet. The involuntary retching continued for several minutes as last night's dinner - what little I ate - came pouring out of my mouth. When the heaving stopped, I felt 100% better. *Anthony's grilled salmon, baked sweet potatoes, and steamed asparagus didn't agree with me!*

I rinsed my mouth thoroughly and looked at myself in the mirror. I didn't look sick. My eyes were bright, my color was fresh, and I did feel much better. I rejoined the group in the conference room after I grabbed one of my favorite pens off my desk. Rashad was back, and he was sitting beside my empty seat. I sat down and looked at Serena who was smiling like the cat who ate the canary. For once, she didn't roll her eyes at me, so I included her in our small talk. I gingerly ate a donut and sipped my coffee. My stomach did not immediately object, and I hoped the previous incident would not occur again anytime soon.

Promptly at 8:00, Mike got right down to business. As always, we went through the meeting agenda quickly, and Mike praised each and every one of us for our hard work. Our sales figures were tops again, and our customer's praises far outnumbered customer complaints. He congratulated Michelle and Serena for being chosen to accompany me on the corporate trip. I spoke briefly about it and answered a few questions.

Mike thanked Rashad for taking my place at the regional meeting in Breckinridge. Rashad spoke briefly about it and asked questions of several managers including me. He questioned me extensively, and he seemed excited to absorb my answers. I watched Serena out of the corner of my eye. She was watching Rashad intently. *Hmm . . . maybe I could help her with that? Maybe he might consider giving her a chance now? Maybe she will start to understand that Rashad is attracted to hard working women?*

The meeting adjourned, and those of us who had to work today scampered to our perspective areas of the store. Serena stopped me to inform me that she would like to leave by 12 and return by 4. I told her that would work just fine. She smiled, thanked me, and walked down the stairs. Michelle witnessed this exchange.

"What in the H E double hockey sticks have you done to her? She's been acting like a totally different person!" Michelle screeched. I ushered her into my office and closed the door.

"My plan is working!" I told her and giggled.

"It sure is!"

"I'll tell you more about it when I cover Serena's spot in juniors today from 12 to 4," I smirked.

"What?!!!" Michelle screamed.

"Shhhhh!!!!" I giggled as I put my hands over my mouth to stifle my laughter.

"You're covering for her today for four hours?!!!" Michelle whisper screamed.

"Yes, I'll tell you why when I'm down there," I giggled and pointed to the clock which warned a few minutes before 9. I waved my hands at her to make her leave. I wouldn't want her to miss any sales on a Saturday morning. She smiled, flashed a peace sign with her fingers and backed out of my office. The rest of the day breezed by without any problems. Michelle and I talked and giggled through the four hours that Serena was gone.

We provided impeccable service to the customers who visited the junior department, and we insisted that Jennifer and Sarah ring up all the sales. They looked at us like we were from another planet. I gave all my sales to Jennifer and Michelle gave hers to Sarah. We straightened the department, cleaned the dressing room, dusted fixtures, and re-merchandised a small section.

We spoke to Vanessa, who was working in intimates, and gave explicit instructions to set up a sale that would last from Wednesday through Sunday. I told her that Dottie would be checking to make sure it was set correctly. Vanessa took in all the information then went to the register, pulled out a small notebook and wrote some of it down. Michelle and I walked away.

"Dottie never checks to make sure the sales are set correctly in my department!" she whispered.

"Right! Because she knows that you know what you're doing. We can't trust Vanessa like that!" I shook my head and Michelle giggled.

Serena returned a few minutes before 4:00, and I told her that I needed her address so I could pick her up. She gave me a strange look. I continued and explained that I wanted us to leave at 10:00 in the morning. She told me the name and address of her apartment complex, Greensborough, on the southeast side of Coronado. She started giving me directions, and I didn't stop her. I wanted to tell her that she didn't even have to explain. I knew the Greensborough Townhouse Apartments very well because this is where I grew up. *Well well . . . Serena and I will have a lot to talk about during our long 4.5 hour road trip, won't we?*

—14—

Control

Anthony spent the entire day moving in, so he was tired and in a funky mood. He had plenty of help, not too much to move and organize, and was able to get it all done in one day. That night, we had a tiny argument. He alluded to the fact that he would not be suspicious or worried if he could talk to me and receive regular texts from me while I was away. I assured him that would not be a problem. I would call and text him regularly.

However, that was not enough to satisfy him. Basically, he wanted to know where I was and who I was with on an hourly basis. I blew up, and he backed down. Now that we have committed to living together, it would not be so easy to get away from him when I'm angry. I usually retreat to the sunroom which would now double as our offices. One wall was strictly windows, and one wall was his which he lined with shelves, a club chair, and a small desk. The other two walls were mine which contain more shelves, a large desk, and my treasured daybed that I've had for years.

After our little blow up, I went in there, grabbed a book and collapsed on the daybed with its large collection of pillows. Shortly thereafter, he came in, grabbed a book, and eased into the club chair. I put my book down, got up and left. I went to the guest room which now contained his bed and bedroom furniture. I plopped down on the bed and stared at the ceiling. He followed me. He came in, opened the closet, and pretended to look for something. I exhaled loudly.

"So, is this the type of husband you are going to be?" I asked in an irritated voice.

"What type is that Amina?" he asked facetiously.

"The type who won't let his wife out of his sight because he doesn't trust her," I stated and glared at him. He kept looking through storage boxes in the closet until he found what he was looking for.

"No baby. I'm sorry. I'm just . . ." he started. He came to the bed and sat down beside me. He had a photo album in his hand. It contained pictures of us during the early stages of our relationship.

"I want this back," he said as he pointed to several pictures of us smiling profusely, laughing, and kissing. We looked supremely happy.

"We can have that baby!" I insisted. He looked at me sadly.

"You have to trust me!" I implored.

"Yes, I do. I have to learn how to do it though because you hurt me terribly back then, and I lost the ability to trust you. I've always been an inquisitive person, Amina; you understand that, don't you?" *Yes, I understand that you are possessive and controlling too!*

"Add jealousy and suspicion to that and you don't get a good combination," he continued. *Not to mention alcohol.*

"Can I ask you something?" I leaned closer and looked him in the eye.

"No baby. I haven't had anything to drink," he answered prematurely.

"How did you know that I was going to ask you that?" I asked, my voice rising in pitch.

"I can tell. You get this worried look in your eye."

"Well, I was going to ask how long it's been since you had a drink?"

"Oh, it's been a long time! Not since that last big argument that we had!"

"You are not counting the days?"

"No! Why should I?"

"Isn't that part of your therapy?" I looked him in the eye, but he couldn't hold my gaze.

"You haven't been going to therapy? Have you seen the counselor at work?" He closed the book.

"Anthony! You promised that you would go!"

"I did. I went once. I told him that I have it under control. I explained how I drink, when I drink, where I drink, why I drink, and how I act when I am drunk. I told him everything. I stopped drinking, so why waste my time going to see him on a regular basis?"

"Because you said you would!" I screamed as I jumped off the bed and swiftly walked out of the bedroom, down the hallway and into our bedroom. He did not immediately follow. He watched television in the living room until close to midnight before he finally came to bed. He didn't say anything to me, and I pretended to be asleep. He knew that I was getting up early to leave, but he made no move to clear the air. Neither did I.

The next morning, I woke up at 7:00 and discovered that he was already gone. I wondered where he went until the smell of freshly brewed coffee wafted from the kitchen, so I strolled to the kitchen and poured myself a cup. Just as I was pouring milk, creamer, and caramel macchiato cappuccino mix into my large cup of coffee, I heard the garage door opening and closing.

Dressed in sweaty gym clothes, Anthony came in carrying my favorite large bouquet of colorful flowers, love spuds donuts, and fresh fruit. My smile almost broke my face in half. We didn't have to apologize to each other. We just knew what needed to be done. He needed to see his counselor regularly and actively participate in the program. I needed to help him learn how to trust me - #1 by being trustworthy *(although he didn't know this part – I had some work to do my damn self)* #2 by being patient and obliging in his little conditions during this trip. It would not hurt me to keep in close contact with him while I was away, especially if it would put his mind at ease.

We ate breakfast, showered together, made love in the shower, showered again, and enjoyed every second of our Sunday morning. By 9:15, I was dressed and ready to go. I dressed comfortably, but I packed several professional outfits as well as the other necessities. Anthony missed my packing and clothing selections because he was pouting in front of the TV. He kept hugging, kissing, and smelling me as I was trying to leave.

"I'm going to miss you baby!" he whispered in my ear. "I'm going to miss you too! The days will go quickly, and then I will be right back here with you," I cooed to him. He smiled and carried my bags to the SUV. It was already packed with the various file boxes and binders that we would need at the corporate office.

I called Michelle to see if she was ready. She was, so I kissed and hugged Anthony several more times, checked to make sure that I was not forgetting anything, and I finally left. I put my favorite CD in, Hits 2000, and turned the volume up. All of a sudden, I felt free. It was a weird feeling, but I shook my head, giggled, and drove quickly to pick up Michelle.

Michelle was waiting on the porch of her parent's home. I turned the music down. The place looked and sounded deserted: except for her little blue PT cruiser, there were no other cars in the drive way, no noises coming from the house and no one peeking out the windows when I drove up.

"Where is everyone?" I asked her after saying hello. She looked at me and laughed.

"Girl, you know my family goes to church every Sunday!" *Duh! That's right Amina! This young lady is very religious!* I jumped out to help with her two bags.

"I call shotgun!" she giggled and bounced into the front passenger seat. Immediately, she picked up the CD case.

"Nice ride!" she admired, "this is one of those cross treks?"

"Cross overs," I corrected her as I backed out of the driveway.

"Well, it sure is comfy!"

"Yes, it is. It will be great for this long drive," I agreed. I was glad that she was in such good spirits. We drove for twelve minutes before we finally made it to the southeast side of Coronado. I drove on the familiar streets of my childhood, past the corner store, past the junior high school, down the long hill that I always dreaded walking up, and into the entry gate of Greensborough Townhouse Apartments. *Hmmph . . . This tall steel prison gate didn't exist when I lived here!* The car in front of us stopped at the gate, the driver entered a code, the large iron gate opened, and the car drove through.

"Do you have the code?" Michelle looked at me quizzically.

"No! Serena didn't even tell me that I would need one!" After only a few minutes, the driver of the car behind us started blowing her horn. I looked at her in the mirror and waved at her. She flipped me off and laid on her horn. I couldn't back up because she was too close. Amidst the loud horn and Michelle's panicking, I called Serena and asked for the code.

"It's 1600," she answered casually. *Can I get an apology? An "Oh I forgot to tell you the code!" Something! This bitch tells me the code as if I already knew it! Sheesh!* I punched in the numbers, the gate creaked open, and finally the bitch behind me got off her horn. I looked at her again in the mirror, and again she flipped me off. *Stupid Bitch!!!* Michelle had her eyes closed in prayer, but my blood boiled for a few seconds.

"Well, that's an interesting start to our trip!" I murmured sarcastically after I calmed down. Michelle burst into laughter and I joined her. I drove around the complex past buildings, a playground, a Laundromat, and a wall of mailboxes until I found building C2. From the information that Serena provided, I knew that she lived in apartment F, but I made no move to leave the car once I parked it. We waited for 5 minutes before Michelle exhaled an exasperated breath.

"She knows that we are here! What's taking her so long?" I didn't say anything. Instead I turned the music back up and tapped the steering wheel along with Outkast's song "Mrs. Jackson." To distract Michelle, I started loudly singing the chorus, and she joined me.

When the song ended, we saw Serena and a girl who looked exactly like her walking down the sidewalk. Serena had a bag on her shoulder, she was pulling a small suitcase behind her, and she had her free arm around the girl. Michelle and I sat in stunned silence. Serena went to the back of the car and knocked, so I opened the trunk. She saw that it was pretty full, so she came to the passenger side's back door and opened it. I had a small crate on the floor behind me that contained a vase with the flowers that Anthony brought me, the donuts, fruit, and some bottles of water. She slid her suitcase and bag across the back seat to rest on the seat behind me.

"I'm gonna miss you Reena," the girl whimpered.

Serena embraced her tightly and said, "I'm going to miss you too Shelby Welby." Michelle and I looked at each other and mouthed "Shelby Welby?" We were both perplexed with this exchange because we had never seen such emotion from Serena.

"Hi Serena, who is this?" I asked after I cleared the shocked look from my face.

"Amina and Michelle, this is my little sister Shelby," Serena introduced. We both said hi and waved at her. She smiled a huge smile and excitedly waved back.

"How old are you Shelby?" I asked nicely.

"I'll be 13 next month!" she answered.

"Wow! You'll be a teenager! I have a niece your age. Her name is Jade, and she's in the 7th grade," I offered. She was about to say something when Serena closed the door and started coaxing her away from the car. *Rude bitch.* Michelle let her window down. I giggled and shook my head. *Dang Michelle! Let the heifer say goodbye to her lookalike in private.*

"Don't forget to bring me something back!" Shelby squeaked to Serena, who promised that she would.

"You behave yourself at Aunt Wanda's house, okay? Jay and Shawn are going to come by and check on you every day," Serena instructed, "I'm going to call you every night." They hugged again, and Shelby walked back up the sidewalk, turned and waved goodbye then she disappeared into the building.

Before Serena got into the car, Michelle and I looked at each other and did a quick eyebrow raise. She got in, and I backed out of the parking spot. Serena broke the awkward silence by telling us that Shelby is the youngest child. Serena and her brothers are all helping raise her. I had not told Michelle all the details behind why Serena needed the four hours off yesterday. *Maybe I should have?*

"Where are your parents?" Michelle quickly blurted. I shot her a side glance, and I could tell that she wished she hadn't asked. I looked in the rearview mirror at Serena. She looked extremely irritated as she exhaled loudly and rolled her eyes.

"Is that what this trip is going to be about? You two interrogating the hell out of me?"

"Absolutely not!" I said and turned the music up. I looked at Michelle and she mouthed, "Excuse me!"

"Any requests? Michelle asked. This CD has a good mix of everything!" She passed the case back to Serena who snatched it out of her hand and placed it on the seat. I looked at Michelle again, and she mouthed, "Bitch!" I changed the song to "Who let the dogs out" and Michelle burst into giggles and started singing along. Serena caught me looking at her in the rearview mirror, and she rolled her eyes after she smirked.

Finally, we made it to the highway, and I increased the speed to 60 mph. The music was bumping, but the ride was uneventful. When "Shake ya ass" by Mystical started playing, I turned down the volume, and Michelle and I talked. I already knew a lot about Michelle, but I asked some general questions which I hoped would make Serena feel comfortable enough to chime in. She was silent. She looked out the window and didn't bother to join our conversation.

I stopped at a travel center/truck stop in a medium sized city after nearly two hours of driving. We all hopped out and went straight to the restroom. As we were washing our hands, I informed them that I had donuts, fresh fruit, and bottled water in the car. They bought coffee and cups of ice; I purchased gum and a cup of ice. My coffee was probably still warm in my travel mug.

We sat in the car and ate donuts and small cups of fruit. Michelle asked me about the flowers, and I told her about how sweet Anthony can be at times. She continued asking me questions, much like I asked her, and I answered. Serena remained silent. We rode in silence for a few minutes, but just as I was about to reach out to turn up the volume on the music, Serena started talking.

"I don't know who my father is. I never met him. I know my brothers' father and Shelby's father, but my older sister and I don't know who our father is. My mother was a drug addict, and she was in a bad way when she had my sister and me. My older sister is only eleven months older than me," Serena paused to drink some of her coffee. "At first, me, my brothers and sisters were torn apart and sent to live with three different foster families. My older sister, Jillian, got the worst family of all. Then, my aunts and uncles managed to get all of us, except Jill back together and my grandmother took care of us until she was too old and sick. My brothers were already grown and out of the house, Jill was living in the streets and no one had seen or heard from our mother. My sister, Shelby and I live in my grandmother's apartment. My brothers help us pay bills, buy groceries, and keep things straight. *Jill? Can't be the same one. I'll save that conversation for later.*

"Sounds like a tight knit family," Michelle replied.

"We are very close now," Serena acknowledged.

"From what you just told us, I can tell that you've had a hard time, but why do you always have such a rough, tough attitude?" I asked directly and braced myself for her smart ass answer.

"I don't know how else to be," she answered honestly. Michelle shook her head in understanding and I glanced at Serena's forlorn expression in the mirror.

"Well, we are not trying to drastically change you, but your manners need some major improvement," Michelle stated.

"I know," Serena quipped. With highly raised eyebrows, Michelle and I looked at each other incredulously.

"I'm working on it," Serena continued. Finally, she loosened up a bit and we enjoyed an informative conversation. She asked me a lot of questions about the events that occurred last year between Anthony, Vickie, and me, and I provided a detailed recap. She seemed impressed that I actually fought back the day that Vickie and I tussled in front of the store. Michelle closed her eyes and prayed when I talked about it because she witnessed the entire fiasco.

They both listened intently when I told them about what happened at my house the day that Vickie killed herself. "Dear Lord, have mercy on her soul!" Michelle whispered as she closed her eyes and prayed again, and Serena simply said aloud, "Damn!"

I quickly changed the subject by asking Michelle about her beau, Kevin. She talked about their relationship for a long time: how they met in church when they were ten, they attend the same college located 45 minutes from Coronado, and how they are focused on accomplishing their goals. She passed the baton on to me by asking if Anthony and I set a date. She noticed the ring a while ago, but decided to wait until I said something. I explained that we haven't set a date yet mainly because he was struggling through the situation with Arielle.

"He has a 13 year old daughter?" Serena asked in amazement. After an affirmative nod, I continued.

Serena shared very little about her love life except to say that she was in a relationship with someone for a long time, but he didn't want to act right. I looked sideways at Michelle; she was looking sideways at me. Serena exhaled loudly. Wow! *She's clueless! Oblivious! I'm sure they broke up because of her behavior!*

"Like I said, I'm working on it," she huffed to us even though we were silent. *Okay, maybe not.*

"Rashad has noticed your recent change in attitude," Michelle timidly suggested. I peeked at Serena in the rearview mirror. She was staring out the window longingly.

"You know that Rashad and I are just friends, right Serena?" I questioned quietly.

"Yeah, I know," she said roughly, "I also know that I don't stand a chance with him after what happened at the restaurant that night."

"What happened?" Michelle wanted to know. She almost broke her neck when she turned around to question Serena, who simply said, "Hmmph," and rolled her eyes.

"Water under the bridge, Michelle, please don't take us back there," I answered.

"I'm going to take a huge step and acknowledge the fact that I started that whole mess. I was wrong, and I apologize," Serena said to me while looking at me in the rearview mirror.

"I accept your apology. I could have reacted differently, but I chose to go the other way," I replied.

"But what happened?!!!!!" Michelle screeched.

"You must not listen to gossip at work? Everybody was talking about it for months," Serena chuckled. I smirked, shook my head, looked at Michelle and calmly said, "Like I said, it's water under the bridge. Let it keep flowing out until it reaches the ocean!" This made Serena laugh out loud. Michelle and I looked at each other and wrinkled our noses because it wasn't really a comical statement.

"So, you said that your older sister's name is Jill, right?"

"Yeah. She's in prison right now. No one in my family has spoken to her in years because she is a lying, thieving, cheating, and conniving crack whore like our mother," Serena answered bitterly. *Damn!*

"Wow, Serena. When I tell you how I know your sister, you might get mad at me all over again," I surmised.

"I doubt it! If you did her wrong, I'm sure she deserved every bit of it," Serena mumbled. For the remaining 80 miles or so to Dayton, I chronicled the story of Tim's terror, how it involved Jill and my cousin Monica. Michelle gasped several times, but Serena remained expressionless.

When I finished, Michelle touched my shoulder and said, "God bless you Amina! I knew you were strong willed, but you are definitely a survivor."

Serena looked at me oddly and asked, "How could you go and visit her after what she put you through?"

"Part of my therapy required me to forgive myself and forgive others for all the terrible things they put me through. Jill wrote me and Monica letters asking for our forgiveness, so I forgave her. It didn't happen automatically, but after we visited her and she told us her story, we both forgave her," I explained.

"Serena, you should visit her," I recommended coolly and again braced myself for a smart ass response.

"You should stay out of my family business!" Serena directed with a point of her index finger.

"Whoa! Serena! Calm down," Michelle declared, "it was just a suggestion! I think it was a good suggestion!"

"Well, there's a lot that you don't know about my sister and what she has done to our family, so just keep your mouth shut about what I should or should not do!"

"Fair enough Serena," I acknowledged, "but let me tell you this: Jill is locked up like an animal. I don't remember the length of her sentence, but she's going to be there for a long time. She doesn't have any support from family or friends. When my cousin and I visited, her face was beaten damn near to a pulp, but she was happy to see us because we were her first visitors since she got locked up. That was many months after the incident. I still write to her, and I believe Monica has visited her again. In a place like prison, sometimes the only thing keeping a woman alive is the hope that when she gets out, she will have somewhere to go and someone to help her get back on her feet," I preached. Michelle was vigorously shaking her head in agreement.

Silence engulfed the vehicle. I was tempted to turn the music back on, but from looking at Serena in the mirror, I could tell that she was processing the information.

"Well, how is she doing now?"

"The last time she wrote, she said that she got her GED and was starting to take some college classes," I answered. Serena shook her head and smirked.

"Jill? College? Get the fuck out of here!" Michelle made a face and sunk down in the seat a little.

"When we get back, would you like to read the letters that she sent me?" I asked thoughtfully.

"I'll think about it," Serena supplied and concluded the conversation about her sister. I turned the music back on, but turned it back down when Serena asked me to.

"I have to tell you something," she confessed, "I knew all about what my sister did to you, at least I heard bits and pieces of it."

"You did?" I murmured in shock.

"Yeah. It's part of the reason that I have such an attitude towards you," she revealed.

"But why? I didn't do anything to her!" I almost screamed. Michelle reached out and touched my arm, and I instantly calmed down. Serena shrugged and gave me a sadly confused look.

"I don't know. I didn't want anyone to know she was my sister, but I'm over it now. I apologized and we are moving on, right?" I glared at the freeway, but I said, "Right."

Finally, we arrived in Dayton, and Michelle read the map directions that I printed from the internet. Traffic was light at 3:30 in the afternoon, so we made it to the hotel without any stops or delays. We turned down the street where USDSI Corporate Headquarters was located and we were awestruck at the enormity of the building. Our hotel was located directly across the street, within walking distance, but we would have to drive across tomorrow to transport the numerous boxes of reports and materials that we brought with us.

We checked in, and a concierge loaded our bags on a cart while a valet parked the car in the parking garage. Michelle and I were smiling at the service, and Serena looked uncomfortable. I noticed her look and I remember feeling the same way once.

"Relax Serena, you belong here. No one knows you, so you have a chance to make a great first impression," I coached. Michelle smiled in agreement. Serena straightened her posture and smiled as she walked with us into the elevator. We followed the concierge to our rooms, waited until he unloaded our bags, and then we entered at the same time. Connie had booked a spacious suite with all the luxuries of home.

Serena didn't even complain when Michelle and I ran and claimed our beds leaving her to sleep on the couch which converted to a bed. She walked around slowly admiring the room, the closet space which we would have to share, and the bathroom. Michelle and I looked at each other and giggled softly. Serena came out of the bathroom and walked slowly to the couch.

"It pulls out into a queen sized bed," I informed Serena and looked at Michelle who had spread eagled on her bed.

"Yeah, I know," she said, "I'm very familiar with these types of couches. I looked at Michelle like she was crazy when she offered Serena her bed. Serena quickly declined and assured us that the couch was fine.

"Hell, I'm the peon in this group. I'm just glad that I don't have to sleep on the floor!" We burst into laughter, mainly because the beds were large enough for us to share, but also because she called herself a "peon." *True, but still funny as hell!*

After unpacking, we ventured over to the shopping strip adjacent to the hotel; then we returned to the restaurant inside the hotel and ordered dinner. During dinner, I made sure they understood what needed to happen tomorrow at the first meeting. They both asked an equal number of questions which I answered without any problems.

I made some phone calls to store managers, VMMs and department managers who would attend the meeting in the morning. I shared my notes and made suggestions about who should be working with whom. Michelle took meticulous notes, and Serena wrote a few things here and there. She seemed more fascinated with the restaurant than anything. Business aside, I started another personal conversation.

"Serena, you are not going to believe what I'm about to tell you," I started.

"Let me guess: you have been in prison too?" she answered obnoxiously. Michelle giggled, and I smiled.

"No! Why would you say that?" I asked, dumbfounded. Michelle giggled some more and sipped her tea.

"Well, I know that Rashad was locked up before," she admitted. Michelle shot her a shocked look and almost choked.

"Actually, you're kind of close," I admitted, "I was going to tell you that I grew up in Greensborough."

"Awww shit! You lying!" she exclaimed loudly which caused the patron at the next table to give her a dirty look.

"The profanity, Serena, is one of the easiest things for you to change!" Michelle scolded.

"Yeah, you're right," she agreed. Serena looked at me and said in a quieter tone, "Nah, I can't believe that you grew up in the projects!"

"Well, I did."

"You don't act like it!"

"Why would I want to?"

"So people know that they can't fuck, excuse me, mess with you," she replied. I told Michelle and Serena a short version of my childhood, and how I learned as a teenager that I did not have to act like I grew up in the projects for people to like me, accept me or respect me.

"That's all part of a messed up mentality that unfortunately exists when you live in poverty," I continued as I forked a plump, juicy grilled shrimp.

"It's called survival," Serena interjected.

"Exactly!" I agreed, "but there's always more than one way to survive!" Serena seemed to agree, but she changed the course of the conversation by asking if I knew this person or that person. I didn't know anyone she named, and I explained to her that I lived there from ages 5 – 12, which was many years ago.

It was getting dark outside when we walked out of the restaurant and back into the hotel. We noticed the pool and hot tub on our way to the elevator. The entire room was full with what seemed like a party for women. Decorations were everywhere and several women wore banners. Champagne and wine bottles were on several tables and a large cake in the shape of a penis was on the main table. Michelle giggled when Serena and I remarked in unison, "Bachelorette party."

Once in our room, Serena darted to the bathroom and started the shower. She came out and pulled items from her bag. Michelle and I followed suit, and then we each sat on our beds and made phone calls.

For the third time, I called Anthony: I called him upon arrival and before we went to dinner. He was pleased that I was keeping him "in the loop." I was kind of irritated, but I obliged like I promised. He was working, but he made a special effort to answer each time that I called. I explained that tomorrow would be extremely busy, but I would call him during the day. I told him that he should call tomorrow evening since he would be at work. He readily agreed to this plan. We talked a few minutes more and then we ended the call. Not surprisingly, Michelle, Serena and I slept like babies after watching a movie and talking in the dark.

—15—

Corporate Chaos

"So you can put faces with names and voices, these are our corporate attorneys: Ashton Webber, Regina Newton, Martha Lewis, Kenneth Hall, and Clayton Burrell," the receptionist of the USDSI Corporate Headquarters announced to me and two store managers and several assistant store managers. We all shook hands, sat down, and waited for the other attendees to join the meeting.

Previously, Michelle and Serena were set up in a large office with several other assistant managers and department managers. Serena looked panicked, lost and confused when I turned to leave, so I pulled her aside and told her, "Don't worry. You can do this. You have my instructions, a checklist, notes and you can ask Michelle about anything you don't understand." She shook her head affirmatively, swallowed her lump of nervousness, walked back to her desk, and got busy with a huge stack of paperwork.

The receptionist fumbled with the conference caller in the middle of the table as I turned to talk to David Gordon from the Breckinridge, Arkansas store. David was a tall, medium brown brother with a shiny bald head, small round glasses and an Adam's apple that was accentuated by his starched white shirt buttoned all the way up to the top. No tie. I couldn't help but look at his shirt and wish that I could unbutton that top button so that lump could breathe. He was very nice though, and I enjoyed visiting his store; his employees were trained well. His store was in compliance, so we had a lot to talk about.

The lady beside me, Judith Cooper, did not have much to say to me. *Looking like Marsha from the Brady Bunch.* She did not want to even look at me, and when she did, her icy stare was cold enough to freeze my blood. Her store in Hollins, Arkansas did not meet compliance standards. Although she wasn't supposed to know, she was terrified when she learned that I was in her store completing the audit. She wanted to talk to me before I left for the day, but company protocol did not allow me to do so. I had to follow the audit procedures to the letter, and she knew this, but that didn't stop her from trying to talk. She was highly pissed when I told her that I couldn't talk to her and promptly left the store.

My presentation today would include footage from her store and David's store. I tried to talk to her before the meeting just to give her a heads up, but she said bluntly, "Just do your job. You don't have to sugar coat it. They all know about the situation at my store and why it existed, but you weren't interested in hearing about that, were you?" I was about to answer, but she cut me off to continue her rant.

"After your visit, we got busy, and I made some changes in staff, so I guarantee you that the next compliance audit will not be a problem at my store." I ate my words, gave her an affirmative nod, and went on about my business. There was nothing that I could say to change what was about to happen at this meeting, so I just kept my mouth shut.

As I sat there chatting with David about nothing in particular, I could feel Clayton's eyes on me. When he shook my hand, I tried not to react, but he gripped me firmly, looked deeply into my eyes and smiled with his familiar, excited question, "How are you doing?" My heart skipped several beats, my breath caught in my throat, and I'm pretty sure that my nipples hardened, but I looked at him and smiled at him in the same manner that I smiled at the others – professionally. I didn't want anyone to know that we already knew each other, but he did not seem to mind at all. I looked at him out of the corner of my eye.

Dammit!!! He looked damn good . . . all straight, muscled, and chocolaty smooth. *Oops, did I just lick my lips?* I couldn't remember the last time we were in the same room. *Ummm, I wouldn't mind having him in a room right now!*

Grasping for composure, I swallowed the hard lump of urges, temptations and regret. David showed me some important paperwork, and I pretended to look at it, but instead I looked over it at Clayton. He was staring right at me. He raised his eyebrows. I raised mine back. *Now what the hell did that mean? Don't look at him anymore. That's what it means! Don't raise your eyebrows at him. Don't smile at him! Don't do anything with him! Pretend he is someone else! Someone you can't stand. Someone you hate! Oh Lord! Give me strength!*

Finally the meeting started, and it dragged on for hours. My nerves tried to get the best of me when I started my presentation, but I took a deep breath, looked at Clayton, stood tensely at first but then he shook his head like he was willing me through my anxiety.

Quickly, I calmed myself down and presented with very few stumbles. I made it through the audit information with zero problems. I made it seem like the stores that were out of compliance would be as simple to fix as bandaging a cut. I answered questions easily, presented ideas flawlessly, and showed examples that had several of the corporate guys smiling and shaking their heads with approval.

When I finished, everyone clapped and started discussing what I had just shown them. I stood at the podium looking around and waiting for the last few questions, but everyone was talking amongst themselves.

I overheard someone say, "Why is she only a VMM? She should be here working as a RMM or in the compliance department."

I stood there listening to the accolades which seemed muted, floating through space, and coming out in slow motion. I glanced down at the podium at my small stack of note cards in my shaky hands, and then I looked up to discover Clayton staring directly at me, but this time I did not look away. Our eyes locked and it was as if I was in a weird, mesmerizing trance.

"She really has it together."

"Her store is one of the top sellers."

"Yes, she's with Mike. Always in compliance, always top sales, always good reviews."

"How long has she held that position?"

A flood of our memories seemed to play in his eyes and in his smile.

Our gazes were completely locked together, and my heart beat steadily as the accolades continued. I could hear my heart beating and my shallow breathing, but for some reason, this did not alarm me.

"Who's the manager of her store?"

"She should be the manager!"

"Oh yeah, Mike made a great choice when he decided to promote her to the position."

A chill raced up my spine and snapped me out of it. The chill quickly melted away when I broke my stare with Clayton and caught the eye of Judith. She was looking at me with what seemed like hatred but not quite as bad.

Conclusion evident, I started walking back to my seat. I smiled at her, and she looked away, embarrassed that I saw her looking at me that way. *Well, damn. Add Judith's name to the list of people who hate me for being great!* Papers shuffled as people referred to reports, but the compliments continued as if I was not even there, and a weird feeling spread all over me.

"He's lucky to have her."

"Wonder what it would take to . . ."

"We might have to steal her away."

"She seems to be keenly aware of what's going on in her entire region."

"Yes, she definitely has a handle on that demographic."

"Isn't there room for her to work as an RMM in her own region?"

"Who is the regional merchandising manager in her region?"

"We could do some reassignments and keep her in her region."

"No, we need to talk about getting her here because her talent could be utilized at the corporate level." *I should be smiling from ear to ear and bubbling over with joy, but I'm feeling weird because Clayton is here, he looks good to me, my heartbeat is out of control, I think I miss him, but I don't even know what I'm feeling!*

Finally the CEO put an end to the chatter by concluding this segment of the meeting. He droned on about sales, profits and revenue . . . blah blah blah. Finally he dismissed us by announcing that he was treating us to lunch at the steak restaurant across the street. He further informed us that our support staff had already been escorted to lunch at a different location, and they would return and get back to work when they finished.

We packed our things and walked back to the office space that the receptionist had provided for us. I told Judith that I was going to the restroom, and I would join them in the lobby. There was a restroom right down the hall, so I started walking toward it. Clayton caught up with me before I could even get started walking.

"It's so nice to see you!" he exuded. I started walking briskly.

"It's nice to see you too," I admitted honestly.

"You did a spectacular job with your presentation. I always knew that you were awesome," he commented. I smiled, remained silent and continued walking quickly toward the restroom. He had no trouble keeping up with me. He didn't even notice that I had increased my speed, obviously trying to avoid a conversation with him.

"How about we go to lunch elsewhere? I would love to talk to you alone, so we can catch up. It's been a long time Amina," he said in his carefully enunciated accent. I stopped just before reaching the restroom.

"I don't think that is a very good idea," I answered in a shaky voice. I looked at his smooth, dark chocolate brown skin, and I almost lost every ounce of my strength.

"Why not?" he asked with genuine confusion and a huge smile. I held up my left hand to show him my engagement ring.

"You're married?" he asked glumly, but he was still smiling.

"No, engaged," I answered with a surprising hint of disappointment in my voice. *Now where did that come from?*

"So, would your fiancé mind if you had lunch with an old friend?" he smiled slyly. *Hell yes, he would mind. He would probably break up with me!* I looked at his upright posture, gleaming smile, and sparkling eyes behind a pair of Armani glasses. *Ummm . . . he always did have great taste. Shit! I need to get out of this spot! He is looking too damn good to me. I need to leave. Now! No! I will not be alone with you! Those festering wounds have finally scabbed over, and I don't want to agitate them or open them up again! Ever!*

"Yes, I think he would," I said and excused myself into the restroom before he could say another word. Hoping that he would give up, leave, and join the crowd as they walked out of the building, across the corporate headquarters campus and into the SUVs waiting in the circular drive at the building's entrance, I took my sweet time in the bathroom. Realizing that I asked Judith and David to wait for me, I hurried out and ran right into Clayton. He was still waiting.

"Whoa! I'm still here!" We were standing close, almost nose to nose, and I looked up at him. My breasts were lightly touching his chest so I stepped backward a centimeter. My breath stopped in my throat, but I mustered the strength to step back an entire inch away from him. He quickly closed the small gap and looked down at me tenderly.

"I'm still here Amina," he said softly. I could feel his breath on my lips and a kiss fast approaching. I shook my head to indicate no, and I turned to walk away from him. Martha, the other attorney was moving quickly down the hallway to go to the ladies room, her dark brown hair flying behind her. She was pregnant, so we understood her urgency, and we moved out of her way.

"David, Judith and Solomon are waiting. It's starting to rain, and the drivers are ready to go," she informed as she strode down the hall. We both smiled and acknowledged her information, and then Clayton and I walked down the corridor that led to the lobby of the massive building.

"When is your wedding date?" he asked nonchalantly. I shrugged, and kept walking. *That's a good question. I don't even know my damn self!*

"You don't have to be that way with me. I will respect your engagement," he offered. I looked at him. *Oh really? Will you stop looking at me like that? Will you stop being my kryptonite?*

"If you want me to?" he continued. *Now that sounds about right! That sounds like the Clayton I use to know. He knows that seeing him again is really affecting me. He knows that I'm feeling vulnerable right now!*

"Yes, of course I do," I answered with a giggle.

"Okay. That doesn't erase the fact that I have missed you," he confessed. My beating heart and my breathing was betraying me again, so I didn't say anything else because we had reached the lobby, and several people from our meeting were waiting for the shuttle.

Lunch was filled with more business talk and accolades. Although he tried to sit next to me, I purposefully avoided sitting beside Clayton by excusing myself to the restroom before sitting. I collapsed on the bench in the ladies room, pulled out my phone, and called Anthony. He answered after the first ring.

"Are you okay?" he asked in a worried voice.

"I'm fine. Why do you ask?"

"You sound breathless. Have you seen him yet?" I rolled my eyes and wondered how I could ever get him to trust me in this situation when I didn't even trust myself.

"Yes, I saw him. No big deal," I lied.

"Anything else?" he prodded.

"Well, you're not going to like it, but I've been assigned to work with him while I'm here," I reported. I could hear him sigh with frustration.

"Don't worry sweetheart," I soothed, "We are both focused on all the work we need to get done."

"Are you two only going to be working at the office? Not at your hotel room? Or his? Is he staying in the same hotel?"

"Anthony, honey, he lives in this area, so I'm sure he doesn't have a room in my hotel. I assure you that all work will be completed at the office. I told you to call me this evening, and I will give you a full report, okay?" Another frustrated sigh escaped from him then silence.

"Okay baby?" I coaxed sweetly.

"Okay. I love you. Please remember that," he pleaded. "Of course! I love you too!" I said just as Martha scurried into the restroom. I got off the phone with Anthony, washed my hands, and left.

When I returned, thankfully, someone had taken the seat beside Clayton, and I was forced to sit across the table. The CEO announced that I would be working with Clayton to compile enough evidence to exonerate USDSI. He continued announcing other partners and groups who would be working together for the next few days. I concentrated on my meal: a grilled chicken, grilled shrimp and grilled sausage medley with pasta, creamy vodka sauce and steamed vegetables. I tried, with little success, to avoid Clayton's eyes. He was a magnet, and I was a ball bearing. There was no escaping my attraction to him.

After lunch, more business talk ensued, and I quickly grew bored. Business and meals always seemed to unsettle my stomach, but today was even more unsettling with Clayton sitting across from me, devouring me with his eyes. I inhaled deeply, answered questions, asked a few of my own, and blatantly ignored Clayton until he addressed me directly.

"So, Amina," he enunciated my name beautifully, and I could feel my spine melt, "if you received a promotion that required you to relocate to the Dayton area, how easy would that be for you to accomplish?"

Although I loathed being put on the spot, I tried not to glare at him when I answered honestly, "It would take some planning and rearranging, but anything is possible." It seemed like everyone around the table stopped what they were doing to hear my answer. I declined dessert, stared at and stirred my tea and sipped on it until lunch was over. I could feel Clayton's eyes on me, but I refused to look back at him.

After lunch, we were driven back to the corporate building. Clayton made it a point to manipulate our seating so he could sit beside me in the third row of one of the SUVs. He asked several business related questions before he reached over and caressed my hand which rested on my leg.

Without looking at him, I answered his questions, slowly moved my hand, turned slightly, and looked out the window. I could feel him smiling, but again, I refused to look him in the eye.

Once at the office, I walked quickly toward the office suite where Michelle and Serena were stationed. Clayton caught up with me and asked me to meet him in his office, so we could get started. We were reconvening with the original group at 3:30 in the main conference room, and I had to present a lot of information to Clayton before that meeting. I gave him a stern look, and he returned it.

"Suite 477, turn left once you get off the elevator and follow the signs directing you to the legal department," he instructed firmly. *Ah ha! He's going to get all stern and business like. Good! That's exactly what I need from him. Otherwise, I won't be able to focus!*

"Thank you. Give me a few minutes to check with my assistants and I'll be right up," I affirmed. Expressionless, he nodded at me before he swiftly walked toward the elevators. I watched him out of the corner of my eye and tried to look past his fine body with its upright stature. I tried to ignore how much I was attracted to him at the moment. *You gave him a chance, and he was a dishonest asshole. He threw it away! Remember that. Focus on business Amina!*

Michelle and Serena were swamped with paperwork and videos, but they were working together nicely. Serena smiled at me when I asked her if everything is okay, and Michelle answered, "Everything is just fine!" They both giggled and I heard Serena say, "See. What did I tell you?" as I walked away. *Hmm . . . what was that about?*

Clayton's office was extremely nice. It was what I aspired to have someday – large, corner office with windows. We got straight to work and collaborated perfectly for about an hour until he started asking questions that I could not answer. He suggested that we take a break, so I could get some answers. I went to the secretary's vacant desk, and I called Mike and asked him the questions that I could not answer. He couldn't answer them either, but he promised me that he would get back to me as soon as he could.

After I hung up with him, I called Anthony on my cell phone. He sounded depressed, so I tried to cheer him up by telling him how much I missed him. He said that he tried to take a nap before work, but he couldn't sleep. "Aw baby, I'm sorry that you couldn't sleep," I said just as Clayton interrupted loudly with, "Amina, let's get back to it."

"Is that him?" Anthony perked up.

"Yes," I answered.

"Let me speak to him!" Anthony demanded.

"No. Not right now baby. We have tons of work to do. I have to go now, okay?" Silence. "Call me tonight when you get a chance, okay?" I coaxed. I visualized the anger on his face.

"Okay, baby. I'll call you. I love you," he answered.

"I love you too," I replied before hanging up.

"So, what can you tell me?" Clayton asked the second I returned to his office.

"Mike, my store's manager, is finding the answers for me," I answered quickly.

"Why don't you have the answers? What I'm asking for is pretty simple. You have all the other bases covered," he announced rudely. I looked at him with narrowed eyes.

"Look, I worked on this project by myself. I planned out everything, put together all the materials, and created the presentation all by myself. The only help I got with this was with phone calls, visiting stores and compiling information," I reported.

"And you did a great job, but perhaps you should have asked for help with some of the finer points," he suggested. *Was he serious?*

"Well, there's always room for improvement, isn't there?" I asked, effectively ending his tirade.

"Yes, there certainly is," he said with an involuntary smile that I tried to avoid, but I couldn't help but see. I smiled back, involuntarily, as well. We finished what we could, and then we walked slowly back to the conference room. Even in his strictly professional manner, he was turning me on, and I could tell that he was feeling the same way. *This is going to be a long damn rest of the freaking day!*

–16–

Once and for all

"This is the life!" Serena giggled loudly as she sipped on her glass of wine. We were in the pool area lounging in the hot tub. She was wearing a hot pink bathing suit with purple polka dots that was more suitable for her little sister Shelby than it was for her 28 year old body. Serena was pear shaped with a round bottom, small waist, and very little up top; she wasn't well endowed or voluptuous. Otherwise, she was thin, but she had a woman's curves. Regardless, she looked ridiculous in those colors.

When she tied up her hair with hot pink elastics before getting into the hot tub, Michelle and I had to look away to stifle our laughter. She saw us and replied, "Amina, you know that you told us at the last minute to bring something to swim in. Hell, how often do you think I swim? I had to search high and low to find this! I haven't needed a swimsuit since I was a teenager! This is one that I wore to a friend's birthday party. It was all I had at the last minute," she explained with a huff.

"Was it her 13th birthday?" Michelle asked with an exaggerated raise of her eyebrows and a choking, gurgling fit of laughter. I leaned back in the hot tub and exploded into giggles.

"Okay! Damn! The next thing I buy with my employee discount at UpStage will be swimwear!" Serena fussed, and then she too started laughing.

Eyes closed, leaned back, enjoying the steamy bubbles of the hot tub, Michelle sipped her ginger ale from a tall stemmed wine glass. She was wearing a black and yellow tankini that Serena said "made her look like a bumblebee." Neither of us laughed because the two piece swim suit only had one asymmetrical stripe of yellow. It was rather stylish, but we both knew that Serena was just trying to snap back because we laughed at her.

I was wearing a royal blue bikini which I tried to keep concealed with a black mesh cover up. It wasn't enough coverage because Serena declared, "Shit! You should have saved that sexy suit for your boyfriend! Titties spilling all out!" Michelle made a choking sound and Serena giggled. She was right. It was quite revealing, but I was in the same boat that she was in. I didn't own a large supply of swimwear, and I grabbed something at the last minute.

After a long, harrowing first day of work at USDSI Corporate Headquarters, we were extremely exhausted, but we vowed to do something every night that we were in Dayton. Going out to the pool was the most that we could manage that night.

Neither Michelle nor Serena expected to complete the sheer volume of work that they completed in one day. They had a rocky start because they didn't know where to begin and how to proceed, but the assistant store managers and some corporate employees helped them organize their efforts, and they were fine.

After a full day of working with him, I definitely appreciated Clayton's workaholic tendencies and desire to excel. Working in the trenches alongside him, I learned a tremendous amount of invaluable lessons. Our day provided little time for socializing or breaks. In fact, after lunch, I was only able to talk to Anthony on my way to the bathroom, while using it, and on my way back to Clayton's office.

The project that we worked on was urgent and intense. Deadlines loomed before us and Clayton demanded perfection. I was shocked at the number of important decisions that I was encouraged to make because each one seemed to live up to everyone's expectations and received approval.

I must have called Mike and Dottie ten to twelve times each to solicit their advice, and I was delighted that they trusted me to do what needed to be done. I kept telling myself to take baby steps, and they kept telling me to jump in and take giant leaps!

Clayton was a hard-nosed extremely demanding, perfection obsessed attorney. Seeing him in action definitely turned me on more than I cared to admit. Instead of calling it a day at 5:30, like everyone else, he insisted that we stay and finish the section that we were working on.

After checking in with Michelle and Serena, making sure they had the car key and knew my plans for the rest of the evening, calling Anthony and talking to him for a few minutes, I trudged back up to Clayton's office. His stern business demeanor was keeping my attraction somewhat in check, and I was grateful for that.

I tried extremely hard to keep my eyes and my thoughts to myself, but I caught myself looking at him with admiration and fantasizing several times and then kicking myself under the table to snap out of his mesmerizing spell. He took several calls while we were working because he was working on another case simultaneously. I tried not to eavesdrop . . . no actually, I eavesdropped like a spy, and I listened for any hints of a personal call. Every call seemed business related. I was so tempted to ask him if he was seeing someone, but I didn't. *Shit! As fine as he is! I know good and damn well that he is probably seeing someone! Damn! Was that a stab of jealousy? YES!* At last, he was satisfied with the work that we completed, so he declared an end to the day. Instantly, he transformed into a gentleman again.

"You're amazing. You know that, don't you?" he smiled at me. I stood up and stretched. My butt, back, arms, legs, neck and shoulders were sore.

"Yes, I've been told that many times before," I answered facetiously. *Must not have been too damn amazing since your ass couldn't tell me the truth and keep me!*

"Do you know what I like to do to unwind after a long day at work?" he quizzed with a naughty smile.

"I can only imagine," I answered evasively as I moved toward the large window to adjust the blinds, so I could see outside. I looked out for the first time and appreciated the magnificent view. Quietly, he stood and moved toward me.

"My gym is close. I love to go there after work, get some good music going in my headphones, and work out until I'm glistening with sweat!" *Oh God! I could listen to him talk forever. His silky mellow voice was like magic. The way those words just rolled off his tongue gave me chills!* It was 7:30, but it was still light outside. He moved closer until he was standing directly behind me. He was so close that my butt was literally touching his legs. "Let me treat you to a nice dinner," he suggested softly. I smiled. *Oh how I wanted to indulge.*

"I've already ordered from the restaurant in the hotel. All I have to do is let my assistants know when I'm on my way. Thanks though." I squeezed my butt in a little, but it seemed like he moved even closer.

"This window is perfect for watching sunsets . . . and sunrises," he whispered into my hair.

"Yes, you have an awesome view of this little side of Dayton," I murmured in agreement. He was completely touching me now, and I wanted to fall back and surrender, but I stood ramrod straight with my muscles tense.

"Yes, I have an awesome view," he murmured and pressed against me. I could feel him breathing down on my neck, and a hot rush engulfed my body. I knew at that moment that I had to leave immediately. First, I scooted away from him, and then I moved quickly and gathered my things.

"So, are you just going to run away from me?"

"Well, it **is** time to call it a day!" I answered shakily.

"Can I, at least, give you a ride to the hotel?" he asked. I laughed aloud, "It's just across the street! I can walk!"

"That bag looks heavy though!" he chuckled.

"It is!" I giggled as the nervousness started to fade away. He moved to lift it, pretended that it weighed a ton, and dropped it heavily onto the table. As I easily picked up the bag and slung it over my shoulder, he made faces and sounds that caused laughter to burst from within me. He laughed too, but soon he was serious as he moved closer to face me.

"I love to see you smile and hear you laugh." I tried not to look up at him, but I couldn't help it because he was looking deeply into my eyes.

Before I could protest, his arms were around me and his lips were on mine. I wanted that kiss – oh how I wanted that kiss – and I let it proceed. I dropped my bag back onto the table, reached up and wrapped my arms around him, melted into his body, and received it, full soft lips, tongue and all until that little nagging voice inside told me to stop. My arms went limp, my mouth became slack, and I turned away abruptly.

"No Clayton. I'm sorry, but I just can't do this!" I said as I wrapped my arms around myself and shook my head. *Amina, you are such a weakling!*

"No. Forgive me. I had to taste you Amina. It's been so long, and I have missed you so much! I thought that time would make me forget you and stop feeling the way that I felt, but nothing has changed."

"Honestly Clayton," I began, searching for the right words, but my mouth betrayed me, "I have missed you too. I thought about you often, and I wondered if you thought about me. Things have definitely changed on my end, but every time it rains, I look out at the clouds or listen to the raindrops and think about you," I confessed somberly.

"Yes! Every time it rains, I think about you too! I convinced myself that I would never get the chance to see or talk to you again, and that was simply heartbreaking! Can you imagine how my heart smiled when I learned that we would be working together?" he exclaimed excitedly.

"Yeah, my heart skipped a couple of beats when I received that information. I kept thinking that there must be another man named Clayton Burrell who is a corporate attorney in Dayton!" He chuckled then stopped suddenly.

"I am so turned on right now," he admitted. I glanced at the front of his pants, and tried not to gasp at the evidence of his desire.

"I'm turned on too," I confessed softly, thankful that he could not see the evidence of my desire.

"Don't say another word! Let's go to my room and take care of each other!" he insisted.

"You have a room at my hotel?" I almost screamed.

"Yes! Corporate has a block of rooms over there at all times. When I'm working on big cases like this one, I usually stay there," he expounded.

"But you live in this area!" I pointed out foolishly.

"Yes, but the commute can be treacherous in the mornings, and nothing disturbs me more than wasting time stuck in traffic," he answered with a direct look into my eyes.

"Well, how does your girlfriend feel about that?" I slyly inquired and looked away.

"No girlfriend at the moment. The last one quickly became too frustrated with the amount of time that I spent at work," he chuckled. I turned back to face him with a smile.

"You haven't changed a bit!" I said as I shook my head, grabbed my bag, and started walking toward the door.

"Nope baby. I'm still hardcore," he said and flexed his arms and shoulder muscles like he was a bodybuilder, and he smiled.

"You're still a workaholic," I smirked.

"That too!" he chuckled.

"When will you ever learn?"

"When you agree to be mine?" he suggested.

"Aw hell! You're just saying that now because you know that I'm not available," I giggled.

"As long as you are not married, you are still available . . . besides, you were mine first!" he pronounced. I looked at him sideways, and we walked out of the office and into the hallway. I hobbled a bit as we approached the elevator.

Alarmed, he asked, "Are you okay?"

"I'm fine. Tired as hell and my feet hurt," I explained, "I haven't worked this long and hard in a long time. I feel like I have walked all over this entire building!" I was wearing a black skirt suit with a shimmery royal blue camisole underneath, sheer black pantyhose, black pumps with 4" heels, and silver jewelry.

After I got dressed this morning, Michelle said that I looked like a "boss." She and Serena opted to wear pantsuits, and I complimented their stylish choices.

"That blue looks so nice against your skin," Clayton complimented.

"Thank you! It's my fiancé's favorite color," I replied with a smirk. We made it to the lobby, and all I had to do was walk out of the elevator door, across the large expansive lobby, out the front doors, down two long sidewalks, and across a quiet side street to get to the hotel. Instead, I lagged behind with him and let him talk me into riding with him.

"Come on. Walk with me to my car. It's in the parking garage. You can tell me all about your fabulous fiancé," he invited. It was extremely tempting to decline, but his harmless nature, the opportunity to tell him about Anthony, how much I loved him, and how excited I was about our pending nuptials was an offer that I could not pass up. I agreed, and we walked slowly through the lengthy corridor that led to the parking garage. It was obvious that neither of us was ready for our time together to end, but we needed to face the inevitable. The path to the garage was hot because it contained a window wall that absorbed the day's sunlight. I wondered if I would be sweaty by the time we reached his car.

Secretly, I was overjoyed to get the ride because the walk would have killed my feet. I vowed to put my black flats into my bag tomorrow. I followed him to his shiny black Lincoln Navigator.

"Nice!" I praised as he opened the door for me, and I was greeted with a new car smell, shiny wood grain accents, and sumptuous beige leather. He quickly walked around to the driver's side, started the car, and turned the air up high. The breeze felt glorious after that hot walk through the glass walled corridor.

Except for a few cars, the garage was vacant, and Clayton made no move to drive as I rattled on about Anthony. Clayton listened intently, and when I paused, he said, "Wow! He's a lucky guy!" I continued and told him about Arielle, and how much I love her, conveniently leaving out our problems that were exacerbated by Anthony's alcoholism. I was laying it on thick, and I knew that Clayton knew that I was sugarcoating my narrative, but I didn't care.

"Do you really love him that much? Or are you in love with what he represents – marriage, family, stability," Clayton inquired seriously. I looked at him and could not help but notice his chest rise and fall as he was breathing, waiting for my answer.

"Both," I answered quickly and definitively.

"So, there's no way that I can talk you out of it?" he joked as he leaned over and touched the tip of my nose. I closed my eyes for a few seconds and smiled.

"No, there's no way that you can talk me out of it. I am going to marry him because I love him no matter what," I answered, again quickly and definitively.

"Okay Amina, I will try my best to respect that."

"Okay," I agreed and breathed a sigh of relief.

"But it wouldn't hurt to get together once more for old time's sake!" he said as he started driving slowly out of the garage. *Why are parking garages circular? Ugh!*

"We are together," I giggled.

"Together in bed would be better!" he suggested. I ignored him and reached out to turn up the music.

"May I?" I politely asked. He nodded and smiled a satisfied smile. "I'm Missing You" by Case billowed smoothly from the speakers and filled the space with sweet memories. I smiled, punched him playfully on the arm, relaxed back in the seat, and listened to the beautiful song that once made me instantly think about him. He drove slowly across the street to the hotel and parked, but neither of us made a move until after the song finished.

"What room are you in?" he boldly asked.

"Room number none ya," I giggled.

"Is that on the 5th floor?" he asked with a snort.

Ignoring him, I unfastened my seatbelt, but he grabbed my arm, and I looked at him.

"Because I'm in room 522," he continued, "Maybe you could visit me after dinner tonight?" *Wait! Not 10 seconds have passed since you just said that you will respect my relationship with Anthony!*

"No can do! And don't investigate to find my room number! And don't come to my room! Remember I'm sharing my room with the two women who came here with me!" I instructed excitedly and shook my arm loose from his firm grip.

"Just the thought of us sleeping under the same roof will keep me up all night!" he persisted.

"Better take some sleeping pills," I suggested.

"So this is goodbye?" he sadly concluded.

"For tonight, yes," I answered and reached for the door handle.

"Wait!" he jumped out, ran over to my side, and offered his hand to help me down and out of the large SUV. What could I do? He was being a gentleman, and every gallant gesture made my heart flutter. We walked into the hotel, through the lobby and to the elevators. He graciously agreed to get on a separate elevator and promised not to follow me.

As the doors closed, he blew me a kiss, and then he was gone. I exhaled deeply, as I waited for my elevator, and marveled in all the tingling sensations that were racing through my body. The hotel room was empty because, according to a text that Michelle sent less than two hours ago, the girls were going to the pool after a quick workout in the hotel's fitness room. I just missed them. We could have run right into each other at the elevators!

Courtesy of the restaurant hotel connection, our dinner trays were on the table; I touched my tray and discovered that it was piping hot. I kicked off my shoes as I made my way to my luggage stand. I put my bikini and cover up on, slipped my feet into my flip flops and walked over to the mirror. Before I zipped up the mesh cover shirt, I admired my body. Working out made a huge difference, I thought as I admired both the tone and the curves of arms, legs, behind and hips.

Suddenly feeling sexy and free, I wanted to go to room 522 and show off my bikini. Of course, I decided against it, and instead I moved my clothes and shoes over to my side of the room. I prayed that Clayton would not show up at the pool, and I grabbed my phone. I called Anthony on the way down despite the fact that I had already talked to him several times today as he requested. Because he was at work, it was his turn to call me; he knew when would be a good time or not. Case in point: he couldn't really talk when I called, but he made sure to question my whereabouts.

"Are you just now getting in?" he asked in irritated disbelief. It was almost 9:00. I started to explain, but he cut me off because he had to go. I turned up the ringtone's volume on the phone and put it in the pocket of my cover up.

Michelle, Serena, I had a blast. Serena and I got a bit tipsy from drinking two shots each and an entire bottle of wine from our hotel room's mini bar, and our volume of speaking and level of laughter intensified. The hot tub became uncomfortable just as we finished our last glass of wine. Michelle was already lounging in a chair, talking to her boyfriend, when Serena and I exited the hot tub. Giggling and chatting loudly, we plopped down beside Michelle as an attendance dropped warm, dry towels on the ends of our chairs.

We relaxed, discussed the day's events, and watched people in the pool until the area became uncomfortably loud and crowded. We left, and Anthony called while we were on our way to our room, so I lagged behind to talk to him privately.

When I told him that we just left the hot tub and we were about to eat dinner, he grumbled, "Wow! This is a hell of a business trip, isn't it?" The sarcasm oozed from his voice, but my slight inebriation caused me to ignore it and reply, "Nope, that hot tub was purely pleasure baby. You know what they say about all work and no play!"

"And you've been drinking too?" he whined.

"Just a few glasses of wine! I'm good baby! I'm on my way back to the room now!" I burbled. He mumbled something that sounded rude, and I loudly requested, "What was that baby?" Speak up! I can't hear you!"

"I'll call you back later," he angrily huffed and hung up before I could respond. Once on the elevator, I pushed the button to go the 5th floor. I got off, walked boldly yet slowly to room 522, stood by the door, and listened closely. I could hear the shower running and what sounded like sports or a news update on the TV.

I smiled. No, he hasn't changed a bit. I wanted to knock, but I knew that if he opened the door, I would have been no good. I would have surrendered to all of the desires that raged through my body at the moment. I would have made my fantasies come true while simultaneously destroying my dreams of having a husband and a family. I turned around and left quickly as I remembered that Clayton said that this floor was booked exclusively for USDSI corporate employees. I didn't want anyone from the office to see me tipsy in my bikini, cover up and flip flops, lurking outside Clayton's room! I scurried away quickly with the sound of my flip flops slapping the bottom of my feet and echoing in the vacant corridor.

In the elevator, my phone rang and I clumsily answered it. Anthony. Suddenly sober, I listened while he apologized for hanging up on me earlier.

"No problem baby. I know how it is when you are working," I stated slowly, trying to erase the drunken lilt from my voice. Silence. The elevator stopped and I walked off slowly.

"Amina, I hung up because I was mad," he confessed.

"Why were you mad baby?" I condescended. I knew damn well why he was mad, and I deserved every ounce of his anger. I was not doing right by him. I deserved his little blow up. I lied to him, and now I was stuck with it. *If only he knew . . .*

"Because you were drinking, and I want a drink so bad right now," he sadly admitted. *What? That's why you were mad? Because I was drinking? I'll be damned!*

"Oh," I answered, disappointed then embarrassed, then totally ashamed because I vowed to help him stop drinking and there I was flaunting my drinking fun in his face.

"I'm so sorry baby," I whispered.

"I'm okay now baby," he assured. *Good because I'm pretty damn relaxed right now and I don't need to be feeling sorry for you or ashamed of my insensitivity.*

I told him about my long day working at corporate. Until he asked, I conveniently left out all mention of Clayton. When Anthony inquired about how I dealt with working beside him, I kept my answers short, clean, and somewhat evasive. He didn't press, and I was delighted because I didn't want to lie too much and have to try to remember what I said while I'm a tiny bit intoxicated.

In the room, Michelle was perched in front of the TV eating, Serena was in the shower with music blasting, and I went over to my bed and flopped down on it.

Anthony talked and I listened: he told me about Arielle's latest problems. Alycia's drug use was escalating, but the custody hearing was still months away. Child protective services lagged dangerously behind, and he feared that they would only take action after something terrible happened to his daughter. What's worse is that he was experiencing difficulty reaching his mother and sister which was unlike them.

He was terribly worried, so much so that I could feel his stress through the phone. I tried to comfort him, but it was no use. He promised to text or call to tell me goodnight later. I told him that I was looking forward to it. Before we hung up, I told him that I loved him; he reciprocated. I sighed heavily and put the phone down.

I warmed my food, joined Michelle in front of the TV, and waited for my turn to take a shower. Afterward, I was so exhausted that I fell asleep as soon as my head hit the pillow. I missed Anthony's call and his text said: I know you are tired sweetheart. I love you. Goodnight.

The next two days were pretty much repeats of the first one. My somewhat guarded attitude toward Clayton gradually dissolved with each minute that I spent with him. This time in Dayton was the most time that I had ever spent with him. Even though we were working to save a corporation millions of dollars in lawsuits and settlements, the sexual chemistry between us sizzled like bacon in a hot frying pan.

The more I relaxed, the more I enjoyed being with him. I started wanting to BE with him, and I tried to hide it with little success. He knew what was happening, and he knew exactly how and when to turn on and turn off the charm.

We got to the office early, worked tremendously hard, stopped an hour or so for lunch, returned and continued with the hard work until we finished. Michelle and Serena finished at a decent hour every day, and they returned to the hotel to relax and wait for me to finish and return. Michelle worked on her school work, and Serena checked on Shelby.

On the second night, we went to a dinner/movie theater located close to the hotel. It was extremely nice and convenient to eat a meal and watch a movie in the same building! Serena loosened up completely and started acting normal.

Michelle and I deduced that she was accustomed to being excluded, so she figured that she needed to be rough and tough to disguise her pain. All she needed was acceptance and inclusion, and she was able to be herself. Although she was extremely rough around the edges, her blunt nature was usually hilarious.

On the third night, we ventured downtown on the train and attended an outdoor dinner concert, a first for each of us. The venue was expertly set up for the event, the music was lively and the menu was exquisite. We spent a bit more than we planned, and I promised them that I would ask Connie if this entertainment was an allowable expense. Since it included dinner, I was sure that we would be reimbursed for it. We stayed late, and danced the night away at the after party, and we surely regretted it the next morning which was our last day at work there.

We trudged into the office at 7:30. Coffee did little to perk us up, but after lunch our energy increased considerably, and we were able to power through the rest of the day. After the morning conference, I spent several hours working closely with Michelle and Serena closing out, packing up, and tying loose ends.

Promotions were inevitable for each of us because we jumped in and expertly handled so much work that was entirely outside of our pay grade. No need to lecture Serena on the importance of visual merchandising and how it was connected to safety and security anymore. My plan absolutely worked. After working behind the scenes and seeing so many audits, she thoroughly understood that VM was top priority.

After lunch, I returned to working with Clayton who was in a weird mood. I did not ask him about it because we had too much to complete by 5:00. We finished slightly before that time, and he asked me if I would please go for a ride with him. Confused, I looked at him. A ride to where, I wanted to know, but he wouldn't tell me.

"It's important Amina. Once and for all, we need to do this," he answered. More confusion from me. *Do what? Haven't we talked about this enough?*

He moved closer and looked deeply into my eyes as he implored, "Please, you have moved on. Help me close this chapter of my life too. Ride with me. Let's talk. We really need to talk, and you know it." I didn't protest. I went with him, and we spent hours closing the door that was left achingly wide open for both of us.

I lied and told Michelle and Serena that I was attending a dinner party that one of the corporate big wigs was hosting. I told them not to wait up because I would be in late, and that much was true. It was well after midnight when I returned to the room, quietly showered, and got into bed. Michelle and Serena's deep even breathing indicated that they were fast asleep, so I moved about the room as quietly as possible.

As soon as I plugged the charger into my phone, it sprang to life with notifications of missed calls and text messages from Anthony. Turning the call volume down, I winced at the elevating anger in Anthony's voicemails. I closed my eyes, listened to several voice messages, and tried not to think about Tim, but it was very difficult. From what I could tell, Anthony wasn't drunk, so it frightened me that he was that angry without being fueled by alcohol. After the voice mails, I looked at the text messages:

6:05 – What am I supposed to think when you don't answer your phone and then you don't call or text me back?

6:37 – Wow! Really Amina?

7:42 - I hope and pray that it's truly business not pleasure that has you so busy that you can't answer your phone or check your texts.

8:04 – Amina, don't you think it's time for a break? I have been calling you like crazy. I even called your hotel room and no one answered. What the hell is going on? It might ease my mind if you would just call or text me back! I'm starting to think that something bad happened. I hope nothing bad has happened.

9:00 – Ok. First I was a little worried, but now I'm mad. Answer your fucking phone.

10:02 – Amina. What the fuck is up?

10:57 – This is breaking my heart. You can't be working this late! And this is your last day there. You are still leaving in the morning, right? You said that you would finish on time and leave in the morning after you checked out of the hotel. If that plan has changed, I'm really going to be pissed. Maybe I should call your hotel room again?

11:28 – I need a drink.

12:05 – You can't even begin to imagine what's going through my head. I can't believe that you are doing this to me. You better have a good explanation for this bullshit, or I don't know what the hell is going to happen to us.

Tim. All over again without the beat downs. At least not yet. The last text definitely seemed like a threat to me. I read it several times and tears spilled out of my eyes each time. A wave of anxiety rippled across my stomach as I laid there, quiet and still, processing the night's events, the voice mails, and the text messages. I contemplated the various ways to respond and wondered if tonight was my glaringly obvious sign that my relationship with Anthony was over. He just moved in! We just hammered out so many important plans: marriage, custody of Arielle, working our way up in our perspective careers, and having children. I squeezed my eyes shut as tears flowed down my face and onto the sheet. I could easily break up with him right now because his behavior is uncalled for, and he knows it.

Oh, how I wish I had not asked him to move in! I can see now that was a huge mistake! I composed a series of long texts, starting with the truth:

1:15 – I am texting you because everyone is asleep, and I don't want to disturb them with trying to talk to you. Today has been a long, difficult, decision filled day, and I have been extremely busy trying to tie up loose ends and finally close the door on this part of the project that I have been working on tirelessly for months. Common sense should tell you that the reason why I have been working so hard, nonstop at times, was to make sure that we can leave as planned tomorrow. Yes, we are sleeping in, eating breakfast, checking out of the hotel, and heading home tomorrow ONLY because we worked like animals to get everything taken care of. That's what we came to do – work until we got everything taken care of.

1:33 - You have really shown your true colors while I was away Anthony, and I do not like it at all. You remind me of Tim so much right now, that I'm actually kind of scared to come home because I fear an ass whooping when I get there. Without reason, your level of trust in me has disintegrated to microscopic, and I just can't deal with that.

At some point tonight, my phone died, and I did not notice it because I was so busy working. I incorrectly assumed that you were busy too, and I was satisfied with that as a reason why you hadn't called me from work. I didn't know that my battery was dead until I was back here in the room. When I listened to your voice mails and read your texts, they upset me deeply. I could not read your texts without crying. I started feeling anxious and shaky like I was about to have an anxiety attack, something that I haven't experienced for a very long time. The last time I suffered through one was when I felt like things were out of my control. Well, Anthony, things are still within my control. I still have control over what happens in my life. You need to think very carefully about this.

Then I lied:

1:43 - Anthony, I haven't done anything to hurt you or destroy your trust in me. I came here and did exactly what I was supposed to do. Work. I called you and checked in and updated you exactly the way you asked me to. The precious little time available to relax, and enjoy myself, I spent with Michelle and Serena. I have pictures to prove it! You talked to me almost every hour on the hour after work! You knew where I was, who I was with, and what I was doing. I don't know what else I could have done to put your mind at ease. Why do I have to jump through so many hoops to please you anyway?

before telling the truth again:

1:58 - I have really tried to support you and commit myself to you, but it's getting to the point where I don't believe that I'm strong enough to continue on this way. It is starting to feel like too much, and I honestly don't know how to handle it. You have to start trusting me; this is imperative. It's been a long day, and I don't want to continue on with this message while I'm upset. I don't want to think about what needs to happen between us while I'm tired and feeling so anxious. This is a terrible feeling that I convinced myself that I would never have to feel again especially when it involved the man that I love. This trip has instantly transformed me from a self-assured, proud, confident, loving woman to one who is full of doubt, questions, guilt and shame. For the record, I feel guilty and ashamed because I want to call it quits, walk away from you, and never look back. If I do that, I'll be admitting that I didn't learn from my first mistake. Am I about to make the same mistake twice? I need to stop now. I'm tired. I'm going to bed. I intend to sleep late, but I will call you when I wake up or before we leave. Good night.

I put the hot, charging phone on the night stand, and I let the cold, silent tears continue falling until I fell asleep.

The next morning, Michelle and Serena woke up at 9:00 or so, got dressed, and went to enjoy breakfast in the hotel's restaurant. They didn't wake me, and I was grateful. My back, neck, shoulders, arms, legs, and hips ached incredibly, but I smiled at the possible reason that might explain why. *Damn hot tub sure would feel good right now!* Still smiling, I rolled over, picked up the hotel phone from the nightstand, and called Clayton's room. No answer. He answered on the first ring when I called his cell.

"Clayton Burrell," he answered in his stern, professional voice.

"Good morning," I purred. Instantly his voice softened.

"Good morning sweetheart! How are you?" I could see his giant smile and his twinkling eyes behind his glasses.

"Sore," I giggled.

"Hmm . . . I wonder why?" he chuckled.

"Don't tell me that you are already in the office working?" I inquired, even though I knew the answer.

"You know me. I'm obsessed with work. I have to get started on another case in the Midwestern region soon," he explained.

"Another one? But you're still working on the Northeastern fiasco!"

"I'm an expert when it comes to multi-tasking baby," he stated with a laugh.

"Yes. Yes, you are," I accepted with a wiggle of my toes and a flutter of butterflies in my stomach. *It's been so long since I felt it that the feeling was almost foreign!*

"So, you're good?" I questioned.

"Are you kidding me? I'm great!"

"I'm surprised that you are okay with this," I quietly pressed.

"Baby, you were mine first. I'm just glad that you are back in my life. I wish it wasn't mainly based on our work relationship, but of course, I'm cool with it. I'm shocked that you agreed to it," he answered.

"I explained why I'm okay with it last night, and after speaking to him and sleeping on it, I'm positive that I made the right decision. I have to do what's right for me," I announced, suddenly feeling empowered, entitled, and free from guilt, shame, and regret.

"I wish I could see you before you leave," he expressed wistfully.

"We already talked about that too," I reminded.

"Yes, we did, but you can't blame me for trying. Have a safe trip back. Drive safely, okay?"

"Absolutely, I will. No looking back. I'm moving forward," I declared.

"So am I baby. So am I."

We ended the call, and I got up, showered, and dressed. As I looked at myself in the mirror, a twinge of guilt surfaced and flashed in my eyes. I blinked it away, and I kept my eyes closed for a few minutes. *Last night is now a part of the past. Close the door on the past Amina. Move forward. Do what makes you happy. You only live once. Either you are going to do what makes you happy or not. Your choice.* I opened my eyes and smiled at myself. *I choose happiness. So what if I go straight to hell afterward? I'll be dead and it will be too late to change anything anyway!* I giggled at my silly thoughts and started thinking seriously and more positively.

I moved around the room and the bouquet of flowers that Anthony gave me caught my eye. Usually, they lasted for a week or so, but after just five days, they were wilted and slowly dying. *Much like our relationship.* It was hard to believe that less than a week ago, I treated Anthony to a special night and we were in a much better place than we were in now. Four days away from each other! My head started to ache just thinking about all the hoops that I jumped through just to make sure that night was extra special for him.

Michelle and Serena burst into the room talking loudly and giggling, effectively interrupting my thoughts. They brought me coffee and a cream cheese pastry which I devoured. *Damn! I didn't realize that I was so hungry! Must have worked up quite an appetite last night.* I giggled to myself, and both ladies looked at me strangely then each other and burst into giggles themselves. We engaged in light, humorous chatter as we packed. I called the valet service to get the car from the parking garage. Within 5 minutes, a valet was knocking on the door to get the key.

"Damn, you better wait until we get completely packed to call the bag boy!" Serena stated. I looked at Michelle who was already looking at me, and we burst into fits of laughter. Serena looked confused, "What? What did I say?" and this only made us laugh even harder.

She was right though. I waited until we were completely packed to call for concierge service. As we were getting into the car, I saw Clayton standing near the circular driveway of the corporate headquarters building. He was on the phone with the one hand in his pocket. He was too far away for me to see his giant smile, but I knew that it was there. He waved at us and we all waved back.

"Umm hmm . . . what did I tell you Michelle? That guy likes her," Serena spilled.

"What did I tell you about rumors and how destructive they are?" Michelle scolded, "Amina is engaged to be married. She and her fiancé will soon be raising his daughter, and I'll bet they will also be starting a family soon too!"

I looked at her with huge eyes. Obviously, during my absence, I had been the topic of many discussions between Michelle and Serena. I was about to say something, but Michelle continued her thorough reprimand.

"Just because a man and a woman work together really well, smile at each other and treat each other cordially and with respect doesn't mean that there's anything more than that. A rumor gets started and it spreads like wildfire! So, we'll both know who started the rumor if this one gets out," she finished.

As far as I knew, neither of them knew about my history with Clayton. I racked my brain trying to remember if I introduced him to all of my co-workers so long ago. I'm pretty sure I did introduce him to Katy, Whitney and Dottie, but I'm uncertain about Michelle and Serena. *Oh hell! Who cares? What did it matter? Anthony made up his mind about it months ago when he highlighted the damn phone bill. As far as rumors flying around the store, Michelle just nipped it in the bud. If I hear Vanessa running her mouth about it, I might just have to kick Serena's ass.*

As we were driving away, I glanced out the window at Clayton who was still standing there talking on the phone. He waved again, I reached up to adjust the sunroof, and I pretended not to notice, but my heart filled to capacity. I wanted to drive over there, race into his arms, and fill his face with kisses, but I had to resist the urge with all my might. I had to be satisfied with what already happened. A huge smile spread across my face. Neither Michelle nor Serena noticed that we had an extra passenger on the return trip home: my little secret.

–17–

Business as Usual

December 27, 2001

Dr. Branson,

*T*his is starting to be a tradition, isn't it? Not too long ago, I gave you the other letter that I wrote a year ago on the same date, and here I am writing again. I've already decided that I won't give it to you immediately, because just as I did with the other letter, I intend to refer back to it often to see how much progress I have made with the "Improvement of Amina." The years 2000 and 2001 were long, difficult years. There were not enough happy moments to drown out the sad ones, at least not enough that I can publicly celebrate. Yes, we'll have to talk about that later.

Sometimes I think that I have changed, but then I analyze some of my haphazard decisions and I realize that I am still the same little girl who wished she had a father who told her that she was beautiful, who grounded her for breaking rules, and who scrutinized the boys she wanted to date. You were absolutely right when you suggested that I open the lines of communication with my father. You also hit the nail on the head when you said that my mother would be okay with everything. She was not the least bit hurt when my father and I reconnected.

In fact, she has been quite supportive of us rebuilding our

relationship. It boggles my mind to even try to understand how she could act this way after everything he put her through. I guess it's true: Time heals all wounds. Imagine my shock when I saw them sitting together at my wedding!

By the way, thank you so much for coming, and quadruple thanks for the wonderful gift. Our honeymoon cruise was spectacular!!! No, I still have not gotten around to hand writing all those thank you cards! Yours was the first and will probably be the only one!

Anthony and I knew that we were not 100% ready to get married, but we committed ourselves to each other and promised to stand strong when the other was weak, and well you remember the rest of our heartfelt vows.

Before I got married, you asked me if my feelings of guilt due to my poor decisions had subsided since my "summer of secrets." Yes and No. Yes, because I don't feel guilty about it even though I know what I did was wrong, and I know that I should feel guilty. No, because I'm still sort of kind of doing it. There, I said it! It's what's keeping me sane! Believe it or not, it's actually helping me love my husband even more. I know that doesn't make a bit of sense, but it's true.

Getting full custody of Arielle brought us closer, and then when I learned that I was pregnant, I was devastated. I'm sure you can understand why. When my bundle of joy, my baby boy A.J. was born, all of my questions were answered and all of my doubts diminished because he sealed the deal for the Wallace family. Arielle and A.J. mean everything to Anthony and me. Arielle seems to be adjusting well despite everything she went through. She is one of the main reasons why we decided to remain in Coronado for a few more years.

Although it was extremely difficult to turn down the job at USDSI Corporate, I knew that living in the Dayton area would be too complicated considering what I had going on . . . Again, that's something that we will have to talk about later. Nevertheless, I'm very pleased with my new position as RMM – Regional

Merchandising Manager of the Southeastern region of USDSI. Anthony hates that I have to travel one to three times a month, but it's okay with me especially since I have such dependable child care and support from my family.

My greatest fear is that I will return home to discover that Anthony has fallen off the wagon. I can handle his little slip ups when I'm home, but when I'm away! Gosh! It's horrible for me to even fathom him sloppy drunk and trying to handle the children. I can't trust him and alcohol because he is so weak. He always uses stress as an excuse. He has had a lot of stress lately, but I've supported him through it.

Holidays are his second favorite excuse. He's usually okay for New Year's, Valentine's, birthdays, anniversaries, Thanksgiving, Christmas, and Easter, and I'm not really sure why it's so much easier for him to remain sober during those holidays. For Memorial Day, the 4th of July, Labor Day, Halloween (yes, the damn trick or treat day!), family reunions, random friends/family gatherings, Super Bowl Sunday and any other sports related celebrations, all bets are off. I have learned to prepare myself for his nonsense by building up a tolerance for his excuses and later his complaints.

It's taking a toll on him, physically, and he is no longer at the top of his game. It's a good thing that he passed the detective exam during one of his sober periods because I doubt he could have done so otherwise.

When he is around my family, he is fine. He is the picture of health and sobriety, but when he is around his family, I can't stand the sight of him because he usually gets wasted. Sadly, he fits right in. His mother's side of the family lives in California, Nevada and Arizona, and they love to drink. His father's side of the family lives in Louisiana, Arkansas, Tennessee, and Oklahoma and drinking is part of their livelihood (they are in the alcohol brewing business). It's no wonder Anthony has such a desire to drink when he has been surrounded by it his entire life!

Speaking of his family, his mother was diagnosed with ovarian cancer in March, but she did not tell Anthony about it until May when she was very sick and suffering through treatment. Recently, she was declared "cancer free," which effectively shut down another one of Anthony's excuses to drink. She moved to Alton, Texas, which is near Dayton, and she finally started working again. Alton is the home of one of the largest cancer treatment centers in the United States, and we were happy to learn that his mother moved there so she could not only be closer to her treatments, but also closer to us.

Anthony's sister Angie has been in two failed relationships in the past year. Both times, she proceeded at lightning speed and moved in with the guy. Both guys were no good, deadbeat, money grubbers, but she was so enraptured by them that she could not see this. In the past year and a half, Anthony helped her move from Scottsboro, Arizona to Burgess, California to Regal, New Mexico to Alton, Texas where she is now living with her mother. The moves were time consuming and expensive; Anthony complained to me about it, but basically said nothing to his sister or his mother about the inconvenience or the expense. However, I know that they know how much a moving truck, gas, and time off work cost him during those moves. Angie is weak in that sense: she falls in love quickly with guys who talk a good game, she works hard to support them, and she acts like she is genuinely confused when the relationship doesn't work. She was even paying her last boyfriend's car note and child support! He bled her dry and left her with no place to stay, a storage building full of her belongings, and a car that needed numerous repairs. Anthony usually learned information about his sister's life after the fact because his mother and sister are very secretive about Angie's mess ups. Hmm . . . I wonder if this is where his suspicious tendencies and trust issue were born.

He learned at the last minute that his sister was broke, ass out, and needed his help moving from New Mexico to Texas. Without talking to me first, he invited her to come and live with us until she got herself together. I heard him talking about the empty guest room during a phone conversation that he was having with her.

Thankfully, she declined. It wouldn't have been a terrible situation, but we have quite a few problems of our own to deal with!

Speaking of problems, I might have to set up an appointment for Arielle. I believe that she is depressed. She is a great big sister, and she loves A.J. tremendously, but sometimes being with him depresses her to tears because she misses her mother so much.

Alycia is quite a mess right now. She is serving time in the Arizona State Prison for a variety of charges including assault and battery, prostitution, child neglect, child endangerment, robbery, possession of stolen goods, possession of narcotics and controlled substances with intent to deliver, and the list continues. Alycia and her boyfriend Jeff became "Bonnie and Clyde" while Arielle was still living with them.

During several weekend crime sprees, Alycia and Jeff broke into her brother's home and robbed him blind. Luckily, he and his family were not there. The next weekend, they broke into her parent's home and beat up her mother and father before robbing them blind. With all the loot that they were collecting, they should have had enough money to pay off their drug dealers, right? Wrong! It all came to a head one drug filled weekend when Jeff passed out, Alycia overdosed, and their drug dealers broke into the apartment and kidnapped Arielle. They kept her for three days.

If it weren't for a nosy neighbor, Alycia would have died, and who knows what might have happened to Arielle. She still has nightmares about the ordeal, but for the past year, she has confessed, little by little, some of the details surrounding her kidnap and escape. She was very brave, but she is extremely fragile because of that experience. Anthony and I are so glad that she is here with us, and I treat her as if she is my own.

However, all the love and attention that we drown her with does not erase her undying love for her mother. We are planning a trip this summer to go and visit her mother in prison. I would definitely like to start her therapy well before the visit. She is somewhat open to therapy, and would be even more so if her father supported it as well, but I intend to keep coaxing her.

Speaking of prison, Serena and I have grown closer as friends for 4 reasons:

1. She finally accepts me as her mentor – I have included her on more business trips. One was to Allentown, Georgia, and we had to fly. It was her first flight, so she had to completely drop all pretenses. She was scared out of her mind! More and more, she is beginning to trust me. She doesn't know that the children's department manager position will be open soon because Liz is moving to Kentucky. If Serena continues to work hard and shed her rough exterior, I will strongly advocate for her to get that position. Aren't you proud of me for overcoming my animosity toward Serena?

You will be even more proud when I tell you about #2. Even though she was adamantly against it, I forced her to go with me to visit her sister Jill in prison. Yes, Jill, the woman who helped my ex-husband kidnap my cousin Monica and terrorize me just a few years ago is Serena's sister! Small world, isn't it?

Jill has really turned her life around, and I'm glad that I was finally able to forgive her and move past all that hurt. I'm even happier that I was able to help her reconnect with her sister, so they can start working through their pain. They have A LOT of pain to work through. It was a rough first visit, but Serena agreed to write her sister. She has not agreed to another visit, but I intend to keep pushing it.

I told Arielle Jill's story, and she reacted favorably. This is a good thing because she has not been able to understand the rationale behind her mother's destructive actions. When I told her about Jill and what she did to me, Arielle seemed to understand the emotional distress and desperation that fueled Jill's behavior. Arielle made the comments, "Yes, I guess people can change their evil ways," and "I understand why forgiveness is so important for both the villain and the victim." Arielle has grown up a lot. Gone is the cute, giggly, innocent girl that Anthony called "pumpkin".

She is now a teenager, who is still extremely sensitive but now she has developed a hard outer core. Sometimes, she rebels angrily, and it surprises her like it came out of nowhere. She blurts something angrily, and then looks embarrassed when she realizes she actually said it.

This brings me to the third reason Serena and I are closer. Serena has a younger sister named Shelby. I introduced Shelby to Arielle, and they became good friends. Shelby's aunt Jill is in prison and her mother was a known drug addict. Arielle's mother is in prison, drugs had a lot to do with her behavior, and both Alycia and Jill are serving time for committing terrible crimes, so Shelby and Arielle have a lot in common. They talk a lot and think through things together. Even though they don't attend the same school, they are pretty good friends. My niece Jade is right in there with them. Jade and Arielle are more like sisters than cousins. Jade spends more time at our house than she does at her own! I have hosted numerous sleepovers for Arielle, Jade and Shelby. While other girls their age are chasing boys, they are simply enjoying being girls and this pleases Anthony, my oldest brother, and Serena more than anything.

Reason #4, and this one is a shocker! Rashad has finally developed an interest in Serena! Michelle is over the moon because she is certain that this happened because of Serena's change in attitude and work ethic. Yes, I agree. Serena is like a totally new person. At first, when I saw them laughing and leaving work together, I felt a huge pang of jealousy. He doesn't joke that much with me anymore unless we are with a group of people. I got over it though because Rashad and I are still friends, and that's all I ever truly wanted from him. It kind of hurts though that we are not as close as we use to be, and I blame Anthony for that, but it's for the best and I'm over it. Yes, Dr. Branson, I'm really over it.

Serena said that she and Rashad are moving slowly, but she is tickled pink that they are even talking and considering a committed relationship. Anthony is very pleased with their budding relationship, and he asks about them often.

Speaking of pleasure, you saw him, my baby boy A.J. He is the joy of my life! I simply can't believe how fast he has grown! He is already trying to walk! Anthony has hinted several times that he wants another baby. The thought would be tempting if being pregnant did not drastically reduce my workload, reduce my pay, reduce my travel schedule and eventually keep me stuck at home for nearly two months! I love being a mother and a wife, but I don't want to be a stay at home mom. Ugh! That's just not me. I admire the women who do it, but I just can't.

Anthony wouldn't ask for anything more if I did agree to be a stay at home mom. He was sober for my entire third trimester, the two months that I took maternity leave and several months thereafter. It wasn't until I got back into the swing of things at work, and I had to go away for a week that he fell off the wagon.

I know that I have avoided talking about what I really need to talk about in this letter – what happened between Clayton and me during the summer of 2000 starting with the time that I took my first real business trip to corporate headquarters. What happened then and what exists now between us is what needed to happen and what we both need to exist.

Right now, all I can really say is that we are both happy with the situation. Yes, occasionally, I do feel guilty about this secret because it's just that, a secret and I know that it's wrong to keep secrets from my husband. I'm doing what it takes to survive a marriage with an alcoholic husband and all the other stressors that exist in my life. Maybe I have an addiction? I'm addicted to secrets. Yes, I think I am.

Yes, we need to talk about this in more detail soon. But the guilt, Dr. Branson, is not eating me alive. It shows up, but eventually it subsides, and then I am okay. I'm in a good place. I'm at peace. When trouble arises, I handle it with very little difficulty because I know that I have something wonderful to look forward to. I look at every new day as a chance to start over. "Leave the past behind" is my new favorite motto.

~+~+~+~+~+~+~+~+~~+~+~+~+~+~+~+~+~+~+~+~+~

Do you want to know what happened between Clayton and Amina during her last night in Dayton, Texas? Read the next book in the series to find out!

~+~+~+~+~+~+~+~+~~+~+~+~+~+~+~+~+~+~+~+~+~

–1–

Anthony James Wallace

November 2002

*T*his meeting was noisy, chaotic even, on the night that he decided to participate. People were walking around talking and laughing like they were old friends. He didn't even want to be there, and it pissed him off that she was forcing him to do this. The original agreement was that he would attend the meetings, and that's exactly what he's been doing once a week for the past two months. Attending. It would have been nice to know that her sneaky ass was planning on attending this one, sitting in the back, and watching him.

The first few meetings that he attended were so quiet that you could hear an ant fart. "Good one Anthony!" he thought, "You will have to tell Amina that joke!" It did not take him long to realize that he had been coming in late and arriving during the moments of prayer and meditation. He actually liked it that way: coming in unnoticed without the obligation of meeting and greeting. Not getting to know anyone at these gatherings made them more tolerable. After all, this set up was supposed to be anonymous, right?

She kept pushing him to get more involved, to participate, to be active in his journey rather than keep making excuses and slipping back into his bad habits. She asked him to tell her all about the meetings after each one, and she excitedly asked, "Did you get to speak tonight?" as if his getting up and speaking will be an automatic remedy or something. "Hell, I need a tall, cold one right now!" Anthony thought.

She stayed on his back though, and after he still hadn't gotten up to speak after two months of attending, she came and spied on him when he once again promised that he would. The meetings were in a large classroom at the hospital. She sat near the back row behind a large, white woman who was loudly chewing gum, talking to herself, swatting imaginary flies, and occasionally rocking back and forth in her seat.

This was the perfect hiding place for Amina because mostly everyone, including Anthony, avoided eye contact with the woman. Anthony never looked in the woman's direction, so he only spotted Amina in the room when it was too late to back out of what he had just agreed to do. He didn't understand what the big fucking deal was! He came, he listened, he agreed with what other people said, he realized that he needed to make changes, and he slowed down tremendously on his drinking.

She told him that she could only tolerate him when he consumed wine or mixed drinks, so that was all he drank nowadays. But guess what? That wasn't even enough! Now, she wants him completely sober. No occasional drinks, no celebratory drinks, nothing. He worked so damn much that drinking was only an occasional act anyway, and it was only to relax and unwind. So what if he got drunk at the last family reunion! He hasn't seen or hung out with some of his family members since he was a kid! Why does she have to hold that against him? He never got that drunk at home in front of her and the kids.

He wrung his hands and looked down at them. His platinum gold wedding band gleamed under the fluorescent lights, and he could hear her threat, "You need to choose. Do you want your booze, or do you want your wife and kids? You can't have both!" He thought about Arielle, A.J. and the twins. They meant everything to him, and he couldn't fathom the thought of losing them. He gritted his teeth and frowned at the thought of her ultimatum. They had argued before, and she threatened to leave and take the kids with her, but she never made good on the threat.

He had her all figured out. She wasn't very good at working through difficulty. Oh, she tried, but when things got really tough, she took the coward's route. She always wanted to run from her problems. "What a hypocrite!" Anthony frowned as he thought about it, "She runs, but she tries to make me face my problems head on." He continued thinking about how distant she had become in the last couple of years, especially after the twins were born.

It was almost as if she poured all of her love on the children, so she had very little left for him. He knew that wasn't the case, but sometimes it sure felt like it. She wasn't as understanding or as patient as she used to be. She seemed like she was fed up, and she was more than ready to call it quits. Anthony frowned so much at this thought that his eyebrows scrunched together and formed a single jagged line across his face.

The meeting proceeded on from the introductions, opening statements, prayer and meditation, and on to the personal confessions. Several volunteers went to the podium and spoke. This group met on Sunday nights, and it was only for alcoholics while the Thursday night group was for people with a variety of addictions. The confessors droned on with their sad stories, and Anthony listened and thought with satisfaction that he was nothing like them.

Neither his family, nor his health had suffered because of his drinking, and neither had his career nor his social standing, so basically his drinking was not a problem. It was only a problem because his wife thought that it was a problem. Even the counselor at the police department agreed that his drinking was not at a point that was beyond his control. That settled it.

He was going to sit through this and continue on the way he has been doing just to shut her up. He has this under control. If she continued on with her nonsense, he would just put his foot down and show her that he was a man in control of his life. He sat back with a semi-smile on his face and wondered how much longer these confessions might take.

At that moment, he turned to look at the large clock on the wall in the back of the room. He noticed a woman sitting near the back row. She was beautiful: smooth brown skin, large brown eyes, and black straight shoulder length hair. She was wearing jeans, a tight boob revealing shirt, boots and a leather jacket. Her arms were folded and she was staring straight at him. Amina! "What the hell is she doing here?" Anthony fumed. The man in charge was beckoning for him to come to the podium. Anthony waved his hand at him to indicate that he wanted to pass tonight.

"Are you sure?" the man asked. Anthony glanced back at Amina again; she was still staring at him with her arms folded, her lips pressed tightly together, and a look of fierce suggestion on her face. Her eyes were forcing him to get up and speak. She meant business.

Anthony rose from his seat and walked slowly to the podium. "Hello everyone," he started. Everyone just looked at him because they were waiting for the rest of his greeting. The noise and the chaos quieted considerably as everyone waited for him to say it.

"My name is Anthony, and I'm an alcoholic." At this the audience came to life and spoke in unison, "Hi Anthony!"

Unchanged, Amina sat in the back row, arms folded, lips pressed together tightly, and she kept her gaze locked on her husband the entire time that he spoke.

*A*my R. Johnson currently resides in Plano, Texas with her husband and two sons. Always passionate about teaching, learning, and helping others, she teaches high school English and College Preparatory Courses.

In her two previous novels, **Never Let Go** and **Never Say Never**, Amy tackled the tough issues of domestic violence and PTSD. Her characters and situations are so authentic and life-like that readers often question her about the parallels of her life and the characters in her novels.

Never Let Go, an eye-opening story about dealing with domestic abuse, is a tribute to her hometown, El Dorado, Arkansas. **Never Say Never** is the second book in the series about the fictional character Amina Jefferson and this book touches on the struggles and harsh realities of PTSD.

"So many people have asked if I based the character on myself and my life experiences. The answer remains yes, no and maybe. Amina is me, you, your mother, your sister, your daughter, your aunt, your cousin, your niece, your co-worker, your best friend, the woman you can't stand, the women that you speak to everyday and the strangers that you pass by without a second thought. There's a part of her in every woman. I sincerely hope that you enjoy her stories," was Amy's remarks at a book signing event for her first two books.

Never Look Back continues Amina's story. Alcoholism is the main topic, and Amina shares the "struggle" spotlight with Anthony, his daughter Arielle, and her coworker Serena. Expanding these characters' stories has led to the promise of another book in the series, **Never Give Up.**

Over the years, Mrs. Johnson's reasons for writing have transformed in many ways, but they basically remained the same: "My purposes for writing are to shine a 'soft and empathetic' light on painful life experiences, provide hope, laughter, joy and promote a 'love affair' with literacy. "If my words can help someone laugh, love, or learn, then I feel like I have contributed something meaningful to the world and hopefully my legacy will live on for many generations."

Printed in the United States
By Bookmasters